Jacob Barker

The Rebellion

Its Consequences and the Congressional Committee, denominated the

reconstruction committee

Jacob Barker

The Rebellion
Its Consequences and the Congressional Committee, denominated the reconstruction committee

ISBN/EAN: 9783337235437

Printed in Europe, USA, Canada, Australia, Japan

Cover: Foto ©Andreas Hilbeck / pixelio.de

More available books at **www.hansebooks.com**

THE REBELLION:

ITS CONSEQUENCES,

CONGRESSIONAL COMMITTEE,

DENOMINATED THE

RECONSTRUCTION COMMITTEE,

WITH THEIR ACTION.

—

BY INVESTIGATOR.

NEW ORLEANS:

COMMERCIAL PRINT, 22 EXCHANGE PLACE.

1866.

Mr. Jacob Barker having been selected to represent New Orleans, the second commercial city in the United States, his opinions will be read with interest; hence, these pages will be confined in the main to the republication of what has appeared from time to time from his pen, and of harmonizing opinions from the pens of others.

THE REBELLION.

Southern efforts to establish a separate Government having failed, its advocates have submitted in good faith, perfectly convinced of the ruinous course pursued by leading politicians, which has entailed on them the penalty of being heavily taxed to pay the enormous debt created to controvert their efforts ; the loss of all their interest in slaves ; deprivation forever of their constitutional right to benefit by slave labor ; the loss of health, limb and life ; and, finally, in most cases, reduced from affluence to insolvency ; to all of which they submitted without a murmur. And while the victors insist that the secession ordinances were nullities, and that they sacrificed billions of money and hundreds of thousands of lives to preserve the Union, that we are cut of it, and to be taxed without representation ; and yet they do not tell us how we got out, or what is the value of their victory if they failed in its preservation.

The great body of those who embarked in the war on the Southern side, particularly the young men, believed they had a right to defend the Southern institutions ; that the North designed emancipation in violation of the Constitution. Hence, they committed no moral offence—motive being the gist of all crime. However unsound their logic, or unwise the policy resorted to for maintaining what they considered their constitutional rights, they believed that they were exposing their lives, their health and their fortunes in the cause of patriotism.

It is conceded that the extreme Abolitionists of the North always intended to bring about emancipation, regardless of the provisions of the Constitution, while the great body of the Union party had no such design; and had the Southern members retained their seats in Congress, no such result could have happened.

Under Mr. Buchanan's administration there was a majority of thirty against the South in the House. By the co-operation of our Northern friends such a revolution had been produced as to give us seven majority in the House which came into power with Mr. Lincoln, and in tne Senate we continued to have a majority of friends; hence, we had the power of defeating every adverse measure. When the Southern members resigned, resorting to force, they threw away the game. Emancipation was the result of the war—brought about to prevent foreign intervention, and the supposed necessity for the aid of colored soldiers in crushing out the rebellion.

Mr. Barker has ever been the advocate of the colored race; he has fought many battles for them, North and South, and in and out of court, without fee or reward beyond the satisfaction of establishing what he esteemed justice. He always considered making human beings property by the Constitution a blemish on our national escutcheon. Yet, it being there, those who purchased or inherited slave property were as much entitled to its protection as the ship-owners of New England were to the protection of their property in ships. The evil of slavery could only be cured by an amendment to the Constitution, wnich has been done—one of the effects of the disastrous war—to which penalty Southerners submit with becoming grace and fortitude. Mr. Barker would not have it restored if he could. On his settling in New Orleans in 1834, finding that the laws of Louisiana prohibited the education as well as the emancipation of slaves, and believing that great benefits would result from their being educated, he purchased and sent many abroad to be emancipated and educated, viz: Harry, Adam, Caledon, Moses, Nathaniel, Sallie, Anna, Robert, Polly and Claiborne—one to Liverpool, who was refused admittance into their schools on account of his black skin ; one to Washington, D. C.; two to Worcester, Mass.; one to Smithfield, two to Nantucket, one to Boston, and the others to New York. Many of them returned, and are now in New Orleans, benefiting by the education they have received.

After more than twenty years' residence in a slave State, Mr. Barker has come to the conclusion that the master is a greater slave than the bondsman ; that slavery operates prejudicially to the agricultural interests of the State ; but it is an evil entailed by our ancestors which cannot be abolished with the means within the power of the State ; that the slaveholders would consent to a general emancipation on receiving the value of their slaves from the Treasury of the United States ; yet they have no belief that their condition would be improved.

Mr. Barker knows that they are more comfortably provided for when in health, better taken care of when sick, and indulged in more rational amusements than are enjoyed by the laboring classes of any other country ; have full religious liberty, and are allowed to intermarry according to their own fancy, and their children are generally treated with the same kindness as those of their masters.

True, there are exceptions, and cruelties practiced in all countries, quite as much so in free as in slave States. When a white man is detected in a crime he is punished in free States according to the nature of his offence ; and Mr. Barker witnessed, when very young, the horrible scene of a white woman being tied to a cart in a public square, and there receiving on her naked back many lashes, which had been imposed by a court for a trifling theft. When slaves are detected in crime they are also punished, but the number of such punishments is not believed to be comparatively as great, or more severe than is inflicted on offenders in free States; yet it is a constant practice of those who are opposed to the institution of slavery to refer to these occurrences as evidence of general cruel treatment of slaves.

These people are greatly deceived, and most of them very honest in their zeal in favor of freedom, and, Mr. Barker is persuaded, would not meddle if they knew the unfavorable influence of their measures, causing much

greater restrictions on the slaves than would be otherwise imposed.

That slavery is contrary to that great principle which
teaches us to do unto others as we would that they should
do unto us, there can be no doubt ; yet it is idle to waste
our substance, our time, and our good feelings for each
other on what is utterly impracticable. How far the
slaves would make a valuable community, if made free,
and placed in a colony by themselves, where their children
could be educated and grow up free from the withering
influence arising from the supposition that they were to
be slaves for life, is problematical ; but without such an
education, Mr. Barker is satisfied they cannot be materially benefited by the interposition of white men at a
distance.

Many free persons of color being subject to great hard-
ships from the police of New Orleans, Mr. Barker frequently interfered in their behalf, creating very considerable prejudice against him. His interference was
constantly misrepresented by interested parties and in the
newspapers. So great at one time was this feeling that
he considered it expedient to make the following publication :

" TO THE PUBLIC.

"My opinions and conduct having been grossly misrepresented, I beg to be allowed to speak for myself.
All my exertions have been and will continue to be confined to sending out of and keeping away from the State

free men of color.. This, when properly considered, will be approved by every slaveholder.

"On the 3d July instant, I wrote to a gentleman at Philadelphia, who had employed me to present to court the proof of the freedom of a man confined in prison, as follows :

" 'You should publish in the newspapers and otherwise admonish all free people of color to keep away from this place, and especially if they have had their freedom established here, they should keep away, as all such persons are notified to quit the State within sixty days, and if they remain or return again after the sixty days, but for an hour, they are sent to the penitentiary for twelve months, and then ordered to quit in thirty days, and if they remain or return again after the sixty days, but for an hour, they are sent to the penitentiary for life.

" 'There is no safety for free men of color not born here, or here before 1825, but to keep away from this place. This community is justly afraid of their contaminating influence on the slaves, and they cannot be permitted to mingle with each other ; and while I shall at all times be willing to aid in securing to free men the exercise of their just right, without regard to color, I advocate all constitutional and legal measures for keeping free people of color away from slaveholding States. I think their friends in your quarter cannot do them a better service than to admonish them not to come here.'

"My conduct has always corresponded with these opinions. I have not, in the whole course of my life, to

my recollection, written or said a word, in or out of court.
at variance therefrom.

"When admitted to appear in the courts of Louisiana.
the laws of the State as well as my duty imposed the obligation of fidelity to my clients, and it is strange that
any one should complain of my having complied with the
requisites of that obligation.   It must have been misrepresentation that has led them to do so.

"My family have a deep interest in slave property,
and no man is more tenacious of, or will go furtner to
protect the rights of slaveholders than myself.

"If any man feels aggrieved, he has but to point out
in what particular, and I will afford him all the satisfaction in my power, when he will discover that he had no
just cause of complaint.

"Why pass laws protecting free men of color if it is to
be considered wrong for counsel to appear in their behalf?
No one will pretend that they are capable of maintaining
in court their own rights.   And if they were, they, at
work in irons on the highway, could not get their cases
before the court with the proper proofs.

"It may be here proper for me to state, for the information of the public, some of the many facts which have
come to my knowledge in relation to the treatment of
free men of color in the prison of the Second Municipality.   Having occasion to visit that prison very many
prisoners poured forth their complaints through the grates
as I was passing through the road, declaring themselves
free, that they were unlawfully detained and kept at work

on the highway in chains. It would have been inhuman to have turned a deaf ear. Many of them appeared to be so white as for the law to presume them free. I immediately represented the case to his honor the Recorder, who had six of them brought up, and pronounced five of them free from their complexson, without argument and without requiring any other testimony; and on my inquiring why they had not been liberated the morning after their arrest, their degree being as visible then as at any other time, his honor replied that they had been placed in the chain gang by the officers of the prison without having been brought up before him for examination. Was it wrong to interfere in behalf of these men?

"Public justice as well as every principle of humanity requires that prisoners, however great their offence, should have free communication with their counsel.

"On two occasions I was denied all access to prisoners in the Second Municipality, in whose defence I had been requested to assist, on the plea that no such persons were confined. After many months' perseverance, by the aid of his honor the Recorder, I had an interview with one of them, and the only excuse offered for his concealment was that I had inquired for Charles Chandler, when his name was Charles C. Chandler; and by the aid of his honor the Mayor, with the other, after less delay; the excuse for his concealment was that I inquired for James Loyd Warner, when they knew him on the prison books only by the name of Warner. Are such practices to be tolerated in this enlightened age? There was not any pretence that either of these men were slaves.

"On a recent occasion I was informed that a colored man, born in my native State, Maine, of free parents, was in the chain gang at work on the highway—had been there since September last, although the driver of the gang knew him to be free, was born in the same town, went to school with him, and had known him from his childhood. I communicated these facts to his honor the Recorder, he had the matter promptly inquired into, and the man liberated, but without a penny's compensation for nine months' services improving the Second Municipality.

"At the prisons of the First and Third Municipality I have been treated with the greatest politeness, and every facility afforded by the officers and keepers in bringing the law to the relief of prisoners.

"Again, it was the practice unlawfully to retain prisoners in the Second Municipality for their board, doctors' bills, etc., after their freedom had been established, until I brought the matter before a higher court; and on one occasion, without crediting on the account rendered the money taken from him when arrested. The public will please to observe that the rule in the Second Municipality was to allow prisoners three picayunes a day for such days as they labor on the public road, and to charge three picayunes a day for their board, in addition to the clothing supplied, the doctors's bills, etc. Hence, as they can not labor on Sundays, holidays, or in stormy weather, they are brought in debt, as soon as confined, the amount of which is augmented weekly, and as these men seldom

have money, and have no means of earning any during
their confinement, their simple arrest, without being
charged with the slightest offence, would amount to a
decree of perpetual imprisonment, if no person, from
humane feelings, had been allowed to interfere, and no
counsel allowed to bring their case before the tribunals
of the country.

"If the police officers of the Second Municipality expect to escape exposure by their attempts to light up the
torch of suspicion against others, and to continue their
unlawful and inhuman conduct towards their prisoners
with impunity, they will be mistaken. The Legislature
is composed of slaveholders, who understand their rights
and their interest too well to permit such abuses. They
will inquire into the matter and make all obedient to the
requirements of the law.   JACOB BARKER.

At a public meeting held at the Orleans Theatre, immediately preceding the election of Gov. Hahn, Mr.
Barker said, among other things, "that the Almighty had
fixed a distinguishing mark on the colored population
which no Christian should wish to obliterate. The object
of that mark short-sighted man cannot divine—whether
it was to elevate them above, or to place them below the
white man's standard, no man knows. They should be
considered architects of their own condition, and if they
could display more virtue and skill than the white man,
let them have a higher position—a straw should not be
laid in their way. So far from doing this, Mr. Barker

said he had always felt kindly for them, and would, if he had the power, set off a large district of country, in a mild climate, and tell them to go there and try their hand at self-government. He was confident that whatever benefit posterity might derive from this uncalled-for and disastrous war, the present generation could reap nothing but bitter fruit therefrom—the colored race more than the whites. As to amalgamation, it could not be tolerated. He said he did not attend that meeting to war with the decrees of his Heavenly Father—landmarks are not to be obliterated."

At the request of the friends of Alfred Hennen, Esq., who had been residing, with his family, on his plantation on the Lake, Mr. Barker, after peace was restored, addressed him a letter inviting his return, which found its way into the public print, and was severely criticised by interested individuals, and defended by others. Vide :

[Communicated.]

Editor True Delta—Mr. Jacob Barker's letter seems unnecessarily to have disturbed some of the new comers. That gentleman knows too well the advantage of patronizing their steamboats, their ships, their money, and other commercial facilities ; and also the comfort derived from their ice, their sperm candles, codfish, etc., etc., to throw any obstacles in the way of those who traffic in such commodities.

The aspect of the letter seems to be *exclusively political.* Mr. Barker inherited a love for self-government, and has

advocated it from childhood. If we are to be blessed
with a king, the privilege of selecting that king.

The letter insists that there was justice in contending
for the rights guaranteed us by the Constitution, it condemns the war, it tells foreign nations of the bravery of
the Confederate army, who now becomes part and parcel
of the army of the United States, it refers kindly to our
lamented President, it ascribes to British influence the
emancipation of the slaves, it proclaims the partiality of
France for the Confederates, it exposes the misfortune
and folly of the resignation of the members of Congress,
ascribes the ruin which has overtaken this community to
those professed friends, and points out how political
offices could be occupied by men of our own choice without any reference to commercial matters ; hence, new
comers should not allow their equanimity to be jostled.
It seems to us that the letter has a State bearing far
above the point which has attracted much attention. Mr.
Barker seems to have the talent of saying much in a few
words.   MENTOR.

[By the Editor of the True Delta.]

The communication of "Investigator," which may be
found elsewhere, will be generally read. It is a very
able, but moderately worded defence of the course our
venerable fellow-citizen, Mr. Jacob Barker, has seen
proper to pursue in regard to sundry important public
matters; and is especially a vindication of his letter to
Alfred Hennen, Esq.—the able and distinguished father
of the bar of the Southwest—published some weeks since,

which attracted much attention and elicited considerable criticism at the time of its publication.   That letter is embodied in the communication referred to ; and of its merits, as well as of the merits of the defence and explanation which follow, the public is fully competent to judge.

If our memory serves us correctly, for we were not "in harness" at the time, the chief objection to Mr. Barker's letter consisted in his application of the phrase "new comers."   It was thought that he meant the future exclusion of meritorious classes of people who have come among us, and who propose, by the use of their capital and industry, to build up the commerce and agriculture of our city and State, until they reach their former pitch of prosperity and grandeur.   Had this been the motive, it would have deserved the severest condemnation.   But "Investigator" says that Mr. Barker only referred to partied who *had* been guilty of dishonest practices at the polls ; and as he is evidently well posted in the premises, it is not incumbent upon us to deny or support his conclusions.

For our part, we gladly welcome all honest and loyal "new comers."   We wish them to come from New England, from New York, from all parts of the North and from Europe.   Let them come with their capital, their skilled and other labor, their general industry and enterprise—and the more the better,   All will be welcomed.   There is an inexhaustible field before them, where all will be protected in their rights, and all respected as they deserve. The man, or set of men, who would infringe upon the one or trespass upon the other, would be indignantly frowned upon by the entire community. As we have frequently before stated in these columns, we do not believe such a field for the investment of capital and labor in commerce, agriculture and manufactures, ever before presented itself upon the surface of the earth ; and we shall be much mistaken if an immense influx of both does not soon cause the South to become as wealthy and prosperous as she is now impoverished and desolate.

[Communicated.]

The following letter of Mr. Jacob Barker to Alfred Hennen, Esq, has been severely criticised :

NEW ORLEANS, June 12, 1865.

Alfred Hennen, Esq.: My Dear Sir—The battle being over, and the victors too numerous and too well supplied with the sinews of war, triumphed over unequaled perseverance, courage and endurance, with which they were resisted for four years, until it became useless to continue the strife ; therefore, it behooves us to make the best of our position, and qualify ourselves to use our rights at the ballot-box.

Our original cause was just, and the battle should have been fought in Congress. Had that been done, the Abolition party would have been left out in the cold.

Our members of Congress threw away the game by resigning their seats, and then the assault on the flag, the forts and the public property, dissolved the moral influence of the Constitution, and induced our friends at the

North generally to abandon our cause and join those they detested, from whom they can be detached by a return, on our part, to the Union, with a becoming reverence for the Star Spangled Banner.

It behooves all our citizens to return at once and qualify themselves to vote. Do this, and we shall assuredly succeed in giving the new comers leave of absence at the next election.

The blemish of slavery has been effaced from the National record. I would not have it restored if I could. If done, it would be a valueless shadow; half the money wasted on the war would have purchased their freedom, and we are in debt to those who professed to be our friends, for the loss—the irretrievable loss—we have sustained.

Emancipation was adopted by the late worthy President, to please England, and thereby prevent foreign interference in favor of the Confederacy. France dared not interfere in opposition to the known wishes of England.

My best wishes await all the members of your family, anticipating the pleasure of seeing them back to the city.

I am, very respectfully, your friend,

JACOB BARKER.

The critics say the author of the letter showed himself a rebel, by saying our original cause was just. How far he merits the sobriquet may be seen by his various manifestations during our political troubles—a retrospective view of which is in course of republication—his reverence

2

for the ballot-box, his universal kindness to the families of absent Confederates, and to the colored population, may have entitled him to be held in that estimation. In a speech made at a public meeting at the Odd Fellows' Hall, immediately before the Ordinance of Secession was passed, he said :

"The canvas of my ships has whitened every sea, unfurling to the breeze of every clime the Star Spangled Banner, the glittering emblem of our Union and independence, of which every American citizen, native and adopted, is justly proud. If compelled to give it up, I would attend its funeral clad in habiliments of woe."

Some who have criticised the letter, object to the remark that slavery was a blemish on our National character. The author always considered the constitutional provision in favor of slavery a blemish ; yet, it having been settled as a matter of compromise, the question was not open for debate, except by amending the Constitution as therein provided. Confiding in this guarantee, the South was induced to invest their all in such property, whence their claim for the fulfillment of that guarantee was originally just, and continued so as long as they observed the other provisions of that sacred charter. They annulled their right to a fulfillment of the guarantee of the slave question, by assaulting the Union, the flag, the forts and the other property of the United States, all of which were equally guaranteed by the Constitution.

Slavery being thus abolished, Mr. Barker would not have it renewed if he could. If done, his letter says it would be a valueless shadow. He might have added that it would be the cause of renewed strife and agitation.

Mr. Barker took an active part in that election. The result, in such of the rural parishes that made returns, although light, indicates the feeling of the permanent citizens. From six, the returns were as follows :

	Successful Candidate.	Conservative Candidate'
Parish of St. Bernard	5	199
" St. James	7	107
" Assumption	24	441
" Lafourche	223	392
" Terrebonne	13	238
" St. Charles	12	37
Total	283	1415

The majorities in the rural parishes were overcome by illegal and fraudulent votes, cast principally in the city of New Orleans, of which the public have abundant testimony furnished by His Excellency Gov. Wells, who says:

PROCLAMATION.

By J. Madison Wells, Governor of the State of Louisiana.

Whereas, according to an official statement of J. Randall Terry, late Register of voters in and for the city of New Orleans, made to me under date of March 6th, 1865, nearly five thousand persons are registered as voters on the books of said office, who do not possess the qualifications required by law to become voters in this State, and whereas, it is made my duty to see that the laws are enforced; and whereas, the only way in which the elective franchise can be purified and the rights of the citizen be protected against those illegal votes, is by a new registra-

tion of the names and residences of all the qualified
electors of the city of New Orleans—an inconvenience
which every good and law-abiding citizen will cheerfully
submit to for the sake of the end to be be accomplished.

*   * ,   *   *   *   *

Those who like to be governed by such a Legislature
and such a Convention as resulted from the last election,
will doubtless disapprove of the exercise of the elective
franchise by our permanent citizens.   How else than by
their votes can the new-comers be prevented from continuing to stuff the ballot-boxes with illegal and fraudulent votes.   Had the ballots then cast been by qualified
voters, they would not have been illegal or fraudulent.
It was to such that the letter referred when it spoke of
leave of absence to new-comers.   His remarks had special
reference to the election.   The whole letter bears that
impress, and it should be considered, as a whole, referring
exclusively to those who were thus attempting to control
the reorganization of our political institutions.

The letter speaks kindly of our late worthy President,
of the bravery of the Confederate soldiers—which may be
considered a hint at enforcing the Monroe doctrine—it
exhibits the disposition of France and England in relation
to the rebellion, what induced the emancipation proclamation, the feeling of the Democratic party at the North
in relation to the Abolitionists, condemns secession and
the war, and says emancipation could have been accomplished by compensation at half the cost of the war ; that
the Southern cause was sacrificed by their representatives

resigning their seats in Congress ; that the battle should have been fought there and not at the cannon's mouth. It urges the ballot-box as our safeguard—the palladium of our liberties—and entreats all to qualify themselves to participate in the coming elections.

Some who have criticised the letter, consider it the effusions of second childhood ; others, that his conclusions are sound, although not palatable to those of either party who do not like to have their errors unveiled.

The letter speaks for itself ; the criticism induces its perusal. As to our returning erring brothers, Mr. Barker is known to entertain similar views to those expressed by General Sickles at Tammany Hall, New York, at the Fourth of July celebration. INVESTIGATOR.

[From the Picayune.]

LETTER OF MR. JACOB BARKER.

The following is a copy of a letter addressed by our fellow-citizen, Jacob Barker, to a friend in Washington to be exhibited to the President :

NEW ORLEANS, August 25, 1865.

The rebellion is happily over, thanks to Gen. Sherman !

The question now presented is, how the vanquished are to be treated ? Their sufferings and disappointments have been too great for the present generation ever to think of again resorting to the cannon's mouth to redress wrongs, real or imaginary ; hence, no necessity to guard against such a calamity, and no Christian can wish to inflict further sufferings on the deluded advocates of secession.

The return of the "prodigal son" was celebrated by killing the "fatted calf."

Subsequently, there was a worthy example of forgiveness, by Nangfu, the Emperor of China, who, being told that his enemies had raised an insurrection in one of the distant provinces, said: "Come, then, my friends, follow me, and I promise you that we shall quickly destroy them!" He marched forward, and the rebels submitted on his approach. All now thought he would take the most signal revenge, but were surprised by seeing the captives treated with mildness and humanity. "How!" exclaimed the first minister, "is this the way you fulfill your promise? Your royal word was given that your enemies should be destroyed, and behold you have pardoned all, and even caressed some." "I promised," replied the Emperor, with a generous air, "to destroy my enemies; I have fulfilled my word; they are enemies no longer; I have made friends of them."

The object of punishment is to prevent offences, not for revenge, leaving the offenders the hope of Heavenly forgiveness, which is an affair to be settled by the Great Author of our being when the vital spark leaves the earthly tabernacle. Hence the wisdom of promptly restoring our deluded citizens to their civil rights, and to such of their property as has not been vested in others. This would greatly resuscitate commerce, restore New Orleans to her merited importance, and redound 'materially to the benefit of the Treasury—objects of the greatest importance.

No palliation can be offered for the political aspirants who brought about the rebellion. It was little short of insanity! Their deluded followers were made to believe that the Constitution was a mere partnership contract, that its violation by one party authorized the other to consider the whole annulled; that the Abolition party had, by refusing to observe the Dred Scott decision, by refusing to surrender fugitive slaves, by their personal laws, and by their removal of Judge Loring for having respected the decision of the Supreme Court, violated the compact. They were made to believe that the North designed emancipation—although it resulted from the war. Such design was entertained only by Abolitionists, who composed a small proportion of the supporters of Mr. Lincoln's first election, and he then lacked more than a million of a majority of the votes cast. These men intend to press us further on the sable question, in which we shall, with becoming exertions, assuredly floor them.

These considerations induced the multitude to believe that they were called upon to offer up their lives, their fortunes and their health in support of what they had been taught to believe was "States' Rights." Hence, deluded.

Long before secession took place, and during its whole continuance, I endeavored, by various publications and otherwise, to impress the public with the belief that it was in the highest degree impolitic, fraught with all the evil consequences we are now experiencing.

I had supposed confiscation of private property on

shore, without conviction for crime, had been exploded
by the enlightened ages. My experience in the war of
1812 confirmed that opinion. Neither Great Britain nor
the United States descended to such degradation, befit-
ting the "dark ages."

Both sides, in the present case, seem equally to blame;
it is believed to have originated without any special law
or authority from either Government; the first that was
heard of it was the sequestration by the United States
District Attorney of the balances in the New York banks
due those residing in the "Confederate States," which
created such a storm in Wall street that the proceedings
were withdrawn before 3 o'clock P. M. the same day they
were instituted. The Confederate Congress took the
alarm, apparently glad of the opportunity, and proceeded
to pass confiscation laws, which were enforced to a frightful extent, when the United States Congress followed
their example.

However, the further inquiry of who was most to
blame for those laws, would not be productive of that
harmony I wish to inculcate. The occasion which called
those laws into being having passed away, they should
be abolished. Our own experience tells us that kindness
begets kindness. Our much lamented President Lincoln
is believed to have entertained those views, and his patriotic successor seems to be carrying them out to a praiseworthy extent. It is considered impossible that any man
can make the necessary investigations on the numerous
applications for pardon pressing for prompt action, to

enable him to decide on the intrinsic merits of each : hence, in justice to himself and the Nation at large, which feels a deep interest in his health and welfare, it would be good policy to issue an amnesty proclamation, embracing all who might not be considered dangerous, on their taking in good faith a prescribed oath, allowing the excepted class to leave the country, as Britain did my lamented friend, Thomas Addis Emmet, who proved a brilliant ornament to the legal profession, and in his social intercourse a charm to all who participated therein.

Unless some such measure is adopted, it is apprehended that the service, together with his other official duties. will be too severe for the Executive. Let him beware of those who wish his downfall. On his successfully maintaining his present position depends the restoration of the Democratic party.

MR. BARKER'S NOMINATION FOR CONGRESS.

Here we have the published opinions of Mr. Barker, which led to his nomination to represent the second commercial city in the Congress of the United States :

CORRESPONDENCE.

[Copy.]

NEW ORLEANS, October 21, 1865.

Hon. Jacob Barker, New Orleans :

Sir—The undersigned, a committee appointed by the Delegates of the Second Congressional District, have the honor to announce to you that you have been selected as their candidate for Congress to represent the Second Congressional District of Louisiana.

Feeling assured that you are ever willing and ready to sacrifice your personal interest for the good of your country, we expect an early acceptance on your part.

We have the honor, honored sir, to remain your obedient servants,   H. D. OGDEN,

P. G. MOHAN,

D. P. SCANLAN.

———

NEW ORLEANS, October 21, 1865.

To H. D. Ogden, Esq., P. G. Mohan, Esq., and D. P. Scanlan, Esq.:

Gentlemen—I have had the honor to receive your letter, announcing my selection by the delegates of the Second Congressional District as a candidate to represent it in the National Assembly.

It is to be regretted that Mr. Rozier declined the honor tendered to him; the important interests at stake require the advocacy of such men. I do not feel equal to the task, yet I cannot decline so distinguished an honor, inconvenient as it will be for me to leave home. If the name of another approved candidate should be presented, I shall cheerfully withdraw.

The great question to be decided will be the recognition of this State, with all her constitutional rights restored, except the institution of slavery, which has been abolished by the war, not to be revived or discussed. The State being recognized, it will become the duty of the Legislature, among other important questions, to pass such laws as will protect the freedmen in their rights to contract with whom they like, and to appropriate the fruits of their labor to the education of their children, or otherwise, to suit their fancy.

My opinions on other subjects are too well known to the electors whose votes I solicit, to require further explanation.

Permit me, gentlemen, to thank you, and those you represent, for the honor conferred on

Your obedient servant,   JACOB BARKER.

———

[From the New Orleans, Times.]

We are requested to give at some length the remarks of Mr. Barker, at the St. Mary's Market meeting last evening:

Mr. Barker, loudly called for, appeared in the midst of enthusiastic cheering. He said his name was not among those who had been chosen by the organizers of this meeting to address it; and that after the display of so much logic and oratory as had been witnessed, it would be presumptuous in him, at this late hour, to expect to detain this immense meeting to hear many remarks from him. The whole ground had been occupied by others— no thunder left for him—yet he would make a few remarks ; and he spoke of the rule of Butler and Banks, and still of another, of whom the people were glad to be rid—Conway. He had borne the intelligence of Conway's removal to Mr. King, editor of the Times. It had the same thrilling effect on the community as the lookout sailor's cry from the masthead, "Land ! land on the starboard bow!" has on the crew and passengers of a ship in a storm approaching our coast after a disastrous voyage. So astonished was the incumbent at that unexpected information, that he induced the editor to contradict the report, in the Times of the following day. Yet, when the fog cleared up, the beautiful land was in view.

The Freedmen's Bureau has been the greatest curse of the war, devastating our flourishing fields, reducing our luxuriant crops from a yield of fifty millions to not more than two millions. In place of the reverend gentleman we now have Gen. Fullerton, whose course promises all we can ask : restoration of sequestered property goes on rapidly under his wise and patriotic administration ; what we heretofore considered a curse is likely to become a blessing, so long as military rule continues over this State.

The great question to be settled is the recognition of Louisiana, not her admission or reconstruction, as she has not been out of the United States. He entreated all to view the approaching canvass to be a National one—the candidates and their election a minor question. He considered that the South should be ruled by Southern men ; so thinks President Johnson. To effect that object it is only necessary to sustain the patriotic views he has put forth. Will you do this? [The crowd answered, "We will, we will!"] Our citizens who have returned to the support of the Union and the Star Spangled Banner have done so in good faith, and can now be considered as forming part and parcel of the most loyal, and entitled to the cordial support of the Democratic party, and they will receive it.

As to the working men, they do not wish any legislative interference with their occupation further that suitable laws to insure prompt fulfillment of such contracts as they may make ; they prefer to do as they please with their own rights.

The freedmen should be protected in their right to appropriate their earnings to the education of their own children, or otherwise, according to their own fancy ; the collections now in progress of a tax to educate the colored children, Mr. Barker said, was considered unconstitutional, because it was not equal ; and unjust, because the scale of appraisement estimated the amount to be paid on the value of the property, while the slaves constituted three-fourths the amount ; for the parties who had thus demolished its value to require a tax on such an estimate from those whom they had impoverished, Mr. Barker said he considered unjust in the extreme, and that on a proper representation to the Government that General Order No. 38 would be abrogated, which was never enforced by its author, issued on the supposition that it would aid in crushing out the rebellion, for which purpose he had been sent here.

Our opponents say the Democratic party is opposed to the Catholics. This is untrue. It is proverbial for its liberality towards all religious denominations ; and as to myself, I am not a sectarian. I consider the avowed object of all is to find a resting place in Heaven. In the attainment of this object Mr. Barker said he wished them all possible success. Religion being an affair between God and man individually, no political interference can be tolerated. So far as the Catholics are concerned, he considered that they have rendered greater service to the civilized world than any other religious denomination.

He said it was not his purpose to refer to either of the candidates, excepting to refute the slander, put forth by one of them, over his signature, in the newspapers, Mr. Overall, accusing us of slandering the fair ladies of New Orleans—which is false. He cannot find a single lady in this city who will say that Jacob Barker ever slandered her. Mr. Barker now sees on the adjoining balconies many of the fair sex, whose presence is an omen of success, to whom he says, he is never happier than when advocating their cause.

To the Editor of the New Orleans Times:

The status of the freedmen seems to engross public attention more than any other subject. The feelings of this community, if we credit the published accounts, have been misrepresented at Washington by Gov. Hahn and others, and we know them to have been grossly misrepresented by the orators at the meeting lately held by the Abolition party at the Orleans Theatre.

The late election for an individual to represent this city in Congress, from the Second District, should put the question at rest. The election was closely and fairly contested. Four candidates were in the field.

B. F. Lynch, Independent, received........ 530 votes.
J. W. Overall,   "   "   216   "
A. P. Field, Conservative,   "   366   "
Jacob Barker, Union,   " 2473   "

Mr. Barker received 1361 more votes than all the others together.

The triumphant vote cast for Mr. Barker establishes that this community approve of his published opinions.

CITIZEN.

The members from the eleven States repaired to Washington, where they were informed that Mr. McPherson, the Clerk of the House of Representatives, would not insert their names on the rolls to be called when the House assembled.

On the previous evening there had been a caucus of the members of both Houses from the other twenty-five States, who had resolved that there should be a Reconstruction Committee, to consist of six Senators and nine members of the House of Representatives; in effect, that all questions relating to the eleven excluded States should be referred to such committee. The members from the twenty-five States assembled, appointed the proposed Reconstruction Committee, refusing to receive the members form the other eleven States, denying to them the privilege of the floor or the right of being heard.

Mr. Barker had an interview with Messrs. Stevens and Kelly, of the House, and Mr. Wilson, of the Senate, and from what they said and from the aforesaid proceedings, he came to the conclusion that they intended to pass bills adverse to the South, which they feared the President would veto, in which case they felt strong enough to override his veto, if they kept out the members from the eleven excluded States, which they could not do if they were admitted.   Mr. Barker, considering the question settled until such bills should be disposed of, left his credentials with Mr. McPherson, the Clerk, and returned home, urging his constituents to patience and reliance on the ballot-box, in the hope that all would be made right as soon as the people of the Great West were sufficiently enlightened on the subject.   He insists that the credentials of the persons elected from the eleven States were of equal validity with those from the other States ; that they should have been allowed to have taken their seats and participated in the organization of the two Houses ; that done, each House had the constitutional right to pass upon the qualifications of its members; but that they had not the right to refer the subject to a committee of the two Houses, or to divide the responsibility with each other.   Aware of this, the committee is denominated the Reconstruction Committee, which covers the question. If the public had fully understood the question it would have been proper for the President to have refused to acknowledge those assembled to be the Congress of the United States.   The necessities of the Nation required appropriation and other laws, hence it was better for the President to wait for the people to demand such a course than to have taken the lead therein without their prompting. The case will be different on the assembling of Congress in December next; before which, if the President proclaims his intention to recognize the members elected from the eleven States in their constitutional rights, the friends of law and order will sustain the measure. His oath of office binds him to do so, as much as to see the other laws properly enforced. These rights are to have the qualification of each individual claiming a seat passed on simply by the House to which he has been appointed or elected. In this way all or any member might, if sufficient cause appeared, be deprived of his seat, constitutionally, but could not be in any other way.

We are a subdued people, and submit in all sincerity, convinced of the folly of the efforts made to establish a separate government; we have suffered too much in life, limb, health, property and commerce, ever again to be found fighting against the Constitution and the Union, or under any other flag than the Star Spangled Banner. The victors know this and know our bravery, and should treat us with becoming magnanimity.

The agricultural, commercial, manufacturing and financial interests of the whole Nation require the cultivation of kindness on all sides. The strife should be, who can excel in that noble work.

———

We are disarmed and driven to the wall, and if pressed too hard, shall be unwillingly compelled to resort to the only retaliatory measures left to our disposal—commercial restrictions—in which the noble ladies of the South

3·

will perform an important part. We have no power to prohibit importations, but when imported we can allow them to lay mouldering on the shelves, of the importers, patronizing foreign ships and steamboats, while we are feasting on the products of the West, attired in the fabrics of Lyons and Manchester, using silver and gold, which will endure until the nature of the female character shall be revolutionized. French shoes and English muslins will be good substitutes for Lynn shoes and Lowell cottons.

Having demonstrated the circumstances which led to the election of Mr. Barker, we shall leave Investigator to go on with his contemplated work of republishing what has heretofore appeared in relation to Mr. Barker's course, pending the question of secession, that the reader may fully understand the feelings and sentiments of the individual elected by the citizens of New Orleans to represent them in the Congress of the United States, and by the Radicals denied a seat.

NEW ENGLAND DINNER AT THE ST. CHARLES.

When the clouds of discontent were bursting forth in every part of the land, Mr. Barker's confidence in the stability of the Government remained unchanged. The privileges of its citizens were so great and the duties so light than none felt the weight of the Government but those who fattened upon its lucrative offices. The liberty of speech and of the press was perfect, our religion was left to our own choice, we pursued our various occupa-

tions without annoyance, making it the manifest interest
of all to wish and labor for the preservation of the Union.

At a New England festival, held at the St. Charles
Hotel in New Orleans on the 22d December, 1859, the
anniversary of the landing of the Pilgrims, many speeches
were made, full of apprehension for the future, and at
which Mr. Barker spoke, the following report of which
we find in the papers at that time :

After many toasts and speeches from members, the
venerable Jacob Barker being called on, remarked that
he had been honored by an invitation from the president.
some days since, to address the meeting, which from age
and other considerations he was constrained to decline,
and came unprepared to say a word beyond offering a
sentiment, which he did in the words following :

"Virginia and Massachusetts—twin sisters—they can
never be separated by the Fanatics of the North nor the
Fire-eaters of the South."

Mr. Barker said—

"Although admonished by the lateness of the hour and
the eloquent appeals to the patriotism of Northerners and
others to adhere to such determination, yet I cannot subscribe to all I have heard this evening, and I beg leave to
detain you a few moments, late as it is, to express my
dissent. The few blossoms—indicating my approach to
the grave—which yet deck my brow, will convince my
brethren from New England of the sincerity of my remarks. First, it appears to me that our worthy president
seems to be unnecessarily alarmed for the safety of the

Union—like his namesake, the elder Adams, he thinks we have fallen on evil times—he seems to sympathise with the sage of Quincy. I have no such apprehension. I witnessed the Whisky Insurrection of the Keystone State under Washington, to quell which our troops were sent, under the advice of Gen. Alexander Hamilton, one of the first men of that age. [Cheers.] The work was accomplished without the burning of gunpowder; not a drop of human blood was spilt, not a crimson spot was to be found on any garment. Then came the administration of Adams, with whom there were sad dissensions. Then came the election of the illustrious Jefferson, which agitated the whole Nation. The pious old women were made to believe that if the French Jacobins, so denominated by their political opponents, and of whom I was one, [laughter,] succeeded, the churches and pulpits would be demolished and their bibles burned. We triumphed, and no such calamity resulted; the churches remained undestroyed, the pulpits continued to be graced with clerical robes, and the sacred bibles circulated as freely as ever. [Laughter and cheers.] Then came the glorious war of 1812, in which I witnessed the flight of our troops through Washington from Bladensburg— fleeing with them myself, [laughter,] carring with me, by the command of Mrs. Madison, the original portrait of Washington by Stewart. [Applause.] The army halted at Montgomery Courthouse, without a pound of beef or bread to subsist on; the United States Treasury empty; Treasury notes and stock dividends maturing, unpaid. Then came the demonstration against the Constitution, at Charleston, S. C., which was snuffed out by the renowned Jackson without shedding a drop of human blood. [Applause.]

"All these lowering clouds have been dispelled without moving a single plank in our excellent Constitution. [Applause.] I could enumerate many other stirring events, were there time, which would admonish us not to be afraid when there is not any danger. I have never been afraid of my fellow-men, and it is too late for me to encourage that feeling. We have only to ' be just and fear not.' [Cheers.]

"Great confidence is felt in the influence of the advice of the immaculate Washington, the inimitable Father of our common country, in his Farewell Address; and also, in the patriotic feelings of all good men—a theme which politicians delight to dwell on. My experience tells me that we have a much more powerful guarantee for the preservation of the Constitution in the influence of the "almighty dollar." [Laughter.] My countrymen have a keen appetite therefor, and know full well that if there should be a division of the Union their ships would be prohibited an entrance into Southern ports, and consequently would become worthless. The Southerners would impose heavy import duties on the shoes, clothes and other fabrics of New England—giving a preference to foreign articles. This would be done for the double purpose of revenue for defraying the expenses of carrying on their new government and for revenge. This would put to sleep the looms, spindles and jennies of New England, and throw out of employment a thousand pretty girls. [Laughter and cheers.] We Southerners also keep a sharp look-out for our interest, and our appetite for gain is equally keen. [Applause.]

"We know full well that our slaves would not be worth the clothes they wear if the Union should be dissolved. Their value consists in the preservation of Southern rights, as guaranteed by the Constitution. Should it be vacated by a division of the Union, the Northern section would imitate their cousins, the British—making all free who would put their feet on their soil. This would depopulate the border States of their slave population, and they would, one after another, become free States, until not one would be left to tell how it happened.

"Mr. President, in that event, our only redress would be war, in which conflict the odds would be in favor of the North, on account of their superior numbers, and the necessity of guarding our slaves; and further, all must admit that our importance as a nation depends on the preservation of the Union. I repeat, we have only to 'be just and fear not,' and all will remain safe."

It must be acknowledged that Mr. Barker placed too high an estimate upon the influence of the "almighty dollar," or of the people's intelligence in calculating the cost and consequences of a war.

SPEECH AT ODD FELLOWS' HALL.

Mr. Barker exerted himself to the utmost of his capacity to avert this unfortunate war, and when declared, to bring it to a speedy termination.

At the great meeting of merchants, mechanics and others at the Odd Fellows' Hall, he spoke in substance thus :

"FELLOW-CITIZENS—I am not come here to denounce any man or any party, or to utter an unkind word—the subject is too grave.

"The canvas of my ships has whitened every sea, unfurling to the breeze of every clime the Star Spangled Banner, the glittering emblem of our Union and independence, of which every American citizen, native and adopted, is justly proud. If compelled to give it up, I would attend its funeral clad in habiliments of woe.

"We are now called on to haul down that glorious emblem of our greatness, bequeathed to us by Washington, Franklin, Jefferson, Madison, Hamilton and other departed spirits of the Revolution, and to substitute therefor an unknown standard called the Palmetto Flag, at the bidding of the State of South Carolina, because the institutions of the South, on the maintenance of which our wealth, happiness and national importance depend, have been outraged by some of the Northern States. However true this may be, and no one disputes it, is it fit and becoming that a single small State, less interested than most of the others, should dictate to all the slave States the sacrifices to be made and the course to be pursued for obtaining security and redress? I say it is not; that it belongs to the people of those States to decide when called on by a convention of delegates from all the slave States to vote on the question.

"If such a convention should mature a plan for a separate Confederacy, and a majority of legal voters should ratify it, the minority would acquiesce and yield a hearty support, when the united power of the slave States would be irresistible. We should continue to hold Washington, and all the machinery of the Government, preserving the Stars and Stripes, leaving the free States to form a confederacy of their own, with a new capital beyond Mason and Dixon's line.

"If a majority of such a convention should decide to endeavor to effect a compromise, before adopting the plan of trying which could do the other the most harm, then in adjusting the terms all the slave States should have a voice—no one should be allowed to dictate.

"If war should be the melancholy result, the people have to do the fighting and to furnish the sinews of war. It is, therefore, right and proper that they should be consulted; hence, I say, let there be a convention of delegates from all the slave States, and the result of their deliberations submitted to the citizens of those States, and so far as I am concerned, I pledge myself to support whatever decision a majority may arrive at, to which every friend of Louisiana will subscribe.

"Fellow-citizens, I bid you beware how you send your Ship of State to sea without rudder, compass or pilot. I have sent too many ships to sea to be willing to recommend the placing of the finest bark in the Confederation in so perilous a position.

"Separate secession cannot be viewed in any other light."

___

AN APPEAL TO THINKING MEN. *

NEW ORLEANS, December 17, 1860.

To the Editors of the Picayune:

Gentlemen—My opinions on the unfortunate, uncalled for and calamitous state of public affairs correspond so exactly with those expressed in the accompanying articles from the Natchez (Miss.) Daily Courier, that I think I cannot do my fellow-citizens better service, on this eighty-first anniversary of my birth, than by having them republished.

Very respectfully, your obedient servant,

JACOB BARKER.

___

[From the Natchez Daily Courier, Nov. 17, 1860.]

HAVE WE EXHAUSTED OUR CONSTITUTIONAL REMEDIES?

NUMBER ONE.

To say the least of it, the right of secession is an extremely doubtful one. The ablest and wisest of the constitutional fathers were against it. Madison, with emphatic exactness, called it "an extra and ultra constitutional remedy." The State of Mississippi, acting in her sovereign capacity, has declared it to be a doctrine unsanctioned by the Constitution. Outside of South Carolina, it is doubtful whether the people of a single Southern State would vote affirmatively that the right of peaceable secession exists. No such right is granted in the Constitution ; no such right can be among the powers reserved to the States or to the people ; for, to use Judge Boyd's expressive language, "a reservation necessarily implies the pre-existence of that which is reserved. The States were about dividing out the powers of Government, a part to their separate State Governments, and a part to the General Government, and they expressly reserved out of the existing mass all the residue. If they were not at that time in being, they were not and could not be reserved. A right to break a contract not yet made, or to destroy a government not yet formed, did not belong to a State before she became a party to such contract or government." Nor is such a right at all compatible with one of the main designs of the Constitution, which was "to form a more perfect Union" out of the "perpetual Union" declared to exist by the articles of confederation.

But even were this right of secession clear and undisputed, would it be justifiable to exercise it, until every remedy for wrong, which the Constitution now gives us, has been exhausted? Grant the fact that half a dozen or more Northern States, under the influence of fanaticism and hatred, have violated the Constitution by their personal liberty laws; grant that many of them are doing all they can to annoy, irritate, and wound the States of the South, and to make the bonds of Union as disagreeable as possible; grant that they have sectionally combined to get possession of the Government, and have so far succeeded as to elect a President and Vice President —grant all this; still, *have we exhausted all the remedies for aggression the Constitution gives us?* and if we have not, then, until we do so, are we morally justifiable in exercising the doubtful right of secession, or even the unquestioned right of revolution? These are serious questions, and must occur to every reflecting mind. If we have exhausted all remedies under the present Constitution, and can no longer live under it honorably and safely, the North must consent to new remedies being given us, and to new guarantees for protection, or the Union must be broken up.

But let us see whether we have or have not so exhausted them. The Constitution is an instrument of checks and balances. For instance: the legislative power of the country, vested in Congress, cannot be exercised without the assent of the Executive; or in case of his dissent, only with the assent of two-thirds of each House, instead of a bare majority. The Executive power can convene Congress; but that body can adjourn without his consent. The President is commander-in-chief of the Army and Navy; but he cannot declare war; Congress alone can do that. The President also commands the militia of the several States, when called into the actual service of the United States; but the calling it forth is given to Congress, as well as its organization, arming and discipline; while the appointment of its officers and the authority of training are especially reserved to the States themselves. The President makes treaties; but only with the concurrence of two-thirds of the Senate. He appoints to office, but only when the Senate confirms his nominations.

The power to convene Congress; to grant reprieves and pardons; to temporarily fill vacancies in office; to give information and make recommendations to Congress, and to receive ambassadors, comprise about all the President can legitimately do, without the concurrence of one or both branches of the Federal Legislature, and for illegitimate acts, he can be impeached by the House before the Senate. The judiciary, it is true, is independent. Its members hold office during good behavior; but the direct operation of their decisions is only on the particular case in issue. The judges cannot legislate at all, and can only execute their edicts by the arm of officers appointed by the President and Senate.

Thus it would seem that by the wisdom of our ancestors, the Constitution was framed to be one of complete checks and balances; to preserve the rights of the States, and the property and liberty of the citizen; to prevent the encroachment of one department upon the other; and to insure that neither States nor people should suffer material injury from the Federal Government, until all three departments united in the wrong; until a Senate merely confirmed executive mandates; until Congress should be a willing abettor of executive wrong, and a venial judiciary should surrender its independence to both the other branches.

Under what wrongs do we now rest, emanating from

the Federal Government? Certainly no legislative enactments; because the South has been for years back
guiding and directing the enactments that have been
passed; nor unless the South deserts its post can these
enactments be touched within the next four years. We
have a stringent fugitive slave law, and even Lincoln says
we are entitled to it, and it shall be enforced. As far as
Federal legislation can do it, Utah, New Mexico, Kansas
and Nebraska, have been opened to our peculiar institutions; nor has any Southern member (except Governor
Brown) asked, nor has the Democracy allowed, that the
adverse legislative action of the Territory of Kansas
should be repealed. So far as Federal legislation is concerned, the South has no just complaint. Nor can it
complain of judicial encroachment. The Dred Scott decision is a tower of strength, and must remain so.

But the secessionist will reply: "Abolitionism has
obtained control over one department of the Government.
It has elected a President." The answer is easy, my
friend. The Constitution was designed to apply to precisely such a case. Not merely is the President powerless
except to convene Congress if he chooses, to grant reprieves and to fill temporarily any vacancies that may
occur in office, but the wheels of Government can also,
under the Constitution, be stopped upon him at once, by
both Senate and House, unless he pursues a National and
conservative course. If to carry out the purpose of the
Abolition faction, he selects his advisers and officers from
its ranks, let the Senate perform its duty firmly, and say,

it shall not be done. If he is a Republican, it is Democratic and Opposition. If he nominates bad men, it can
reject them. It can sit in the Senate Chamber from
March 4, 1861, until the day of its next session, and
President Lincoln cannot free himself from its constitutional control. If he is true to faction, let the Senate be
true to the country. It should be the glory of its members that they are sentinels on the watchtower, and only
traitors will desert their post in the presence of the
enemy. Let the Senate tell the President frankly, "You
must nominate conservative and National men, or we will
reject your nominations. If it leaves you without a Cabinet, and the country with only a part of its officers—so
be it."

He cannot remove one from office during the session of
the Senate, except by appointing another to office, and
that can only be done with the Senatorial consent. Here
is the very check the Constitution provides; here is one
safety of the South. Let it be cherished and exercised ;
not abandoned or neglected! Mr. Lincoln is then powerless for mischief, without the Senate's consent or conni-
vance, until December, 1861. He may have the empty
honor of being commander-in-chief, but he cannot declare
war or call out the militia; he may nominate, but cannot
appoint; he may negotiate, but cannot make a treaty.

We are also safe after December, 1861. At that time
he meets an anti-Republican Congress. For legislative
purpose he and his faction are powerless during its term.
Nay, more; should he persist in using executive influ-

ence to carry out the combination which the North has attempted to make against the South, besides refusing to repeal existing legislation, or to listen favorably to legislative recommendations he may make, Congress can, if necessary, adopt that last and most efficient check which a British Parliament has upon an administration it detests —*it can stop the supplies.* If it stop the wheels of Government temporarily—better that, than to dissolve the Union, while one reasonable chance is left for its maintenance. The President and the North must give way, or the Government will be compelled to pause; it can go on again when, and only when a spirit of justice and Constitutional equality resumes its sway in executive councils and in Northern legislative halls.

These are checks, legitimate, constitutional, allowable; which the South now holds; which she voluntarily abandons, if she secedes. Has she exhausted them? Has she yet tried them? If she has not, is she justifiable in at once adopting the last resort of sovereigns? It will be folly; it will be madness; it will be criminal, if she does.

But we shall be told that these doings will only postpone the issue two, or perhaps, four years, and then the South will be weaker. It is a great mistake. The South will then be stronger, because she will be united. Nine millions of intelligent people never can be weak. Resist now, secede now, and we are divided here at home! It will not do for forty thousand men, by a popular vote, to declare thirty thousand fellow-citizens traitors, or to make them unwilling or dissatisfied friends. To be strong, we must be united; to be united, we must be right; and we cannot be right in making a revolution until we have exhausted all the remedies the present Constitution gives.

But we shall be stronger another way. In the meantime, a convention of all the States can be called; not a sectional, but a National body. There the rightful demands of the South can be presented; there the fifteen States can tell their eighteen sisters that under the Constitution the latter have no right to combine, and will not be allowed to combine, against them; that the combination, while it lasts, shall be resisted, within the Union and under the Constitution, by every means the latter allows. They can tell them that it is not the man, Lincoln, they fear, but the principle, combination to aggress, which they resist; that Government must and shall stop unless the President acts Nationally; that if that combination goes further, and obtains possession of the legislative department, as well as of the executive, then, the present Constitution having proved inefficient to protect the principle of equality among the States, new guarantees must be yielded by the North, or the compact of Union must be dissolved by joint consent. In these and such measures, we shall be united at the South; we shall present one firm and united front to the North, instead of as now jarring and distracted counsels.

Nay, more; the popular majority of Republicanism at the North, over all its opponents, is but small—perhaps hardly 300,000, in a poll of nearly 3,500,000. Will not the conservative men there again rally, when they realize what we are doing under the Constitution to resist aggression, and that if those endeavors fail, what we shall do outside of its influences and commands? Precipitation and rashness will weaken our cause and our influence. A manly determination to resist within the Union, and under the great organic law, as long as resistance can be efficacious, will commend itself to every patriot heart that respects the Constitution and loves the Union, and that does not desire the Government to become a final wreck.

We shall be no worse off then than now, as far as the North is concerned. At home, we shall be better off, because we shall be united. We shall have the glory and the pride of being right; of having exhausted all the protective, peaceful and legitimate means the Constitution affords, before resorting to those extra and ultra constitutional remedies which only become rightful when absolutely necessary.

These ideas have been thrown together hastily. We ask for them a patient and attentive perusal. We all owe our country much; and most of all, to think well and listen to all that can be said before we strike a blow at her continued existence. We hope to be able, on Tuesday next, to present to our readers other thoughts in connection with the above, and in a more carefully prepared and elaborate form.

4

[From the Natchez Daily Courier, Nov. 21, 1860.]

HAVE WE EXHAUSTED OUR CONSTITUTIONAL REMEDIES?

NUMBER TWO.

THE AGGRESSIONS WE COMPLAIN OF.

The South, we fear, (or at least too large a number of its good and thinking men,) is acting upon an impulse, rather than from sound judgment and clear deliberation. Rash men are getting ahead even of their own States; inflaming public sentiment, rather than reasoning with it; and driving it on, rather than guiding it. While yet no State has acted in its sovereign capacity, we find members of Congress and United States officers throwing up their offices, raising colonial flags, wearing colonial cockades, and doing every act possible, short of actual treason, to show their contempt for the authority or the perpetuity of the Union. Here, in the Southwest, the great danger is not that Mississippi or Louisiana will of themselves prefer revolution, but that the secession of one State will almost unavoidably drag others into the vortex of disunion. The lower tier of Southern States is so linked together in feeling, and so excited at the stand the North has seen fit to take, that however diverse or antagonistic their interests may hereafter be, should they attempt a new and distinct government for themselves, the ordinary sympathy that aggression ever produces among those who are its subjects, is having a tendency to place the South, from Georgia to Texas, by the side of Carolina. Deeply as it may be regretted, as a single spark often causes the explosion of a mine, so one single rash movement may convert a half-dozen of yet conservative States into open and avowed revolutionary organizations.

Can this be avoided? We believe it can. How? By good men avoiding extremes, by counselling prudence instead of rashness, and by a careful examination of the question as to whether we have yet remedies within the Union, and under the Constitution, for the evils that at present surround the country. If we have them, as yet untried but still powerful, let us not give up a country that a Washington founded, and a long line of patriots, consecrated to "Liberty and Union, now and forever, one and inseparable."

To ascertain precisely the nature of the aggression made upon the South, and the means within the Constitution for its successful overthrow, our readers must permit an historical retrospect.

Comparatively a few years have elapsed—hardly more than a generation—since undeniably the sentiment of the Christian world was against the institution of slavery. England and France abolished it within their dominions. Here in the United States, even at the South, it was generally acknowledged to be an evil—made the best of rather than encouraged—excused, rather than justified. The anti-slavery sentiment commenced its attack upon the institution by appealing to the religious feeling, and by denying that Christians could rightfully hold or enjoy that species of property. The self-interest of the Christians and church members of the South at length prompted their examination of the subject—to know whether this was so or not. And what was the result? Let us answer it in the words of Dr. F. A. Ross :

"Speaking, then, from that region where '*cotton is king*,' I affirm, contrary as my opinion is to that most common in the South, that the slavery agitation has accomplished and will do great good. I said so to ministerial and political friends, twenty-five years ago. I have always favored the agitation—just as I have always countenanced discussion upon all subjects. I felt that the slavery question needed examination. I believed it was not understood in its relations to the Bible and human liberty. Sir, the light is spreading North and South. The political controversy, however fierce and threatening, is only for power. But the moral agitation is for the harmony of the Northern and Southern mind, in the right interpretations of Scripture on this great subject, and, of course, for the ultimate union of the hearts of all sensible people to fulfill God's intention—to bless the white man and the black man in America. I am sure of this. I take a wide view of the progress of the destiny of this vast empire. I see God in America. I see him in the North and in the South. I see him more honored in the South to-day than he was twenty-five years ago; and that that higher regard is due mainly to the agitation of the slavery question. Do you ask how? Why, sir, this is the how: Twenty-five years ago the religious mind of the South was leavened by wrong Northern training, on the great point of the right and wrong of slavery. Meanwhile, powerful intellects in the South, following the mere light of a healthy good sense, guided by the common grace of God, reached the very truth of this great matter—namely, that the relation of the master and slave is not sin; and that, notwithstanding its admitted evils, it is a connection between the highest and the lowest races of man, revealing influences which may be, and will be, most benevolent for the ultimate good of the master and the slave—conservative on the Union, by preserving the South from all forms of Northern fanaticism, and thereby being a great balance wheel in the working of the tremendous machinery of our experiment of self-government. This seen result of slavery was found to be in absolute harmony with the Word of God. These men, then, of highest grade of thought, who had turned in scorn from Northern notions, now see, in the Bible, that these notions are false and silly. They now read the Bible, never examined before, with growing respect. God is honored, and His glory will be more and more in their salvation. These are some of the moral consummations of this agitation in the South. The development has been two-fold in the North. On the one hand, some anti-slavery men have left the light of the Bible, and wandered into the darkness until they have reached the blackness of the darkness of infidelity. Other some are following hard after, and are throwing the Bible into the furnace—are melting it into iron, and forging it, and welding it, and twisting it, and grooving it into the shape and significance and goodness and gospel of Sharpe's rifles. Sir, are you not afraid that some of your once best men will soon have no better Bible than that?

"But, on the other hand, many of your brightest minds are looking intensely at the subject, in the same light in which it is studied by the highest Southern reason. Ay. sir, mother England, old fogy as she is, begins to open her eyes."

Self-interest thus taught Christians at the South to examine. Examination of the Bible; of history, sacred and profane; and of the moral economy of the races, convinced them not merely of the lawfulness of the institution of slavery, but that it was one of the instrumentalities of God in enabling man to work out the great problem of humanity. The Southern mind became a unit upon the question. From doubting, it learned to assert the morality and the positive utility of the relation, and by degrees, that feeling has operated upon the North also, until some of its leading minds have been led to the same conclusions.

Fearing the extensions of these views, the anti-slavery sentiment of the North resolved to arouse new agencies. It at once entered the field of politics; and well has it played its game. It has managed to bring within its meshes finally the great majority of the North, and unite almost every Northern State in a combination against the South. Such a combination is the direst blow they could have struck against the Government of their country. Say what we may, the principle of equality among the States is preserved throughout our great organic law. In the Senate, all the States are equal. In the election of a President, Delaware has her two Senatorial added to her one Representative vote; precisely as New York has only her two Senatorial, added to her thirty-three Representative votes. In the House of Representatives, Delaware has only the thirty-third part of New York's influence; in the Electoral College, she exercises one-twelfth part of that influence; in the Senate she is New York's equal. To preserve these rights of the States and these rights of the people; to let sovereign organizations have their due weight in one body, and popular numbers their due weight in another, while the influence of both should be combined in a third, the complex composition of the executive and legislative departments that distinguish our Government was determined on.

Nor can it be doubted that this principle of combination of some States against others—of one section of the Union against the other, (no matter for what purpose,) is the highest attack that can be made upon the spirit of our Constitution. View the case irrespective of the question of slavery! Nine States out of the present thirty-three cast 160 electoral votes of the 303 composing the college—a majority more than sufficient to elect a President. Suppose that those nine should combine together for local or special purposes of their own, to run a Presidential ticket, irrespective of the views and in direct opposition to the wishes of the other twenty-four States, and by their numerical force be able to elect it—parceling out the offices, and avowing that they intended to continue their organization until they—the nine—controlled all legislation over the thirty-three, and then suppose, in addition, that this was done in positive hostility to domestic institutions upon which the twenty-four States depended, and in which their every-day interest was vitally concerned—would not the twenty-four minority States exclaim that this combination was in defiance of the spirit and meaning of the Constitution, and that it must be remedied? Has the North ever looked on the question in this light? It was to such a combination that Mr. Fillmore so eloquently referred in 1856, in his speech at Albany. Said he:

"We see a political party presenting candidates for the Presidency and Vice-Presidency, selected for the first time from the free States alone, with the avowed purpose of electing these candidates by suffrages of one part of the Union only, to rule over the whole United States. Can it be possible that those who are engaged in such a measure can have seriously reflected upon the consequences which must inevitably follow, in case of success? Can they have the madness or the folly to believe that our Southern brethren would submit to be governed by such a Chief Magistrate? Would he not be required to follow the same rule prescribed by those who elected him, in making his appointments? If a man living south of Mason and Dixon's line be not worthy to be President or Vice-President, would it be proper to select one from the same quarter as one of his Cabinet council, or to represent the Nation in a foreign country? Or, indeed, to collect the revenue, or administer the laws of the United States? If not, what new rule is the President to adopt in selecting men for office that the people themselves discard in selecting him? These are serious, but practical questions, and in order to appreciate them fully, it is only necessary to turn the tables upon ourselves. Suppose that the South, having a majority of the electoral votes, should declare that they would only have slaveholders for President and Vice President, and should elect such, by their exclusive suffrages, to rule over us at the North. Do you think we would submit to it? No, not for a moment. And do you believe that your Southern brethren are less sensitive on this subject than you are, or less jealous of their rights? If you do, let me tell you that you are mistaken. And, therefore, you must see that if this sectional party succeeds, it leads inevitably to the destruction of this beautiful fabric reared by our forefathers, cemented by their blood, and bequeathed to us as a priceless inheritance."

But where would the twenty-four States go for a remedy? To the Constitution itself; and they would be encouraged in the search by the writings of the Fathers of that great instrument. Those Fathers saw the tendencies of majorities to usurp power; to aggress upon the spirit, while they adhered to the letter of the law; and they made the Constitution, for this very purpose, a system of checks and balances; so that the rights of the States could be preserved through the Senate; those of the people through the House; and that the usurpations that a combination of States might attempt through the Electoral College, could be overcome by the power the representatives of the State and the people could exercise in the two Houses of Congress, singly or collectively.

In answering the question as to the expedients possible for practically maintaining the necessary partitions of power among the several departments of Government, James Madison, in the Federalist, (No. 71,) *after demonstrating that all provisions exterior to the Constitution were inadequate*, laid down the principle that the defect should be supplied "by so contriving the interior structure of the Government, as that *its several constituent parts may, by their mutual relations, be the means of keeping each other in their proper places.*" And in substantiation of this, he says :

"In the compound Republic of America, the power surrendered by the people is first divided between two distinct governments, (the Federal and the State,) and the portion allotted to each, subdivided among distinct and separate departments. Hence, a double security arises to the rights of the people. The different governments will control each other; *at the same time that each will be controlled by itself.*

"It is of great importance in a republic, not only to guard the society against the oppression of its rulers, but to guard one part of the society against the injustice of the other part. Different interests necessarily exist in different classes of citizens. If a majority be united by a common interest, the right of the minority will be insecure. There are but two methods of providing against this evil; the one, by creating a will in the community independent of the majority, that is, of the society itself; the other, by comprehending in the society so many separate descriptions of citizens, as will render an unjust combination of a majority of the whole very improbable, if not impracticable. The first method prevails in all governments professing an hereditary or self-appointed authority. This is, at best, but a precarious security, because a power independent of the society may as well espouse the unjust views of the major, as the rightful interests of the minor party, and may possibly be turned against both parties. The second method will be exemplified in the Federal Republic of the United States. Whilst all authority in it will be derived from, and dependent on the society, the society itself will be broken into so many parts, interests and classes of citizens, that the rights of individuals, or of the minority, *will be in little danger from interested combinations of the majority.*

With what perfectness of comprehension did the mind of James Madison grasp this difficult question and its only true solution! An hereditary, or absolute authority on the one hand, and a Federal Republic of United States on the other. The former precarious, because independent of society; the latter safe, because derived from the various interests of society itself. Thus derived, each part is a check upon, each part a balance to the other. Shall we give this Federal Republic up, without trying those checks, or resorting to those balances, with the certain prospect before us, that if we do, the only other resort is a monarchy, or a military despotism?

The end no man can foresee. A dark and gloomy cloud hangs over the gulf on whose overhanging edge the Republic now stands. The eye cannot trace its depth ; the judgment fails in resolving its gloom. Nor is the peril of the hour lessened by the reflection that a single arm can precipitate us into the chasm ; nor is the danger less felt, when it is already announced by the Hotspurs of the hour that out of the seceding States is to grow one nation, with State lines obliterated, and of course, monarchy and absolutism at its head.

But of all this, and of further reflections with regard to remedies still existing and untried, under the Constitution and within the Union, we shall have to speak in another article.

[From the Natchez Daily Courier, Nov. 22, 1860.]

HAVE WE EXHAUSTED OUR CONSTITUTIONAL REMEDIES ?

NUMBER THREE.

THE NATURE OF THOSE REMEDIES.

In previous articles we have referred to remedies against Northern Republican aggression, still existing within the Union and under the Constitution ; so far untried, it is true, but yet, for the present at least, entirely efficacious. We allude to the control the Senate has over every appointment to office, and over every treaty negotiated ; and also to the entire control the Congress has over the legislation of the country, embracing every appropriation of money.

These checks upon the executive department are con-

ferred in express and positive terms by the Constitution
upon the Senate and Congress. "The President shall
nominate, and by and with the advice and consent of the
Senate, shall appoint," etc. "All legislative powers
herein granted shall be vested in a Congress of the United
States," etc. "No money shall be drawn from the Treasury, but in consequence of appropriations made by law."
The existing appropriation bills expire with the current
fiscal year; and as it is only during the recess of the
Senate that the President can fill a vacancy by temporary
appointment, and as he cannot dispense with or shorten
the sessions of the Senate, but that body can sit, if it
choose, from March 4, 1861, till the very hour of the
commencement of the next session of Congress, so, in
fact, the whole power of nomination and appointment,
and the whole expenditure of the Government, can be
checked during Mr. Lincoln's term of office, or during
such portion of it as a Senate or a House shall remain
firm in their opposition to the aggressions of the North
upon the South.

It is true that these checks were not given to the Senate or to Congress, to be exercised on trivial occasions,
or for factious purposes; *but they were given, and they are ·
unlimited.* They were confided to the sound discretion of
the Senate and Congress, and the extent, the occasion and
the continuance of their exercise, must be suited to the
emergency of the case. Severe diseases require powerful remedies; and the representatives of the States and
of the people, as they are the sole, so are they the right-

ful judges of when the emergency arises, how great is
that emergency, and the extent of its duration. The
Senate cannot appoint to office; nor can Congress by
itself appropriate money. They are both checked by the
President, who alone can nominate, and whose signature
is essential to the making of a law, except where a two-
thirds majority is obtained in each House of Congress.
That power of nomination and of vetoing, is unlimited;
applies to all cases, and rests with executive discretion
alone. So the power of rejection of nominations, and of
passing appropriation bills, is unlimited in the Senate and
in Congress, and rests solely on *their* discretion.

Says Judge Story, in his Commentaries on the Constitution, § 1531 :

"The President is to nominate, and thereby has the
sole power to select for office ; but his nomination cannot
confer office, unless approved by a majority of the Senate.
His responsibility and theirs is thus complete and distinct.
He can never be compelled to yield to their appointment
of a man unfit for office ; *and, on the other hand, they may
withhold their advice and consent from every candidate who,
in their judgment, does not possess due qualifications for
office.*"

And in the next section Judge Story adds :

"It will be principally with regard to high officers,
such as ambassadors, judges, heads of departments, and
other appointments of great public importance, that the
Senate will interpose to prevent an unsuitable choice.
Their own dignity, and sense of character, *their duty to*

their country, and their very title to office, will be materially dependent upon a firm discharge of their duty on such occasions."

The authors of the Federalist, in No. 76, express their ideas upon the same subject:

"To what purpose, then, require the co-operation of the Senate? I answer, that the necessity of their concurrence would have a powerful, though in general, a silent operation. It would be an excellent check upon a spirit of favoritism in the President, and would tend greatly to prevent the appointment of *unfit characters from State prejudice,* from family connections, from personal attachment, or from a view to popularity.

"He would be both ashamed and afraid to bring forward, for the most distinguished or lucrative stations, candidates *who had no other merit than that of coming from the same State to which he particularly belonged."*

And the author might well have added, *"from the same section!"*

Whether the Senate should have a negative on Presidential appointments, was a question upon which the members of the convention were much divided. John Adams was opposed to it; and a friendly correspondence took place between him and Roger Sherman upon the subject. It is to be found in Pitkin's History of the United States. (II Pitkin's Hist. pp. 285 to 291.) To the objections of John Adams, Roger Sherman (one of the framers of the Constitution) replied, that he esteemed "the provision made for appointments to office to be a matter of very great importance, on which the liberties and safety of the people depended, nearly as much as on legislation. If that was vested in the President alone, he might render himself despotic.

"It appears to me," continued Mr. Sherman, "that *the Senate is the most important branch in the Government, for the aid and support of the Executive, for the securing the rights of the individual States, and the liberties of the people.*" *The Senators being chosen by the Legislatures of the States, and depending on them for re-election, will naturally be watchful to prevent any infringement of the rights of the States.* And the Government of the United States being Federal, and constituted by a number of sovereign States, for the better security of their rights, and advancement of their interests, they may be considered as so many pillars to support it, and by the exercise of the State governments, peace and good will may be preserved in the places most remote from the seat of the Federal Government as well as the centre. I believe this will be a better balance to secure the Government than three independent negatives would be."

The power of the National Legislature (the other check alluded to) is eloquently summed up by the distinguished author first quoted. · (I Story's Com. § 531.)

"The latter (Legislative) has and must have a controlling influence over the executive power, since it holds at its own command all the resources by which a chief magistrate could make himself formidable. It possesses the power over the purse of the Nation, and the property of the people. It can grant or withhold supplies; it can levy or withdraw taxes; it can unnerve the power of the sword by striking down the arm which wields it."

But it may be said that an entire obstruction of the power of appointment, or a stopping of the wheels of Government by refusing supplies, would be factious and in the nature of a revolutionary proceeding. Not at all, *whenever the emergency requires such a remedy to be applied.* Here we have a sectional party endeavoring, under the forms of the Constitution and the letter of the law, to get possession of the Government for sectional purposes. We see a combination of Northern States to annoy and oppress their Southern sisters, in defiance of the spirit of the Constitution, of the objects of the Union, and of the great doctrine of the equality of the States, enunciated in the composition of the Senate and the Electoral Colleges. We see that combination—we might almost say, conspiracy—so far successful as to have obtained control of one department of the Government, and to be intent on obtaining control over the others. Here is a great emergency that must be met; and how? Not by destruction of the Government, or by an extinguishment of the Constitution, but by exercising every power and check under the Constitution, given for our protection.

The North says to the South, "Mr. Lincoln is constitutionally elected, and we avail ourselves of the forms of law (even if against its spirit) to oppress you." Let the South reply, "And we will use the forms of the law, preserving too the spirit of the Constitution, to prevent

5

that oppression.   Mr. Lincoln may be constitutionally elected, but it shall be

" 'A barren sceptre in his grasp,
No son of his succeeding.'

His power of appointment shall be negatived, and supplies refused to carry on the Government, (and it shall be done constitutionally, for the Constitution has given us these checks and these appliances to make your combination and conspiracy fruitless,) until the North returns to its senses and abandons its aggressions, its insults and its outrages.   If you can combine to constitutionally elect a President, we in self-preservation, will exercise the powers granted by the Constitution to check your conspiracy.   You cannot call our conduct factious, for we are fighting faction.   You cannot call it a revolutionary proceeding, for we will but suspend the operation of Government, not extinguish or change it.   You cannot call it a violation of the Constitution; for we are using its letter to check your violations of its spirit."   Thus let the North be answered by the South.

Where do we derive in a great measure our theory of Government, and system of checks and balances.   From the British Constitution; and in its operation there has been many an instance where the House of Commons has fought, and fought successfully the battles of the people. "These are my prerogatives, said Charles I, and I shall exercise them."   They may be your prerogatives," replied the House, "but if you exercise them, it is equally our prerogative to vote or to refuse the supplies."   And for eight years they thus peacefully fought the Crown, and the Crown succumbed; and when, after succumbing and obtaining a vote of the supplies, the Crown again claimed its prerogatives—a revolution cost the monarch his head. Shall we set less value on the undoubted right of the Senate to reject nominations, and of Congress to pass bills or refrain from passing them?

Here, then, the South and its friends have a complete check upon the Republican party. Even in the hour of their triumph, the latter will find themselves chechmated. The Government can be made to pause, only to move on when the rights of the South are acknowledged, and the unfriendly combination of Northern States is surrendered. Such a clogging of the wheels of Government will cause us inconvenience, it is true; but far less than to the North; office holders will have to go without their salaries; but so they would, and their offices too, were there secession and revolution. Private enterprise would, in ninety days, convey mails better than the Government now does, and upon private enterprise would we have to depend in case of secession. We would have in no event greater inconveniences under a suspension than under a dissolution of the Government, while we would be spared the evils of revolution, and the sad reflection that, however justifiably it was done, our hands had destroyed the great work of Washington.

The North could not stand this peaceful, legitimate and constitutional clogging of the wheels of Government. Their commercial and manufacturing interests would be made to feel instantly the power that even a minority possesses. As in the case of the South, self-interest would teach them to examine more closely the Bible and the Constitution, and that the examination would oblige them to be willing conceders of every right the Constitution guarantees, and to become peaceful neighbors and friends, instead of disturbers of domestic quiet, and enemies.

Nor is this idea of a temporary suspension of the active powers of Government strange or novel. There is now a provision by law, authorized by the Constitution, saying what officer shall act as President in case of removal, death, resignation or inability of both President and Vice President; but there is no such provision, (nor in all probability would the Constitution warrant one,) in case a President and Vice President elect should die before the time of taking office, or should decline to accept the offices to which they have been chosen. The official term of the old officers would have expired, and the terms of the new officers would not have commenced; so it would not be a vacancy by death, removal or resignation, but by expiration of the official term of office. Speaking of the possible non-election of President and Vice President at the period prescribed by the Constitution, Judge Story observes: (Vol. II Com., § 1482):

"No absolute dissolution of the Government would constitutionally take place by such a non-election. The only effect would be a suspension of the powers of the executive part of the Government, and incidentally of the legislative powers, until a new election to the Presidency should take place at the next constitutional period; an evil of very great magnitude, but not equal to a positive extinguishment of the Constitution."

In case of the checks to which we have referred, there would not be even a suspension of the powers of Government, but only a clogging of the wheels; an evil far less than that of the extinguishment of the Constitution and the dissolution of the Union.

Let us first exhaust all these constitutional remedies, before we declare for open revolution. If the former are found to be of no avail, then—but not until then—in the language of Madison's letter to Edward Everett, (August, 1830,) "In the event of a failure of every constitutional resort, and an accumulation of usurpations and abuses, rendering passive obedience and non-resistance a greater evil than resistance and revolution, there can remain but one resort, the last of all—an appeal from the cancelled obligations of the constitutional compact, to original rights and the law of self-preservation."

How foolish, then, to see the South throwing away the checks and remedies 'it possesses; to see Senators and Representatives resigning; giving up the Union at once, and letting Black Republicans take possession of the Senate and Congress, as it will have of the Executive! These resigning men are unfaithful to the South; these seceding States are untrue to the Constitution. South Carolina ought not thus to precipitate us into a revolution, or drive us into abandoning faithful allies at the

North; giving up remedies laid down in the Constitution and destroying the great fabric of Government, merely to drift upon a stormy sea of revolution, unprepared, and ignorant of the future.

The words of the Good Book are most applicable: (Acts xxvii : 30, 31):

"And as the shipmen were about to flee out of the ship, when they had let down the boat into the sea, under color as though they would have cast anchors out of the foreship,

"Paul said to the centurion and the soldiers, *Except these abide in the ship, ye cannot be saved.*"

[From the Natchez Daily Courier, Nov. 23, 1860.]

HAVE WE EXHAUSTED OUR CONSTITUTIONAL REMEDIES?

NUMBER FOUR.

THE DISEASE AND ITS REMEDY.

The crisis demands something more than mere temporary remedies. In common parlance, we may as well "meet the bull by the horns." But our grievances are misunderstood; or at least, the main outrage is almost altogether overlooked by us. For instance : we complain of negroes being allowed to vote in Ohio. But have we forgotten that the only objection we can urge is, that they are not citizens of the United States, and that the same legal rule will exclude the unnaturalized white residents of Illinois, Wisconsin and other States, who, with the sanction of law, have been controlling the votes of those States for many years? We complain of the per-

sonal liberty laws of the Northern States, as violative of
the United States Constitution; and so they are; but then
do we recollect that Mississippi has upon her statute book
one law at least (in relation to banks and assignment of
debts due them) which has been declared by the United
States Supreme Court to be unconstitutional, and which
Mississippi still neglects to repeal? Is it a doubtful
matter—this attacking "sovereign States" for establishing or declining to repeal laws? The Federal, if not the
State courts, will do final justice in individual cases; and
it may as well, and truthfully, be at once acknowledged,
that a Vermont creditor can as justly complain of Mississippi for a non-repeal of certain of her laws, as a Mississippi slaveholder can complain of Vermont for her citizens
not looking at the cars on the "underground railroad,"
as they pass by their houses or fields! We complain of
juries in Boston and Chicago, for not being able to convict in fugitive slave cases; but we forget that Charleston
juries also fail to convict in foreign slave-trade cases.
We complain of Northern judges interposing or in-
veighing against the Fugitive Slave law; but we forget
that United States judges in Southern States, after charg-
ing the grand juries on the subject of the foreign slave-
trade, immediately after the adjournment of their courts,
have announced from the same stand, that they should
address their fellow-citizens in opposition to the laws
prohibiting that trade, at candle-light the same evening!
"They who live in glass houses must not cast the first
stone."

We waste time when we talk about the mere annoyance to which our individual property is subjected at the North, when we claim the right to subject property to what inconveniences we please at the South. The principle, and not the amount of the aggression, governs the case. It may be unpleasant for us to have our neighbor wink at, or frown on us, at a distance; but it is the positive attack that compels resistance! The real aggression that has been made upon the South is, not that a man not of its choice has been elected; not that he will distribute offices against its wishes; nominate those it does not like; negotiate treaties it may not approve; recommend measures it may not sanction; *but that the Northern States have entered into a combination among themselves to obtain control over the Government.* We cheerfully submit to the rule of the United States; but not to the rule of a portion of those States. The majority should rule, we grant, and the minority should yield. But the principle upon which this idea is founded is that the assent of each one of the minority has already been given to the act of the majority. A law is binding upon every citizen, not because he personally assented to it, or joined in its enactment, but that the act of all the citizens of a common society is construed to be the act of each one of that society, even if one individual, or the whole ten thousand, is in the minority. "Governments are instituted among men, deriving their just powers from the consent of the governed." It may be an actual, it may be an implied consent; but it can be neither when imposed by one section of a community upon another, even if done by the whole of that section, and they composing a majority. We are, of course, talking about white men. Neither Revelation, the Old or the New; nor history, sacred or profane; nor experience, ancient or modern, ever elevated the black man to an equality with the white.

The people of the several States, in their various State organizations, formed our present National Government. They did so upon the basis of the equality of the States. The people of each State were originally equal,,so far at least as regarded their sovereign capacity to treat, to agree, to negotiate, to adopt, or to consent. They did consent; but it was to a government by the *United* States. The equality of those States entered into the whole structure of the Government. It fashioned the entire composition of the Senate ; it entered into the basis upon which the executive power was erected. That equality is destroyed when a sectional President is elected. Were we a minority in every State—the candidates being run on National issues—we could have no word of objection. Florida only assented to a government in common with New York, when votes, *pro or con*, for the men who were to form the government, could be cast in Florida as well as New York; but who supposes a Lincoln ticket could have been formed in Florida? Hence Florida, and so with all the Southern tier of States, feel that their assent has not been given. They can submit to being in a minority ; but it is destructive of their equality to think that the whole of the majority which is to take the executive, and the legislative, and finally the judicial departments of the Government away from them, reside in one section and they in another.

The idea that a sectional election would be inimical to the continuance of the Union has been long and often acknowledged at the North. It is no new idea. It is a principle that comes home to the North as to the South. Were the cases reversed, how quickly would the cry come up of Southern aggression! Look again at Mr. Fillmore's eloquent expostulation in 1856. Oh, well! but in deep regret that they had not flocked to his standard, may Southern men look to the words of one that then so freely denounced, but who struck with the battle-axe of truth at the very root of the tree of sectionalism, whose leaves are now extending over them, and whose blossoms and fruit they are now trying to avoid!

Abraham Lincoln was not elected by the people of the *United* States as their President. He was elected by the people of seventeen of the States, combined against the institutions of the other fifteen States. Here is the grievance, and here the outrage. His election was the result of a combination—a conspiracy almost—(for the North may as well hear hard words from a Union source as hear them from a secession paper,) among the non-slaveholding States, to obtain control over the slaveholding States. We have no fear but what Mr. Lincoln will make a fair executive officer; he may not purjure himself; he may carry out the fugitive slave law; but all that is not the question. His sectional notions about the Territories and the District can all be overcome by National majorities in Congress. Nor do we regret even if his election should stimulate examination into the great question of slavery; whether it be of Divine institution and permission; whether it be consonant with the law of love to our neighbor, and the Golden Rule; whether it be adapted to the circumstances of human condition, and one of the stones in the great foundation of its structure. One thing we know; neither examination of the Bible, nor of history, nor of physiology, nor of law, nor of ethics, has ever resulted in aught but a conviction that the institution of slavery was permitted by Divine rule, and approved by human experience as a necessary law of races.

But none of this is really material to the purpose. The election of Mr. Lincoln is the consummation of a political conspiracy, undertaken partly for partisan, partly for sectional, and partly for fanatical purposes; but all with the intent that eighteen Northern States should rule over fifteen Southern States. The principle upon which the assent of the minority is presumed to be given to the acts of a majority, was ignored in his election; because the people of each State were admitted into the Union as the equal of the people of each other State; and no election ought to be consummated where the assent of Florida, Texas and Arkansas could not have been as well implied to the election as that of New York, Pennsylvania and Ohio. Except just upon the border, no Lincoln ticket was attempted to be run in the Southern States. The

Chicago nominations were announced as sectional; they were advocated as such. No tint of Nationality was given to the picture. Thank God, we are personally without the stains of having advocated a sectional or secession ticket. If such there were, it came under the same ban, and was objectionable on the same principles; and it died the death it should have done. But that does not prevent us warring against sectionalism at the North. We have few tears to shed over the grave of the one, and nothing but sorrow and indignation to express as the car of the other passes along in its triumph.

The position we take is above that of mere disappointment. We have endured men we as little liked personally as Mr. Lincoln. We know, with a Senate and House opposed to him, he can do but little mischief, comparatively; but the principle established in his election is, that a combination or conspiracy of States can be formed to obtain possession of the Government, and it has already consummated its triumph in Lincoln's election. Against such a principle we fight, and shall fight ever. We fight it within the Union, while it lasts, (and may it last always!) and we think the Constitution enables us to fight it successfully. The wisest and best men of the North, unless we resort to rash measures, will make war for that principle alongside of us of the South. It is not a sectional, but a National principle. It appeals not exclusively to the slaveholding, but as well to the non-slaveholding region. If our forefathers would not consent to taxation without being represented in the taxing body,

so we are unwilling to be represented by a President not
elected by or with the consent, express or implied, of all
the States. It is a principle we cannot surrender; one
that rises above the personal qualifications of Mr. Lincoln,
the probabilities of his adherence to his oath of office, or
the promises or assurances made to us of the South, that
State liberty laws shall be repealed, or United States
laws be enforced.

There are but two ways within the Union that this
great difficulty can be met. The one is by the Northern
electoral colleges being made to see the error of their
path. The Constitution never designed the electors to
be the mere tools of party, nor does the morality of par-
tisanship force them to obey the edicts of a faction, when
the ruin of a country is certain to ensue. They were
elected as State electors, not as Lincoln electors; and if
there is patriotic spirit enough left in twenty-four of
them, they will reject the party ties that bind them, and
yet vote for their country. *It is within the power now of
the electors for Northern States to give peace to the country.*
We ask them neither to vote for Breckinridge, or Bell, or
Douglas; but they can so vote collectively for two men,
from different sections, and irrespective of caucus or convention arrangements, as will break the force of sectional
combinations, and render them hereafter impotent. What
a glorious monument would they erect to their own fame!
Let them give to their country the trust committed them
by party! "More honored in the breach than in the
observance," their votes deposited for a conservative man,

irrespective of party or of section, would crown their names with unfading laurel! "Not that I loved Cæsar less, but that I loved Rome more," would be their full justification. .

The only other way to meet the difficulty is the resignation of the sectional President and Vice President; or in case they assume the reins of Government, the assumption by the Senate and House of every power, and to its fullest extent, that the Constitution affords. We have already shown what those powers are, and that they are ample for the purpose; that they are given, and are unlimited; that they were given for use, and to an extent commensurate and co-extensive with the exigency of the time and the occasion; that a sectional President must be taught that he can be controlled by a National House and Senate, and that he will be so controlled; that nominations can remain unconfirmed; appropriation bills unpassed; and all the ordinary machinery of Government suspended, unless he and his party unconditionally surrender the sectional position which they hold.

All this can be done within the Union, and under the Constitution, agreeably to its forms and in obedience to its spirit. We need not secede; we need not revolutionize. No standing armies are necessary; no unconstitutional laws justifiable. We have a full and perfect control over the sectional madness of the day, and we are mad ourselves unless we exercise it.

Let us say to our Senators, you were placed there as

were the Consuls of the Roman Republic—"*Ne quid Respublica detrimenti capiat;*" to see that the Republic shall receive no harm, during his term of service, is the Senator's bounden duty. The great principle of the equality of the States is confided to his keeping. If he neglects or abandons it,

> "May life's unblessed cup for him
> Be drugged with treacheries to the brim."

[From the Natchez Daily Courier, Nov. 24, 1860.]

HAVE WE EXHAUSTED OUR CONSTITUTIONAL REMEDIES?

NUMBER FIVE.

WHERE ARE WE HURRYING TO?

We have written the previous articles under the general heading, "Have we Exhausted our Constitutional Remedies?" to very little purpose, if the reader has failed to perceive the two great objects we have in view —*first*, to show tersely and clearly the nature of the grievance the Southern States complain of, in the election of Mr. Lincoln; *secondly*, to point out the ample remedies provided in the Constitution and under the Union, which the South and the Nation have for precisely such a grievance.

First—The aggression rises above and beyond mere annoyances, obstructions to law, unkind words, or election of men we do not like, and upon principles we do not approve. It reaches the very heart of the Government itself. It is, that a conspiracy has been formed by certain of co-equal States to get possession of the Government for their own peculiar purposes. It involves the question of the equality of the States. It is one that the North is equally interested in with the South; that Rhode Island has the same stake in determining rightfully, that Arkansas or Florida has. Can certain States, great or small, combine and conspire together, for any objects whatever, to obtain possession of the Government, and thus lord it, under the Constitution, over the remaining States? Ask the comparatively feeble New England States, if the West and the Southwest thus conspired to strike at their peculiar interests, whether they would not consider it violative of the spirit of the Constitution, and to be resisted to the very extent of all the checks against such a combination that the letter of the Constitution gave? The greatest and wisest men of the North, without reference to their peculiar views on the subject of slavery, have already testified to the strength of this position. Some of them, who brought to the subject the strongest prejudices against our domestic institution, stand with us and by us upon the great principle that States ought not to combine against States, their equals in the Union, nor section against section. Ours is the National position; *let us not abandon the Nationality of that position.* It is a position which a million and a half of voters in the North have already virtually taken. They stand by the side of thirteen hundred thousand voters in the South in asserting the principle that States must not combine against States, nor section conspire against section. Why leave this to stand on lower or less National ground?

However much and rightfully the South may object to Mr. Lincoln's views, or to the views of the party that sustains him, it cannot be united in resistance to his inauguration, because they know that his election was and his inauguration will be in compliance with every form of law. But they can and will say, unanimously, and every fair-thinking and right-minded man at the North, free from mere fanatic prejudice, will join them in asserting that the State combination against State, or sectional combination against section, is violative of the spirit of the Constitution, subversive of its aims, and destructive of the very principle upon which alone it can, or ought to work successfully. Such a combination, if allowed to succeed, neither forms a more perfect Union, nor establishes justice, nor insures domestic tranquility, nor provides for the common defence, nor promotes the general welfare, nor secures the blessings of liberty to ourselves and our posterity—the great and noble objects for which the people of the United States ordained and established the Constitution.

Second—The remedy we propose is not secession or disunion, nor an extinguishment of the Government. This is to abandon at once, and without a struggle, the citadel of freedom to foes who now only have possession of the outer gate. "Fight on and fight ever," should be our motto. If we give up—and secession and disunionism are only giving up the contest—what have we in prospect? We now have a powerful minority in the North, almost a majority—we make them hostile foreigners.

6

We now have rights and property under the Conststution —we abandon them all. We now have a self-supporting Government—to commence a new one we insure the necessity of a taxation, at once unnecessary, onerous and excessive. We have a border on the Ohio river, north of which the laws we think necessary for protection are executed as far as Federal authority can execute them, and with the assurance that if we only exert the checks the Constitution grants, the pressure on Northern public opinion will make those laws observed as far as State authority can influence—but if we dissolve the Union there is no Federal law to operate, no Northern opinion to influence. We give the advantage to the North of saying—

"We held but slack allegiance to this hour,
But now our sword 's our own."

Shall we give up all, or shall we stand by our flag? Secession is submission and abandonment of our rights. Resistance in the Union is standing by our colors. Will we allow our Senators and Representatives thus to abandon their posts? How beautifully comes over the remembrance of the reader of Sir Walter Scott the tribute paid to the faithful dog of Sir Kenneth :

"It was midnight, and the moon rode clear and high in heaven, when Kenneth of Scotland stood upon his watch on St. George's Mount beside the banner of England—a solitary sentinel, to protect the emblem of that nation against the insults which might be meditated among the thousands whom Richard's pride had made his enemies. Beside the banner and staff lay the large stag hound, on whose vigilance Kenneth trusted for early warning of the approach of any hostile footstep. The noble animal seemed to understand the purpose of the watch."

Kenneth left. "Watch thou here, and let no one approach!" But when he returned he found that the standard of England had vanished, but that the spear on which it floated lay broken on the ground, and that beside it lay the faithful hound in the agonies of death!

Shall the Senate of the United States prove less true to the banner of the Constitution and the Union than the hound to that of England? "A dog who dies discharging his duty is better than a man who survives the desertion of it."

But what have we proposed as a full remedy? Simply that the Senate and the House shall remain faithful to their trust. If the people, who made the Senate and the House, abandon for a time the standard of their country, let that Senate and House watch and ward it till the people—their masters—return from their delusion. Let the hound of Sir Kenneth again, even in his dying moment, point out to his loved owner the only post of duty —the true path of glory.

Let the Senate, which meets the very instant of Lincoln's inauguration, tell him, frankly, "We are at our post; we will not confirm your sectional nominations; we will not ratify any treaties you negotiate. It is an ultra remedy we propose to administer; but the disease involves the very life of the Constitution and the existence of the Union. The remedy will be efficacious, and we will administer it in heroic doses. A combination has elected you, in defiance of the spirit of the Constitution. The principle of the expressed or implied consent of the minority to the action of the majority we cannot surrender, and that principle was violated in your election. It is a fundamental principle, and we will not abandon it. We can, within the letter of the Constitution, emasculate the virility of your appointing power, and it shall be done until the legislative power of the country meets."

Let Congress tell Lincoln, when it meets in December, 1861, "What the Senate has done in the recess, we shall repeat, and continuously, till March 4, 1863. We lie beside the flag of our country, and the hour of desertion shall be the hour of death. We vote no supplies; we pass no laws. Our position may be passive, but no sectional man touches the staff on which that banner floats, while life survives."

These are remedies within the Union and under the Constitution. Let the Government pause, but not be destroyed; let its functions be suspended, but not extinguished; let the flame grow dim, but not be altogether quenched!

If we abandon these remedies we have under the Constitution, surrender the protection of the Union, or give up the rights that we have under it—what is left to us? What does secession forebode? What does disunion promise? View it in its most favorable light! Grant that all the border States, Maryland, Kentucky and Missouri, follow the banner we bear, and from which so many stars will have to be erased. Ah! well did the gifted Prentiss prophesy that all the stripes would remain behind! Let fifteen Southern States unite in forming a Southern Confederacy! Will Delaware, Maryland, Virginia, Kentucky or Missouri, grant us of the "Cotton States" a representation for three-fifths of our negroes? Will the interests of Baltimore, Richmond, Louisville, St. Louis or Memphis, be identical with ours? Will the rule that Charleston will impose, either for foreign commerce or for domestic relations, be that which the Southwest will relish? How long will mutuality of interest in one species of property, keep together those who are dissimilated with respect to all other species?

When Charleston demands free trade, and New Orleans a duty on sugar; and Kentucky and Missouri a duty on iron or hemp; when Louisiana, Mississippi and Missouri are taught to feel that theirs are democratic States, and South Carolina an oligarchical one; that universal suffrage controlls the West, but that in the East of the new Confederacy, the people are not permitted to vote except on property qualifications, and then never for their Governors or Presidential Electors; when they realize that a purely aristocratical State has made them rashly surrender undoubted rights, powers and property, in a great Government; how long will the Southern Confederacy last? "*Millions for defence, but not a cent for tribute,*" is a great maxim; but where shall we get our millions for war, when we can secure the results for which we fight, within the Union, and without the expenditure of a dollar? How will Mississippi feel in being taxed a million or two, for expenses she could have avoided by remaining in the Union, and by fighting for the Southern cause under the Constitution, and that successfully; when by abandoning that cause she surrenders the objects she is called on to fight for?

A thousand such reflections come over the mind, that neither editorial time nor our readers' patience will admit further dwelling upon. In the Union we can fight for our rights; by going out of it we surrender. Under the Constitution we have remedies; by passing from under its ægis we refuse them. In vulgar parlance, we cut off our nose to spite our face. We commit suicide, for fear we shall die a natural death.

The newly confederated South will soon become dissatisfied. The Northern tier of States will find their interests diverse from those of the Southern tier. The former will become the Northern States of the new Confederacy. The passions of the hour will soon pass away, and self-interest will dictate political action. The slaves of Maryland, Virginia, Kentucky, Missouri, will be sent South for sale; the present line of the Ohio river will be transferred to waters or imaginary lines fully four degrees lower; and then the same conflict, which by our own action we shall have consented to be called "irrepressible," will be transferred to the fields and plains of the extreme sunny South. Could William H. Seward wish any better "Helper," to say nothing about his book, than the aid our secessionists are lending him? And what will be the final result? another split and a second secession! If the border States now refuse co-operation, this final result will be only the more quickly consummated.

The end, at any rate, will be a Confederated Government of the Southern tier of States. The cotton States (to use Mr. Yancey's phrase) will have been precipitated into revolution, for it is with them only that the effective movement he has been so long designing, can be hoped for. Self-preservation will necessitate the employment of the severest measures. Where will the framers of the new Government find the model for their political action? Upon what, if any, green spot amid the waste of waters, will the dove from their ark of safety rest? Upon none, if it seeks a republic! It will return home—and what a home!

The old Confederation will have proved to be a failure. The Union and the Constitution will also have proved to be a failure. Freedom will have fled, or else have stood aside,

> "——as if, in plaintive notes,
> To weep her own decline."

And what is left? Well may we shudder when we reflect! From the angry waters of revolution, made to boil and bubble up by fires of passion and of rage, there can only arise the dim spectre of despotism. The interests of the "cotton States" will be one; but if the

Union, the Constitution, and a Southern Confederacy shall have alike failed, (and the latter must fail if the other two be abandoned,) these States can only be kept together by a stronger force than Constitutions will vouchsafe or popular will sanction.   Yes, out of the seething mass of revolution will arise that spectre of despotism—and as all the characteristics of our people are military, it will be a military despotism—glorious it may be in its luminosity, as it breaks upon the sight, but degenerating into the darkness of the political night to which it will inevitably hasten.

Men of the South!   Are you prepared for such results? Are you willing to give up all to accomplish nothing? Our fathers built up a great temple of liberty.   Its aisles reach from ocean to ocean.   Its courts are wide and large enough to embrace the people of the earth.   Upon the dome of that temple the smile of the Almighty has so far given the effulgence of His rays.   Within that temple stands the altar of freedom, and daily and hourly the smoke of sacrifice arises.   Shall *we* put out the light upon those altars?   If we do, we can never reillumine it.

The great master of the human heart has told how this idea operated upon the husband who fancied himself injured, but who was not injured in reality.   He came into the bedchamber of his wife, as she lay sleeping with the light beside her ; and we quote his words :

"Put out the light, and then—put out the light!
If I quench thee, thou flaming minister,
I can again thy former light restore,
Should I repent me :—but once put out thine,

Thou cunning's pattern of excelling nature,
I know not where is that Promethean heat,
That can thy light relume. When I have plucked thy rose,
I cannot give it vital growth again ;
It needs must wither."

Men of the South, "let us smell it on the tree !"

————

"DON'T GIVE UP THE SHIP !"

The following communication from the pen of Mr.
Barker, first appeared in the Picayune in December,
1860, shortly after the close of the memorable political
struggle, the result of which entailed on us our present
calamitous condition. The communication was univer-
sally read at the time, and commanded very marked
attention :

[Communicated.]

"DON'T GIVE UP THE SHIP !"—We proudly proclaim
to the world the justice of our cause. Nothing should
be done to tarnish its lustre.

We have had a severe political contest, in which, owing
to the peculiar organization of our Confederacy, we were
defeated, but not vanquished, as a majority of near one
million of legal voters cast their ballots against the candidates elected for President and Vice President, while a
majority of both Houses of Congress was secured to the
friends of law and order.

For this we are greatly indebted to our Northern
friends, who fought our battle valliantly. Can we abandon them to the tender mercies of our opponents without
committing an act of direct, palpable injustice ? I say
we cannot. As patriots, men of honor and lovers of

justice, we are bound to fight on with them, side by side, until we can form a separate Confederacy of the slave States. Seceding singly would be to leave our opponents a majority in both Houses of Congress, in possession of all the funds, property and machinery of the Government, obliging us to appeal to them for a fair participation therein.

Our opponents are the seceders, by their opposition to the decision of the Supreme Court, and their personal liberty laws.

If they do not repeal those laws, and carry the provisions of the Constitution into full and fair effect, they should not be allowed to have a representative in either House of Congress or to vote for a President or Vice President.

In place of withdrawing from the Confederacy singly, we should fight on and demand a law for a convention to amend the Constitution, giving the election of President and Vice President to the people.

All free white citizens of the United States over the age of twenty-one, who are entitled to vote for State legislators, to be entitled to vote therefor; one of the candidates to be a citizen and resident of a slave State, the other of a free State, to hold office for ten years, and not to be eligible for a second term.

This latter clause would give what we most want, stability to our institutions, avoiding those frequent convulsions which always prove destructive to business of every description.

New Orleans has suffered many millions of dollars from the anticipation of a dissolution of the Union; what would be the ruinous effect of the reality no man can tell; time only can solve that question, if so dire a resort becomes necessary.

If the advocates of secession would enlighten the public mind as to how the proposed change will restore those losses, and how the mechanics and laborers who are thrown out of employment are to be fed, under the separate organization of the States, they will better know how to estimate such a measure; and if they will inform the friends of our domestic institutions how we are to get better security under a separate government, or under a Confederacy of the slave States, than we have under our present Constitution, we shall better know how to estimate their patriotic labors in bringing about a change.

The slave States, if they consult their own interest, will adhere together and take no separate action.

Whatever a majority decide on, the minority will agree to, and thus present an undivided front, which cannot be resisted; while any other course will greatly weaken our position.

It is too late to inquire whether slavery be a blessing or a curse. It was entailed on us by Great Britain contrary to our wishes; it cannot be abolished, and we have to submit to it. Our slaves—four millions—are the most religious, industrious and happy class of workingmen in the world. To change their position would do them incalculable mischief.

The prosperity of the South depends on its existing institutions, hence our jealousy at all interference.

                                        JACOB BARKER.

New Orleans, Dec. 20, 1860.

———

It had been determined by the advocates of secession that a Convention should be called. An election for delegates was held. The contest was close. Mr. Barker took a very active part against secesssion. It resulted in their favor, in the city of New Orleans, by about four hundred majority. Had it been otherwise, it is believed that the vote of the city members, with its moral influence, would have induced the Convention to reject the fatal ordinance. Notwithstanding the decided majority of those elected, it is believed that the popular vote of the State was averse to secession—the returns never having been published, we are unable to speak with certainty.

Near eight thousand registered voters declined to attend the polls. They were mostly those who worshiped at the churches of the Rev. Dr. Leacock, of the Episcopal, and of Dr. Palmer, of the Presbyterian faith. Those two gifted and eloquent divines preached very impressive sermons immediately preceding the election, which were well calculated to prejudice the public mind, and, beyond all question, decided the fate of the State, and consequently the great National question at issue. We have no disposition to take a mistaken view of those sermons, and if we could put our hand on them, would give them in full in these sheets—to which end we have made many inquiries, without finding a single copy. They will be added in an appendix, if they come to hand in season.

The Convention met, and made hot haste to pass the secession ordinance. It was resisted by the Hon. Mr. Jas. G. Taliaferro, a member from the parish of Catahoula, and the Hon. Mr. J. Ad. Rozier, a member from New Orleans, who made very able although ineffectual speeches against secession; and, on the final passage, the members of the Louisiana Convention voted *seriatim* and in the alphabetical order of their names. The Honorable James. G. Taliaferro, the delegate from Catahoula, when called in his turn, made the following remarks :

Mr. President—Several of the gentlemen who have preceded me took occasion to express their strong attachment to Louisiana, and the deep interest they feel in her prosperity and welfare, and offer these as the leading reasons which induce them to support this monstrous measure. Sir, I have lived in Louisiana more than fifty years, and from early childhood. All my interests, associations and feelings are closely connected with her well being. All that I have of worldly goods, and of worldly hopes and aspirations are centered in Louisiana. The soil of Louisiana covers the bones of very many of those who were near and dear to me; and her soil, at a day not now distant, will envelope my own. Sir, I am behind no man in attachment to Louisiana. I am unable to see that higher and grander position which gentlemen say Louisiana is to assume by the act of secession. Clouds and darkness, rather, are before me. The dimness of age, perhaps, prevents me from penetrating the gloom and seeing the bright skies and green fields beyond. In the exercise of my best judgment, and under my honest convictions of the ruinous tendency of this measure, I must pronounce it an act of madness and of folly. Sir, I vote *nay!* And, presenting the following protest, asked leave to have it spread on the journal, which was refused:

PROTEST.

The delegate from the parish of Catahoula opposes, unqualifiedly, the separate secession of Louisiana from the Federal Union, and asks leave to place upon the records of the Convention his reasons for that opposition. They are as follow:

I oppose the act of secession because, in my deliberate judgment, the wrongs alleged as the cause of the movement might be redressed under the Constitution by an energetic execution of the laws of the United States, and that, standing on the guarantees of the Constitution, in the Union, Southern rights might be triumphantly maintained under the protection and safeguards which the Constitution affords.

Because, in secession, I see no remedy for the actual and present evils complained of, and because the *prospective* evils depicted so gloomily may never come; and if they should, the inalienable right to resist tyranny and opression might then be exercised as well and successfully as now.

Because I see no certainty that the seceding States will ever be confederated again; none that the border States will secede at all; and if they should, I see no reliable ground for believing that they would incorporate themselves with the Gulf or cotton States in a new government. I see no surety, either, that Texas will unite with them.

Because the Gulf or cotton States alone, were they to unite in a separate confederacy, would be without the elements of power, indispensable in the formation of a government to take a respectable rank among the nations of the earth.

Because I believe that peaceable secession is a right unknown to the Constitution of the United States; that it is a most dangerous and mischievous principle in the structure of any government; and when carried into the formation of the contemplated Confederacy of the Gulf States will render it powerless for good, and complete its incapacity to afford the people permanent security for their lives, liberty and property.

Because it is my solemn and deliberate conviction that the distraction of the Southern States by separate secession will defeat the purpose it is intended to accomplish, and that its certain results will be to impair instead of strengthening the security of Southern institutions.

Because the proper status of Louisiana is with the border States, with which nature has connected her by the majestic river which flows through her limits; and because an alliance in a weak government with the Gulf States east of her is unnatural and antagonistic to her obvious interests and destiny.

Because, by separate secession, the State relinquishes all its rights within the Government, it surrenders its equal rights to the common territories—to the vast public domain of the United States, and to the property of every kind belonging to the Nation. And for this reason I oppose secession as being emphatically submission.

Because secession may bring 'anarchy and war, as it will assuredly bring ruinous exactions upon property, in the form of direct taxation, a withering blight upon the prosperity of the State, and a fatal prostration of all its great interests.

Because, the act of dissolving the ties which connect Louisiana with the Federal Union is a revolutionary act, that this Convention is, of itself, without legitimate power to perform. Convened without authority from the people of the State, and refusing to submit its action to them for their sanction in the grave and vital act of changing their government, this Convention violates the great and fundamental principle of American government, that the will of the people is supreme.

JAMES G. TALIAFERRO,
Delegate from the Parish of Catahoula.

Mr. Barker witnessed with deep regret and serious apprehension the frightful secession feeling which continued to pervade this community, yet he did hope until the last moment, that the horrors of war might be avoided. For the purpose of staying, if possible, the wild storm that threatened to desolate the whole country, and considering that the first hostile gun fired would kindle a quenchless flame, immediately before the fatal attack on Fort Sumter he caused to be published in the Picayune, of the 17th of January, 1861, the following article:

Editors of the Picayune—Your remarks about blockades and embargoes may lead your readers to apprehend further embarrassments in the commerce of New Orleans than await us.

It is not believed that those in power, or coming into power, at Washington in March, will resort to either, or cause a hostile gun to be fired unless attacked. They will doubtless allow free importation as well as free exportation from the seceding States, requiring all vessels from foreign ports with dutiable goods to call at a port where the laws of the United States are recognized, and pay the duties on such goods, after which to be allowed to pursue their voyage as originally intended. Beyond this, it is understood the seceding States will be allowed to pursue their own course.

As to France, England or any other Power permitting a blockade, their views will not be consulted, or allowed to weigh a feather in the scale with any party that hopes to gain or retain the approbation of the American people.

MENTOR.

Every effort to avert the calamity of war failed. The Confederates commenced it by the attack on Fort Sumter. It raged thereafter with uncommon pertinacity on both

7

sides. Mr. Barker, considering himself a non-combatant, did not take part therein, confining himself mainly to vindicating the rights of sufferers, and particularly of those of the ladies of New Orleans. His father, Robert Barker, of Nantucket was a rebel, who, on account of the exposed situation of that island, retired therefrom with his family at the commencement of the Revolutionary troubles, locating on Swan Island, in Kennebeck river, where his son, Jacob Barker, was born on the 17th December, 1779, and where his father died in April, 1780. After our independence was acknowledged by Great Britain, and peace restored, Jacob's mother, Sarah Barker, born Folger, at Nantucket—a blood relation of Doctor Franklin—returned to that Island with her family in 1785. Jacob, during his minority, was under the care of the religious Society of Friends, denominated Quakers. Although not a member by birthright, from their tuition he imbibed an aversion to war which has continued through his long life. That good lady taught her son how to secure independence by telling him, when thirsty, to take a glass, go to the pump and help thyself.

During the administrations of Jefferson and Madison he advocated commercial restrictions as the best manner of obtaining redress for national wrongs. The peaceable principles of the said society may be seen by the perusal of the following memorial :

THE NORTH CAROLINA QUAKERS' MEMORIAL.

The Raleigh (N. C.) Standard gives the following :

"At a stated Meeting for Sufferings, representing Yearly Meeting of Friends, held at Deep river, on the 14th of Fourth month, 1862, the subject of our present sufferings, on account of our conscientious scruples against bearing arms, claiming the deliberate consideration of the Meeting, and believing it right to embrace our privilege to petition those in authority, we therefore adopt the following :

"*To the Convention of North Carolina,*
in Convention assembled :

"Your petitioners respectfully show that it is one of our fundamental religious principles to bear a faithful testimony against all wars and fightings, and that in consequence we cannot aid in carrying on any carnal war.

"This is no new principle of our society, but one which was adopted at its rise, as the doctrine taught by our Saviour and followed by his disciples for more than two hundred years, and has ever been and is now held as one of our fundamental and vital principles, and one that we cannot yield or compromise in any degree whatever.

"We would further show that the whole number of our members in the Confederate States is less than ten thousand, while in the United States the number probably exceeds two hundred thousand, who bear the same testimony against all wars and fightings ; and that in every nation and clime where our society exists, it is at this day, as heretofore, maintaining this precious principle of peace, and that we everywhere in this respect speak the same language and mind the same thing.

"We may further show that, according to the best information we can obtain, until the present time, Friends of North Carolina have not been called on to aid in the battle field or military camp; but now our peaceful principles are in a measure disregarded, and many of our members are drafted to take part in the conflicting armies, while we understand that our brethren in the United States are not.

"We have enlisted under the banner of the Captain of our souls' salvation, Jesus Christ, the Prince of Peace: therefore, in obedience to His express command, we cannot fight, or aid directly or indirectly in any carnal wars. But your petitioners would represent to you that we believe it to be our moral and religious duty to submit to the government under which we live, and to the laws and powers that be, or suffer patiently their penalties.

"We love our homes and our country much, but at the same time we love our religious principles more; therefore your petitioners would most respectfully ask that you grant us the enjoyment of this important religious principle.

"We own to no god but the God of love, truth, peace, mercy and judgment, whose blessings we invoke, and whose wisdom we implore to be with you in your legislative deliberations.

"Signed on behalf and by direction of the meeting.

"NATHAN F. SPENCER, Clerk."

Mr. Madison, near the close of his first term, recommended a declaration of war against Great Britain, and an embargo, as a preparatory measure. The embargo was adopted, for ninety days. Mr. Madison was nominated for a second term. A majority of the Democrats of the State of New York preferred DeWitt Clinton for the Presidency. The Federalists, despairing of their ability to elect a member of their own party, resolved to support Mr. Clinton.

A majority of the Democratic party of the State, including Chief Justice Spencer and Martin Van Buren, united, they insisting that war should be declared against France, or against both France and England. Mr. Clinton considered the recommendation of war against Great Britain a political device to secure the re-election of Madison, and that he had no belief that Congress would adopt the measure he recommended. They were disappointed by a declaration of war against Great Britain, which took place on the 16th June, 1812. On the happening of that event, Chief Justice Spencer, and many other of Mr. Clinton's personal political friends, urged him to withdraw his name as a candidate for the Presidency, to which he had been nominated by the Democratic party of the State. This, being assured of the support of the Federal party, he refused to do; which caused an estrangement between the brothers Spencer and Clinton, which continued until after the close of the war, when a reconciliation took place by the interposition of Mr. Barker; from which time until the day of their death, those two distinguished men continued the devoted friends of each other and of Mr. Barker, although the political views of the Chief Justice often differed from those entertained by Mr. Barker, and both fearlessly put forth their opinions, and severally sustained the political parties to which they were attached, with uncommon zeal. Mr. Clinton and Mr. Van Buren both sustained the war. They differed in their views in relation to the measures adopted for carrying it on, which estranged them from each other. Mr. Van Buren, sustaining the administration, became the opponent of Mr. Clinton's political views. The political campaign progressed with great ardor. The parties became very violent. The legislature met for the appointment of electors. Mr. Barker was, with Colonel Rutgers, Colonel Willett, and others, appointed, at Tammany Hall, delegates to attend a Democratic convention at Albany for the nomination of electors. The friends of the two candidates in the legislature, held separate meetings. According to the best of Mr. Barker's recollection, Mr. Van Buren presided at the meeting of the friends of Mr. Clinton ; and Nathan Sanford, a Senator from New York, presided at that of the friends of Mr. Madison. The former, having a majority, and assured of the support of the Federalists at the election, declined all propositions for a compromise, and nominated an entire ticket friendly to the election of their chief, who were elected by the aid of Federal votes.

Mr. Van Buren was esteemed the master-spirit of the whole affair. Mr. Barker remonstrated with him against their course, remarking that he would, if they persisted, plan a pamphlet, describing their coalition with the Federalists, in every hamlet in the State. This had no influence. Mr. Van Buren was not to be diverted from the course he had adopted, vainly imagining that it would be successful.

Pending the debates in Congress on the question of war, Dr. Mitchel, a member from the city of New York, being opposed to war, addressed a letter to the Tammany Society, in the hope of having his views sustained by that patriotic body. He asked them, among other things, if they were prepared to abandon their fruitful maritime pursuits in exchange for the frozen regions of Canada. To which they promptly replied, in effect, that the Nation's honor must be sustained at every hazard.

About the same time, Mr. Barker received from a correspondent in England, letters which indicated that the British ministry would very soon rescind the orders in council, when he drafted a petition asking Congress to continue the embargo and defer a declaration of war for a short period, which was signed by men of both political parties, of the greatest respectability, to whom he exhibited those letters. The petition was presented to the Senate by Mr. Smith, a member from New York, the day before war was declared; which, on motion of Colonel Taylor, of South Carolina, was ordered to be printed. The petition and speech of Colonel Taylor in relation thereto were as follows :

[From Niles's Register, Vol. II, page 278.]

TWELFTH CONGRESS.

In Senate—*Monday, June* 15, 1812.—Mr. Smith, of New York, presented the following petition of sundry inhabitants, merchants and others, of the city of New York, praying that the embargo and non-importation laws might be continued as a substitute for war against Great Britain :

MEMORIAL.

To the Honorable the Senate and House of Representatives
of the United States of America in Congress assembled,
the memorial of the subscribers, merchants and others,
inhabitants of the city of New York, respectfully sheweth :

"That your memorialists feel, in common with the rest of their fellow-citizens, an anxious solicitude for the honor and interests of their country, and an equal determination to assert and maintain them ;

"That your memorialists believe that a continuation of the restrictive measures now in operation will produce all the benefits, while it prevents the calamities of war ;

"That when the British ministry become convinced that a trade with the United States cannot be renewed but by the repeal of the orders in council, the distress of their merchants and manufacturers, and their inability to support their armies in Spain and Portugal, will, probably, compel them to that measure.

"Your memorialists beg leave to remark that such effects are even now visible ; and it may be reasonably hoped that a continuance of the embargo and non-importation laws, a few months beyond the fourth day of July next, will effect a complete and bloodless triumph of our rights.

"Your memorialists, therefore, respectfully solicit of your honorable body the passage of a law continuing the embargo, and giving to the President of the United States power to discontinue the whole of the restrictive system on the rescinding of the British orders in Council.

"The conduct of France, in burning our ships, in sequestrating our property entering her ports expecting protection in consequence of the promised repeal of the Berlin and Milan decrees, and the delay in completing a treaty with the American minister, has excited great sensation, and we hope and trust will call forth from your honorable body such retaliatory measures as may be best calculated to procure justice.

After the same was read Mr. Taylor said that "the respectability of the subscribers to a petition presented to this body, and the importance of the matter therein contained, had, on various occasions, been used as inducements to us to give such a petition a respectful *disposition* in the course of our proceedings. He recollected a case in point. It was the case of the petition of an eminent merchant of Massachusetts, presented by an honorable Senator from that State, and which, at the suggestion of that honorable gentleman, was by the Senate ordered to be printed. He was of opinion that the petition just read ought not to be treated with less attention; that he had seen the petition and inquired into the character of its subscribers, and had been informed that the fifty-six subscribers to it were among the most respectable, wealthy, and intelligent merchants of the city of New York. There are to be found in that list the names of two presidents of banks, three presidents of insurance companies, thirteen directors of banks, besides other names of pre-eminent standing in the mercantile world. They had all united in the sentiments contained in the petition, notwithstanding that there existed among them a difference of political opinions, for he understood that of the petitioners forty-two were Federal and sixteen Republican. Mr. T. added that he considered some of the sentiments contained in the petition as of the highest importance. He hailed it as an auspicious occurrence that these honorable merchants, in praying that the evils of war might be averted from them and from the Nation, had, nevertheless, held fast to the principles of resistance to the aggressions and unhallowed conduct of Great Britain towards our Nation; and had exercised the candor and frankness to bear testimony to the efficiency of the restrictive system for obtaining a redress of our wrongs and, of course, the integrity and honor of those who had imposed this system for that purpose. He hoped that the example of these petitioners would tend to counteract those strenuous and unremitting exertions of passion, prejudice, and party feeling which had attempted to stamp upon the majority in Congress the foul and unjust censure of being enemies to commerce; that, however unfashionable and obstinate it might appear, he still believed that the embargo and non-importation laws, if faithfully executed, were capable of reaching further than our cannon. We are, at this very time, tendering an urgent argument—an argument to be felt by each city, village and hamlet in England. This, touching to the quick the vital interests of that empire, would demonstrate to the people, at least, the folly and absurdity of the orders in council. The ordeal of the twenty weeks of scarcity which the people of that unhappy country are undergoing, to relieve which, but for the madness and folly of their rulers, every yard of American canvas would be spread to the gales; the thousands of starving manufacturers thrown out of employ for want of our custom, which custom, but for the injustice of their *masters*, we were willing to give, *now feel* the efficiency of the restrictive system. These matter-of-fact arguments want no sophistry nor long speeches to give them weight. But Great Britain is proud and will never yield to this sort of pressure. *Hunger has no law.* Where was her pride during the last war, when she exported to her enemy on the continent more than eleven millions of pounds sterling for provisions, and, meanly truckling to her enemy, consented to buy the privilege of laying out her guineas for bread, and actually submitted, on the compulsion of Napoleon, to buy the wines, brandies and silks of France, which she did not want. This restrictive system, when commenced under the former embargo law, encountered every opposition among ourselves which selfish avarice, which passion and party rage, could suggest; and so successful were its assailants that, while it was operating with its fullest effects, (which the prices current of that day will show,) some of its greatest champions in the National Legislature abandoned it; *yes, sir*, in the tide of victory they threw down their arms. How are the mighty fallen and the shield of the mighty vilely cast away. The disavowal of Erskine's arrangement was the consequence of this retreat. But it may be said that the sentiments in the petition were extorted by the apprehension of a greater evil—*war*. In all our trials those who had not predetermined to submit to Great Britain must have anticipated this alternative. Let those who, by their acrimony, sneers, and scoffs, have thrown away this chief defence of our Nation be held responsible for the compulsion they have imposed on us to take this dire alternative. He said that though he was unwilling to abate a single pang which we might *legally* inflict upon our enemy, and might, at the proper time, oppose anything like the swap proposed of one system for another, when we had the power and the right to impose upon our enemy both the one and the other, he nevertheless thought the petition was deserving of the attention which he now moved it should receive. He *moved* that the petition should be printed; which was agreed to."

———

The petition came too late ; the war party could not recede or delay the measures they had resolved on. The war was declared on the 16th of June, 1812, and the orders in council were rescinded on the 7th of July following, before news of the war reached England, thus establishing the power of the restrictive measures. Congress, on a previous occasion, empowered the President, in case the orders in council should be revoked during the recess, to annul, by proclamation, the non-importation law; and so confident were the British ministry that he would suspend the war as soon as he heard of the repeal of the orders in council, they having been repealed before the war was known in England, they did not send a fleet to our coast for more than three months—ocean steamboat navigation being not then known.

In this confidence the United States minister at London participated to such an extent as to authorizing the loading of all the American ships then in England with British fabrics for the United States. They sailed under British licenses and arrived in the United States safe. A great drought occurred at the same time in China, interrupting the navigation of her rivers, so that teas and other of her products could not reach Canton for a long time; this detained a large fleet of American ships at Canton until after the news of the war reached that place.

These measures combined saved the insurance companies, the ship owners, and the importers of British fabrics from ruin, which seemed to be their impending fate when the war was declared.

Mr. Madison did not feel authorized to suspend the war, or relax the non-importation law. He said the war having been declared, it must be continued until other matters were settled.

When these ships arrived they, with their cargoes, were forfeited to the United States by the provisions of the non-importation laws, which remained in full force.

This immense amount of property was released on bond, and these bonds were cancelled, on the payment of the duties, by an act of Congress, which passed, after a hard struggle, by the casting vote of the Hon. Langdon Chevis, of South Carolina, then the Speaker of the House of Representatives. To the very great and praiseworthy exertions of that distinguished man the merchants in general were indebted for their escape from ruin.

War being declared against Great Britain, Mr. Barker thought a vigorous prosecution of it the most likely way to procure an honorable peace, furnishing the empty treasury with more than. five millions of dollars in specie or its equivalent, while most others, particularly the New England banks, drew tight their purse strings. So well satisfied were the citizens of New York with the course pursued by Mr. Barker that they, immediately after the close of the war, elected him a member of the Senate of that State. At that time, among the required qualifications of voters for Senators was to be a freeholder. A majority of that class had never before been had for a Democratic candidate in the Southern district of New York.

————

Soon after the commencement of the late war New Orleans was blockaded. Commerce had been very much depressed, and certain individuals seemed to set all law and authority at defiance. Among other things they attempted to close the establishments of those who dealt in gold, silver, stocks, etc., in which they were partly successful. Mr. Barker resisted, and continued his business, when the following articles appeared in the New Orleans Picayune :

THE BROKERS.

[From the New Orleans Picayune. March 9, 1862.

We are informed that certain individuals took upon themselves to circulate an anonymous placard denouncing the dealers in gold and silver obnoxious to public indignation, and to call on them personally, demanding that they should discontinue their business, which they were conducting under license from the State and city authorities, for which license they had paid large sums of money.

This assumption of power is highly reprehensible. If the business is deemed prejudicial, the Governor or Mayor should issue a proclamation suspending the operation of the license, returning to the dealers a due proportion of the money they have paid therefor.

If the Board of Currency, the Governor, Mayor, or a committee from the Chamber of Commerce, had called on the dealers in coin, suggesting to them that their traffic was considered injurious to public credit, they would, with one accord, have cheerfully discontinued that business. This would have been far better than for anonymous individuals to have attempted to overthrow it by mob law.

However praiseworthy the motives of these individuals

may be, they may not have well considered the operation of the interdiction they wish to enforce.

The question to be considered is, when the public find that they are not allowed to exchange their bank or currency notes for gold or silver, on any terms, will they be more willing to sell their merchandise for currency notes than if no such obstacle existed?

If the dealers are not allowed to purchase, they cannot supply those who wish to convert their paper into gold and silver. They are not men who hoard it up; the profit of their business consists in turning it over rapidly.

Monopolizing salt, flour, pork and other necessaries of life, and supplying the army, as well as the poor, at five or ten prices, is far more objectionable than dealing in gold and silver.   A.

REMARKS BY MR. BARKER.

Certain individuals object to the dealing in gold and silver by persons duly authorized, under licenses from the State and city authorities, to conduct such business. Suppose they succeed in annulling such licenses, the effect will be to place those in moderate circumstances, who have laid by a few dollars in gold or silver to use in case of need, at the tender mercy of street runners, who do not pay rent, and others who act without license, and who monopolize every article necessary for convenience or consumption.

How are the poor women, who have been provided with gold for the support of their families during the absence of their husbands on military duty, to overcome the exorbitant price of bread, pork, salt and soap, if they are not allowed to sell their gold?

As to stopping the traffic, it is not possible, any more than it would be to stop the course of the Mississippi. These men were told by an article, authoritatively published in the Picayune on Sunday, the 9th of March, 1862, that the licensed dealers would cheerfully discontinue the traffic, on the suggestion of- the Governor, Mayor, Board of Currency or the Chamber of Commerce, that it was deemed prejudicial to public good. Further than this they could not go, without sacrificing that individual independence which every citizen of this Confederacy should maintain, as also all reverence for public authority. Martial law being now proclaimed, the subject may be referred to Gen. Lovell, or to the Provost Marshals. If they should think that public good required a discontinuance in dealing in gold and silver, their wishes will be complied with.

The price of gold and silver, like that of all other articles of necessity, depends on supply and demand. This great regulator of trade cannot be successfully resisted. The precious metals are not made scarce by the purchases made by the dealers. They do not purchase to hoard, but to resell. The profits depend on the rapidity with which they turn it over. .

———

These proceedings were reported to the Hon. John T. Monroe, Mayor of the city of New Orleans, who had co-operated with Mr. Barker in opposing secession. He

8

approved the resistance made, and promised to send a police force to protect his bank, which was done on the following day. After the surrender, he was sent to Fort Pickens by General Butler, when, on the application of Mrs. Monroe, Mr. Barker gave a certificate in the words following:

"CERTIFICATE.

"These are to certify that my bank was placarded at night, on or about the 12th April ult., by a lot of men who had combined together, styling themselves the Southern Independence Association. On the following day they presented themselves at my bank, demanding that I should discontinue my business, saying it was injurious to the Southern Confederacy. I defied them, and continued my business, and called on Mayor Monroe for protection against the threatened violence of the mob. The Mayor approved of my course, advised me not to yield to their unlawful requirements, and promised to send police officers to protect me, which he did on the following day, and thus were these men restrained from further action in the matter.   JACOB BARKER.

"*New Orleans, 23d May*, 1862."

———

Being disappointed in his efforts to avert the great calamity, Mr. Barker, with the co-operating party to a man, went in for a separate Confederacy as preferable to a continuation of the war, although he never believed we could get as good security for the institution of slavery as we had under the old Constitution. And he supposed, if granted to the then few seceding States, they would, after a few years' trial, return under the Star Spangled Banner; and vainly supposing he could promote the cause of peace and good will to his fellow-men, he procured from the authorities of this city a pass from New Orleans to New York and back.

With this pass he travelled in Pennsylvania, New York, Connecticut and Massachusetts, pointing out to those deluded men the mischief they were doing the colored race ; the certainty there was of a long war if they meddled with the slavery question; the folly of wasting countless millions, and sacrificing the lives of thousands of the flower of the Nation, entreating them to agree to a separate Confederacy.

It was all in vain, and he returned, telling his fellow-citizens that our dependence for recognition must be on the bravery and skill of our soldiers ; that the public mind at the North was equally decided as that at the South ; that the question must be decided on the field of battle ; that the sooner they abandoned the Quixotic notion of foreign interference the better.

On or about the 1st of May, 1862, the Star Spangled Banner was again unfurled in New Orleans by Admiral Farragut and General Butler. The panic which ensued can be more easily imagined than described. Steamboats, ships, cotton, sugar, molasses, tobacco, were given to the flames or otherwise destroyed. Fearing confiscation or mob violence, most of the banks had the folly to send their specie—countless millions—into the Confederacy, where it was lost. Our late worthy fellow-citizen, J. D.

Denegre, Esq., who was then president of the Citizens'
Bank, and his associates, were too wise thus to sacrifice
the institution entrusted to their management, they retained its specie—near four millions of dollars. To their
sagacity is to be ascribed the present sound condition of
the bank.

———

On the arrival of Gen. Butler, he issued the following
PROCLAMATION:

HEADQUARTERS DEPARTMENT OF THE GULF, }
New Orleans, May 1, 1862.   }

The city of New Orleans and its environs, with all its
interior and exterior defences, having been surrendered
to the combined naval and land forces of the United
States, and having been evacuated by the rebel forces in
whose possession they lately were, and being now in
occupation of the forces of the United States, who have
come to restore order, maintain public tranquility, enforce
peace and quiet under the laws and Constitution of the
United States, the Major General commanding the forces
of the United States in the Department of the Gulf,
hereby makes known and proclaims the object and purposes of the Government of the United States in thus
taking possession of the city of New Orleans and the
State of Louisiana, and the rules and regulations by
which the laws of the United States will be for the
present and during a state of war enforced and maintained, for the plain guidance of all good citizens of the

United States, as well as others who may heretofore have been in rebellion against their authority.

Thrice before has the city of New Orleans been rescued from the hand of a foreign government, and still more calamitous domestic insurrection, by the money and arms of the United States. It has of late been under the military control of the rebel forces, claiming to be the peculiar friends of its citizens, and at each time, in the judgment of the commander of the military forces holding it, it has been found necessary to preserve order and maintain quiet by the administration of Law Martial. Even during the *interim* from its evacuation by the rebel soldiers and its actual possession by the soldiers of the United States, the civil authorities of the city have found it necessary to call for the intervention of an armed body known as the "European Legion," to preserve public tranquility. The Commanding General, therefore, will cause the city to be governed until the restoration of Municipal Authority, and his further orders, by the Law Martial, a measure for which it would seem the previous recital furnishes sufficient precedents.

All persons in arms against the United States are required to surrender themselves, with their arms, equipments and munitions of war. The body known as the "European Legion," not being understood to be in arms against the United States, but organized to protect the lives and property of the citizens, are invited still to co-operate with the forces of the United States to that end, and, so acting, will not be included in the terms of this order, but will report to these Headquarters.

All flags, ensigns and devices, tending to uphold any authority whatever, save the flag of the United States and the flags of foreign Consulates, must not be exhibited, but suppressed. The American Ensign, the emblem of the United States, must be treated with the utmost deference and respect by' all persons, under pain of severe punishment.

All persons well disposed towards the Government of the United States, who shall renew their oath or allegiance, will receive the safeguard and protection, in their persons and property, of the armies of the United States, the violation of which, by any person, is punishable with death.

All persons still holding allegiance to the Confederate States will be deemed rebels against the Government of the United States, and regarded and treated as enemies thereof.

All foreigners not naturalized and claiming allegiance to their respective Governments, and not having made oath of allegiance to the supposed Government of the Confederate States, will be protected in their persons and property as heretofore under the laws of the United States.

All persons who may heretofore have given their adherence to the supposed Government of the Confederate States, or have been in their service, who shall lay down and deliver up their arms and return to peaceful occupations and preserve quiet and order, holding no further correspondence nor giving aid and comfort to the enemies of the United States, will not be disturbed either in person or property, except so far, under the orders of the Commanding General, as the exigencies of the public service may render necessary.

The keepers of all public property, whether State, National or Confederate, such as collections of art, libraries, museums, as well as all public buildings, all munitions of war, and armed vessels, will at once make full returns thereof to these Headquarters; all manufacturers of arms and munitions of war, will report to these Headquarters their kind and places of business.

All rights of property, of whatever kind, will be held inviolate, subject only to the laws of the United States.

All inhabitants are enjoined to pursue their usual avocations; all shops and places of business are to be kept open in the accustomed manner, and services to be had in the churches and religious houses as in times of profound peace.

Keepers of all public houses, coffee houses and drinking saloons, are to report their names and numbers to the office of the Provost Marshal; will there receive license, and be held responsible for all disorders and disturbances of the peace arising in their respective places.

A sufficient force will be kept in the city to preserve order and maintain the laws.

The killing of an American soldier by any disorderly person or mob, is simply assassination and murder, and not war, and will be so regarded and punished.

The owner of any house or building in or from which

such murder shall be committed, will be held responsible
therefor, and the house will be liable to be destroyed by
the military authority.

All disorders and disturbances of the peace done by
combinations and numbers, and crimes of an aggravated
nature, interfering with forces or laws of the United
States, will be referred to a military court for trial and
punishment; other misdemeanors will be subject to the
municipal authority, if it chooses to act. Civil causes
between party and party will be referred to the ordinary
tribunals. The levy and collection of all taxes, save those
imposed by the laws of the United States, are suppressed,
except those for keeping in repair and lighting the streets,
and for sanitary purposes. Those are to be collected in
the usual manner.

The circulation of Confederate bonds, evidences of debt,
except notes in the similitude of bank notes issued by
the Confederate States, or scrip, or any trade in the same,
is strictly forbidden. It having been represented to the
Commanding General by the city authorities that these
Confederate notes, in the form of bank notes, are, in a
great measure, the only substitute for money which the
people have been allowed to have, and that great distress
would ensue among the poorer classes if the circulation
of such notes were suppressed, such circulation will be
permitted so long as any one may be inconsiderate enough
to receive them, till further orders.

No publication, either by newspaper, pamphlet or
handbill, giving accounts of the movements of soldiers

of the United States within this Department, reflecting in any way upon the United States or its officers, or tending in any way to influence the public mind against the Government of the United States, will be permitted and all articles of war news, or editorial comments, or correspondence, making comments upon the movements of the armies of the United States, or the rebels, must be submitted to the examination of an officer who will be detailed for that purpose from these Headquarters.

The transmission of all communications by telegraph will be under the charge of an officer from these Headquarters.

The armies of the United States came here not to destroy but to make good, to restore order out of chaos, and the government of laws in place of the passions of men; to this end, therefore, the efforts of all well-disposed persons are invited to have every species of disorder quelled, and if any soldier of the United States should so far forget his duty or his flag as to commit any outrage upon any person or property, the Commanding General requests that his name be instantly reported to the Provost Guard, so that he may be punished and his wrongful act redressed.

The municipal authority, so far as the police of the city and crimes are concerned, to the extent before indicated, is hereby suspended.

All assemblages of persons in the streets, either by day or night, tend to disorder, and are forbidden.

The various companies composing the Fire Department

in New Orleans, will be permitted to retain their organization, and are to report to the office of the Provost Marshal, so that they may be known and not interfered with in their duties.

And, finally, it may be sufficient to add, without further enumeration, that all the requirements of martial law will be imposed so long as, in the judgment of the United States authorities, it may be necessary. And while it is the desire of these authorities to exercise this government mildly, and after the usages of the past, it must not be supposed that it will not be vigorously and firmly administered as occasion calls.

By command of   MAJOR GENERAL BUTLER.
GEO. C. STRONG, A. A. G., Chief of Staff.

———

Soon after the restoration of the authority of the United States over New Orleans, to wit: on the 18th May, 1862, the following publication, from the pen of Mr. Barker, appeared in the True Delta, with the approbation of General Butler. It bears its own comment:

INTERESTING COMMUNICATION.

To the Editors of the N. O. Daily True Delta:

Gentlemen—At the particular request of several of my fellow-citizens who are interested in the question of cotton, I have to request that you publish the article "Don't give up the Ship," which appeared in the Picayune of the 23d December, 1860, together with my opinion on the question of destroying the cotton.

I had supposed that King Cotton had been dethroned of its vaunted influence with foreign nations, on the blockade question, it having, according to the report of the Hon. Mr. Yancey, on his return from Europe, proved valueless. It, therefore, becomes a question of property.

A great objection to presenting the cotton question in an imposing light is the motive it induces for extraordinary exertions to procure the article from other quarters, thus permanently injuring those who cultivate here.

It is believed that the soil and climate of Australia are favorable to its culture, so important to Great Britain that she went to war with China to populate Australia with millions of her people to cultivate cotton; and after expending countless millions, and sacrificing lives without number, terminated a very expensive war without a single word being said in the treaty of peace favorable to her interest, except that the emigration of the Coolies should not be restricted.

Those who advocate the destruction of cotton say: "Better destroy it than allow the enemy to have it." However true this might be if they intended to confiscate it—which is not the case—the assumption cannot be sustained, inasmuch as they, from the first, respected all they found on land; and Major General Butler assured the bank presidents, with whom he had a meeting last Monday, that cotton had not been taken at any place without payment therefor, and that he should not only respect cotton and sugar in the hands of the planter and his factor, but, whenever required, would send a guard to protect it against the mob.

Cotton is not like corn, an article of necessity to England or any other Power. Wool, flax, hemp and furs, although far more expensive, are all-sufficient for every other purpose than the employment of millions of their subjects ; and to employ them in digging canals and then filling them up, would not cost half as much money as a war with the United States.

Another important consideration may be found in the fact that if cotton should be· admitted by crowned heads to be an omnipotent power, it might, on another occasion, be effectually arrayed against crowned heads, all of whom seem willing to see the present war continued, that the growing power they have so long dreaded may be broken to pieces, or so much exhausted as to be harmless.

If the cotton question could influence them, burning the last crop and refusing to raise another would be considered a hostile act leveled at them, and he who expects to coerce Great Britain into a friendly intervention by open hostile proceedings, knows little of the character of that proud nation.

Such of our banks as have parted with their gold and silver have to depend on their portfolios to meet their bank notes, pay their depositors and dividends. If the planters destroy their crops they cannot pay their debts, and will finally be relieved by a bankrupt law. Thus, destroying their crops becomes a war against the banks, the bill holders, the depositors, the stockholders and the factors, and all this for the single purpose of throwing the operatives in the factories of the world out of employ— a result too remote to have any beneficial effect on the operations of the war.

I would ask how the planters who destroy their crops are to procure food and clothing for their slaves, and how the retired men, the widows and the minors, whose all is invested in bank stock, thus cut off from dividends, are to be supported? And, finally, I would ask, how are we to get a sound currency if the banks are to be thus ruined?

The Common Council are endeavoring to afford relief against the shinplaster currency; which relief must of necessity be temporary, as for all their issues they get only Confederate securities, leading to heavy taxation to pay the notes they issue; independent of which the property holders are already taxed as much as they can bear. Thus, burning our crops may be likened unto the act of a man putting out both his eyes, in the vain hope of injuring only one of his enemy's eyes.

Circumstanced as we are, it has become necessary that all should return to their accustomed occupations. Our families must be fed and clothed; we cannot expect any change in our rulers during the war; and if our brave soldiers, who have fought as men never before fought, do not win for us a satisfactory peace, we must fall back on the ballot-box, the sure palladium of our liberties, when properly respected.

When President Lincoln came into power, he could not

have procured a dinner at the public expense without our consent, nor could any office have been filled by a person not approved by us, nor could they have organized an army or navy; consequently, could not have blockaded our ports. We had, thanks to our political friends at the North—they having elected a majority in both Houses—the game in our own hands, which was thrown away by the resignation of our members of Congress.

Come what will, the Constitution should be so amended as to allow the people to vote directly for the President; a majority should be required to entitle a candidate to the office. This alteration made, all will be safe:

Your obedient servant,　　　　　　　JACOB BARKER.

GOVERNOR ANDREW AND THE WAR DEPARTMENT.

A Washington Dispatch of 23d May, 1862, was as follows, which we insert here as a presaging chapter in the history of subsequent events:

The folowing letter from Gov. Andrew, of Massachusetts, has been received at the War Department:

"BOSTON, May 19, 1862.

"*Sir*—I have this moment received a telegram in these words, viz:

" 'The Secretary of War desires to know how soon you can raise and organize three or four more infantry regiments, and have them ready to be forwarded here to be armed and equipped. Please answer immediately, and state the number you can raise.

" 'L. THOMAS, Adjutant General.'

"A call so sudden and unexpected finds me without materials for an intelligent reply. Our young men are all pre-occupied with other views. Still, if a real call for three regiments are made, I believe we can raise them in forty days. The arms and equipments would need to be furnished here. Our people have never marched without them. They go into camp while forming into regiments, and are drilled and practised with arms and muskets as soldiers. To attempt the other course would dampen enthusiasm, and make the men feel that they were not soldiers, but a mob.

"Again, if our people feel that they are going into the South to help fight rebels who will kill and destroy them by all means known to savages as well as civilized men; will deceive them by fraudulent flags of truce and lying pretences, as they did the Massachusetts boys at Williamsburg; will use their negro slaves against them, both as laborers and fighting men, while they themselves must never fire at the enemy's magazine, I think they will feel the draft is heavy on their patriotism. But if the President will sustain General Hunter and recognize all men, even black men, as legally capable of that loyalty the blacks are waiting to manifest, and let them fight with God and human nature on their side, the roads will swarm, if need be, with multitudes whom New England would pour out to obey your call.

Always ready to do my utmost, I remain, most faithfully, your obedient servant,

JOHN A. ANDREW."

THE SEQUESTRATION ACT—INSTRUCTIONS OF THE ATTORNEY
GENERAL.

—

DEPARTMENT OF JUSTICE,   }
RICHMOND, 12th September, 1861. }

*Instructions to Receivers under the Act entitled "An Act for
the Sequestration of the Estates, Property and Effects of
Alien Enemies, and for the Indemnity of Citizens of the
Confederate States, and persons aiding the same in the
existing war against the United States," approvnd 30th
March, 1861.*

I. The following persons are subject to the operation
of the law as alien enemies :

1st. All citizens of the United States, except citizens
or residents of Delaware, Maryland, Kentucky, or Missouri, or the District of Columbia, or the Territories of
New Mexico, Arizona, or the Indian territory south of
Kansas.

2d. All persons who have a *domicil* within the States
with which this Government is at war, no matter whether
they be *citizins* or not : Thus, the subjects of Great
Britain, France, or other neutral nations, who have a
domicil or are carrying on business or traffic within the
States at war with this Confederacy, are alien enemies
under the law.

3d. All such citizens or residents of the States of Delaware, Maryland, Kentucky or Missouri, and of the Territories of New Mexico, Arizona, and the Indian Territory
south of Kansas, and of the District of Columbia, as shall
commit actual hostilities against the Confederate States,

or aid or abet the United States in the existing war against the Confederate States.

II. Immediately after taking your oath of office, you will take possession of all the property, of every nature and kind whatsoever, within your district, belonging to alien enemies as above defined.

III. You will forthwith apply to the Clerk of the Court for Writs of Garnishment, under the 8th section of the law, and will propound to the Garnishees the interrogatories of which a form is annexed. These interrogatories you will propound to the following persons, viz :

1st. All attorneys, and counsellors practising law within your district.

2d. The presidents and cashiers of all banks, and principle administrative officers of all railroad and other corporations within your district.

3d. All agents of foreign corporations, insurance agents, commission merchants engaged in foreign trade, agents of foreign mercantile houses, dealers in bills of exchange, executors and administrators of estates, assignees and syndics of insolvent estates, trustees, and generally all persons who are known to do business as agents for others.

IV. In the first week of each month, you will exhibit to the judge a statement showing the whole amount of money in your hands as Receiver, and deposit the same for safe-keeping in such banks or other depository as may be selected for that purpose by the judge—receiving only such amount as may be required for immediate expenditure in the discharge of your duties as Receiver.

9

V. You are very strictly prohibited from making personal use in any manner whatever, or investing in any kind of property, or loaning with or without interest, or exchanging for other funds, without leave of the court, any money or funds of any kind, received by you in your official capacity.

VI. You are prohibited from employing, except at your own personal expense, any attorney or counsellor to aid you in the discharge of your duties, other than the District Attorney of the Confederate States for your district; and you are instructed to invoke his aid, under the 9th section of the law, in all matters of litigation that may arise under the law.

VII. You will take special care to avoid the loss or deterioration of all personal property perishable in its nature, by applying for the sale thereof under the provisions of the 12th section of the law.

VIII. You will keep an account showing exactly all sums received by you as allowances of compensation under the fifteenth section of the law, setting forth the date and amount of each receipt of such sums; and as soon as the amount received by you in any one year shall reach the sum of five thousand dollars, you will pay over to the Assistant Treasurer of the Confederate States most convenient to your domicil all further sums allowed you as compensation, taking duplicate receipts therefor, one to be retained as a voucher by yourself, and the other to be forwarded by mail to the Secretary of the Treasury.

IX. Whenever, in the discharge of your duties, you

discover that any attorney, agent, former partner, trustee, or other person holding or controlling any property, rights or credits of an alien enemy, has willfully failed to give you information of the same, you will immediately report the fact to the District Attorney for your district, to the end that the guilty party may be subjected to the pains and penalties prescribed by the third section of the law.   J. P. BENJAMIN, Attorney General.

THE "NATIONAL ADVOCATE."

Mr. Barker had free communication with General Butler. The General professed to be in favor of sustaining Southern institutions—for which purpose Mr. Barker, believing that a lasting peace could not be otherwise obtained, established, on the 11th day of June, 1862, the NATIONAL ADVOCATE, with the emblem of the Stars and Stripes, and the following announcement :

"This paper will advocate the political doctrines of Jefferson and Jackson, relying implicitly on the ballot-box to correct all the evils to which we are now and have been subject, terminate the present war, and restore the ascendency of the Democratic party, when there will not be any further interference with the institutions of the South. It should be considered treason to debate in Congress the subject of slavery. The States should be left to regulate that question in their own way. All that the South wishes is to have the terms of the Constitution fairly and promptly carried out.

"Our motto being, 'Enemies in War—in Peace Friends,' we shall exert ourselves to the utmost to calm the angry passions of men who have been opposed to each other. Most of those who have erred knew not what they had been doing. Let the past be forgotten, and all go forward with their accustomed occupations, and sin no more. Kindness and forgiveness are the best means of cultivating a Union sentiment, which is now most wanted to promote the prosperity of New Orleans. This feeling, however, must be mutual, or it cannot have any beneficial effect.

"The proclamations of Fremont, Phelps and Hunter have done much to weaken the cause of the United States. The President's proclamation annulling those of the three Generals is doing much good. What is most wanted is the exclusion of politics from the pulpit. The reverend gentlemen occupying the different pulpits should confine their labors to spiritual matters, allowing all men to go to heaven in their own way. This terrible war was brought about by those wearing clerical robes at the North, and if those of similar calling at the South had not been provoked into a course equally adverse to common sense and public good there would not be that misery which pervades the whole community, North and South."

———

[From the Advocate, June 15, 1862.]

Our creed is universal education and universal suffrage. The people are entitled to the services of their best citizens, without regard to their place of birth; it should not be a subject of inquiry. That is an affair in which they took no part; their own actions, capacities and virtues should be the only test of their fitness for public employment, while the road to fame as well as to fortune should alike be open to the adopted as well as to the native citizen. They were invited here by our laws, and their rights secured by those laws should be carefully watched over and protected. We should recommend them to be tenacious to use their rights fully and promptly in selecting the best men, to avoid as much as possible taking office themselves.

They may rely on it that but few men leave office as well off as when they entered it, and they uniformly accustom themselves to a course of life which disqualifies them from returning to the occupation they left when they took office.

A farther objection is to be found in the fact that office holders are always slaves. Although their skins be not black, their time is not their own, and they become targets for the pen and the tongue of the slanderer whom they cannot serve, or who has been disappointed.

[From the Advocate, June 18, 1862.]

Mr. Jacob Barker, in his connection with this paper, seems to attract the attention of our neighbor of the Delta. In our first number we stated that he had not any new opinions to bring out. The height of his ambition is to obtain from the public a consideration of what he has heretofore promulgated. We shall, therefore, from time to time, republish articles which came from his pen.

He is particularly anxious to impress on the public mind opinions which he believes to be in accordance with the best interests of the public. He insists that they are capable of governing themselves, if properly educated.

He had the pleasure of the acquaintance of Jefferson, Madison, Jackson, Armstrong, Hamilton, Clinton, Clay, Webster, John Quincy Adams, Van Buren, Lowndey, Calhoun, Cass, Emmett, and other distinguished citizens, whose many brilliant talents and exemplary virtues for a long time guided the destinies of this Republic.

Mr. Barker would be glad to see luminaries of similar brilliancy bursting on the world in these dark days. They, however, are no more, and it is very much to be feared we shall not see their like again.

———

TEST FOR OFFICE—*Honesty, Sobriety and Capacity to Discharge the Duties thereof.*—We have the utmost confidence in Gen. Butler, Gen. Shepley, and the Collector of the Port, and confidently expect them to be guided by this standard. In doing this, they have of necessity to obtain information from others. Therefore, we say to all, beware how you sign petitions or recommend or solicit office for any man not thoroughly qualified to discharge promptly all the duties of the office he seeks to fill.

Our greatest fears are that the powers at Washington will allow themselves to be deceived by fawning hypocrites or treacherous friends, in their selections for this State and city.

We stated in a past number that Gen. Harrison and Gen. Taylor were not qualified for the duties of President of the United States. The national feeling was so decided in favor of those who had obtained military glory that availability was the only question considered by the Federal party. It triumphed over all other considerations, inducing their leaders to overlook the superior qualities of Messrs. Clay and Webster.

The same consideration induced them to subscribe to the nomination of Gen. Taylor, which had been made by the independent Democrats Nine men out of every ten who voted at the Philadelphia Convention for the nomination of Gen. Taylor, preferred Mr. Clay, yet they had not sufficient independence to stand up to the chalk and meet the question like men.

Disappointment and mortification hurried these great men to their graves.

[From the Advocate, June 21, 1862]

PURCHASING GOLD TOO DEAR.—How shall we improve our present condition? is the great question to be considered. To do this, it becomes necessary to ascertain what it is, and to compare it to what it was before this unfortunate war took place. Comparison is the only power conferred on man by which to decide on all earthly things material to health, prosperity and the condition of society. Small things are a safe standard by which to guide his judgment in relation to those of magnitude.

With this view we should take a retrospective glance of the past, and each individual should consider what he was suffering under the Constitution of the United States as it was administered before the war, how many slaves he lost, and how much tax he had to pay to support the Government, remembering that we must have a Government of some sort, and that no government can be sustained but by a tax of some description; and, further, what rules and regulations to which he had to submit were oppressive and uncomfortable. These things ascertained and compared with his present condition, will enable him to decide whether or not the medicine administered to correct those evils has not been far greater than was necessary to cure or correct them.

The same course of thinking will be equally applicable to all matters of State, however momentous. Look at the banks, their present condition, their business and future prospects, and compare them to what they were before this war took place.

Look at the situation of the planter, and compare it to what is was before this war took place.

Look at that of the shipowner, and compare it to what it was before the inception of this war.

Look at the factors, and compare their present business and prospects to what they were before the commencement of this war.

Look at the condition and prospects of the owners and employes of steamboats, and compare them to what they were before this war took place.

Look at the present business of the mason, carpenter, painter and laborer, and see the difference in their business and future prospects, and see what it was before this war took place.

Look at the business of the stevedore and drayman, and compare it to what it was before this war took place.

Look at the present business of those who dealt in or employed slaves, and compare it with what it was before this war took place.

Look at the business of those who relied on the profession of the law to support their families, and compare it to what it was before the war took place.

Look at the estimation in which the United States was held by foreign nations before this war took place, and compare it with what it now is, or what it will be, in case two Confederacies should be established.

Let these comparisons be made, and we risk nothing· in stating that all parties will unite in the opinion that the attempt now making to change our form of Government is purchasing gold too dear.

This, however, we admit, is not a very appropriate use of the term gold, there not being any such commodity embraced in the boon contended for.

Consider the gay attire, the beautiful wreaths, ribbons, flowers and feathers, which adorned the numerous fine ladies who promenaded our streets, and who are now, or who will soon be shrouded in the habiliments of woe, and tell us if this is not purchasing gold too dear.

Consider the numbers who have or will return from

the battle-field despoiled of an eye, an arm, a leg, or otherwise maimed or disfigured, and tell us if this is not puachasing gold too dear.

Look at the storehouses going to decay and dwellings destitute of tenants, taxes, insurance and interest going on, and tell us if this is not purchasing gold too dear.

Consider the increase of taxes which of necessity must result from the lavish expenditure of money incident to a state of war, and tell us if this is not purchasing gold too dear.

Imagine how half a million of penniless soldiers, when disbanded, without pay and without occupation, are to be supported or provided for, and compare this with their former industrial pursuits in private life, and say whether or not it is not purchasing gold too dear.

The greatest of all the evils of this war is the desire for 'military occupation it has inspired in the rising generation.

[From the Advocate, June 23, 1862.]

LET THERE BE PEACE.—There not being any good reason for continuing this unfortunate war, we say let there be peace. Once concluded, we shall be slow to embark again in a strife likely to prove so disastrous; an unprofitable contest of trying which can do the other the most harm.

The difficult question seems to be how this desirable end is to be brought about. Our very popular Military Commandant, Gen. G. F. Shepley, has opened the way, by his admirable General Order No. 13, inviting all those absent from their families in the military service of the Confederate States, to return home, guaranteeing to them safe conduct and protection after their arrival.

They made a vigorous effort to establish a separate Confederacy, expending the wealth and best blood of the Nation, in the hope of accomplishing what they have been taught to believe would be considered a great work in the cause of self-government. They have failed, and have not the adequate resources for continuing the strife with any prospect of success ; therefore, let them return to their homes, and to their accustomed occupations, as gracefully as possible, forgetting the past, devoting their time and talents to the support of their families, and the resuscitation of the commerce of the city and their own fortunes.

THE BALLOT-BOX.—This palladium of our liberties must and shall be protected and sustained from the abuses, violations and frauds to which, for many years, it has been subject.

So great has been this abuse that it has induced many good citizens to despair of this Republic, and be willing to return again to a monarchy, the worst of all remedies. Military rule is a good substitute for a monarchy. This, of necessity, must be temporary, and before it is withdrawn we hope the ballot-boxes will be open to our fellow-citizens, and that they will profit by so good an opportunity to place competent men in authority to r.it over the city affairs, which have been sadly mismanaged for many years.

This reformation cannot take place if the property-holders, bankers and merchants will not take part in forming good tickets and supporting the candidates thus selected.

If those most deeply interested will not take the troube and make the necessary contributions to select and elect good rulers, they should submit without a murmur to the impositions which are sure to follow their lukewarmness and neglect.

In the place of.contenting themselves with finding fault with and cursing others, they should remember that such a course irritates and drives the voters into the ranks of their opponents. The adopted citizens having been invited here by our laws, they should be allowed freely to enjoy the privileges guaranteed by those laws.

Reviling naturalization laws, universal suffrage, and the adopted citizens, is the most impolitic course which can be pursued. Rules and laws regulating universal suffrage, universal education and naturalization, cannot be disturbed. Respect all rights acquired under them, treat the recipients with becoming respect and kindness, and we shall assuredly benefit by their votes. Kindness and respect are sure to win a return of those heavenly qualities.

————

GENERAL PHELPS.

The friends of the Union, residing in Louisiana, are

not satisfied with President Lincoln's continuing General Phelps in command. They consider him an enemy to the Constitution of the United States, and therefore it is impossible for him to harmonize with our citizens, who are determined to maintain their rights as defined in that sacred 'charter; while Major General Butler and General Shepley are taking great pains to protect us in our rights, as an evidence of which we have General Butler's order that none save those employed should be received or be allowed to remain within the lines of the army, and General Shepley's order warning the marines of the consequences which would attend their aiding the escape of slaves.

These wholesome regulations are counteracted by the adverse course of General Phelps, which the President should not tolerate, if he wishes to have the confidence of the people of Louisiana.

[From the Advocate, June 30, 1862.]

Our neighbors of the Delta said that this was to be a pro-slavery paper, and could not succeed. Strictly true as this is as to the design of this paper, the question of its success remains to be tested. One thing is certain, that no other than a pro-slavery paper can succeed in any part of Louisiana. Opposition to the institutions of the South have brought on us and on all Europe the present disastrous state of things, which can only be relieved by a return to our former pursuits, which we must be allowed to do quietly and peaceably.

It seems to us to be impossible that the whole world should acquiesce in the course pursued by the fanatics of the North, who know not what they have been doing, nor the consequences of what they wish to do. Their course is a war on the peace, happiness and contentment of the colored race. Honest zeal misleads most of them. They vainly imagine that they are serving God. Short-sighted mortals! They overlook the great fact that God is omnipotent, omnipresent, and competent to do His own work without their aid. He has not any attorneys, nor does He require any. Our flag is nailed to the mast on this subject.

The sooner the better the editors of the Delta come to the conclusion that in order to promote and cement a Union feeling in this community, confidence must be inspired in the stability of their property and their occupations, which can only be done by frankness, kindness and the fulfilment of all friendly professions.

There are far too many, we admit, who require rigorous treatment, while the great bulk of the people would be won over by gentle measures, and it would be much better to let the others escape without feeling the penalties their transgressions richly merit, than that the whole community should be agitated and kept hungry and in a state of alarm. We say, let there be peace at home and abroad.

The manifestations on the issuing of our late extra were unmistakable. They emanated from a desire for peace, believing that a foreign recognition would open the door to negotiation, and thus would lead to a measure much wished for by all. Negotiation once commenced will assuredly result in peace. Mistaken as this notion may have been, it was that which pervaded the public mind. We are all so tired of the war that we are panting for peace, and become excited at the least glimmering of such an event.

———

[From the Advocate, August 21, 1862.].

OUR SLAVES.

Great complaints are made at the demoralizing effects on the colored race by the measures pursued by the United States. No one can disapprove of their interference with Southern rights more than we do. We are equally opposed to placing arms in the hands of uneducated men who are not accustomed to use them. When our State authorities organized a regiment or company of blacks, commissioned its officers, and when Governor Moore, by a general order, complimented them, we supposed the public would sooner or later have cause to regret, deeply regret having set so mischievous an example.

Our opposition to all interference with Southern institutions was and is based on four considerations :

1st. That any change would be destructive of the happiness and comfort of the colored race.

2d. That it is impossible to abolish slavery in the Southern States without the interposition of Divine Providence.

3d. That the rights secured by the Constitution cannot be violated without putting the whole afloat.

4th. That emancipation would depopulate the South of its white population, and prove ruinous to the commerce of the world.

The Abolition portion of the Republican press are scolding the President because he does not declare universal emancipation, evidently believing that the avowal of such a measure would end the war, by inducing insurrection among the slaves, etc.   That is another of the phantasies of the one-idea men.   The President, or no other observing man, believes anything of the kind. It would complicate still further the present difficulties, and produce no earthly good.   It would not liberate a slave—because we must first conquer a State before laws can be practically given to it, or emancipation effected. What the people want, and what they are giving their blood and treasure to accomplish, is the preservation of the old Union, under the old Constitution—and it can be done by white men, if at all!   The way to do it, is to respond promptly to the call for aid, which the President makes on the people, and let slavery take care of itself!

[From the Advocate, August 22, 1862.]
FOREIGN INTERFERENCE.

Our opposition to foreign interference, resting as it does on the immutable principles of independence, we could not suppress our feelings of indignation on reading the article from the Baltimore correspondent, by the British steamer Arabia, about the French force landing at Mobile—supported by a large fleet of iron-clad steamers.

This thing is more easily said than done. If such a mad scheme should enter the far-reaching mind of Louis Napoleon, the little business he has to attend to at home would divert him therefrom ; if not, his neighbor, John Bull, would have to be consulted ; and if so hopeless an enterprise should be .undertaken, the happy effect would be to cause all parties in the United States to put on the shelf their domestic differences, to be settled hereafter by themselves, and to unite in a war against the invader, whose soldiers would embrace the opportunity which would be presented for them all to become citizens of the United States, with a snug little farm of one hundred acres, to which they could bring their families as soon as peace took place.

[From the Advocate, August 23, 1862.]

We gave some important documents from the Delta of yesterday, without undertaking to criticise the ungenerous remarks of the learned editor in introducing them.

The attachment of the editor of this paper to the Union and the Constitution is too well established to be shaken by anything that can be said by new comers ; yet he may be allowed to repeat a remark or two which he has made publicly and privately a thousand times :

1st. That the North refused to carry out the Constitution according to its letter and spirit.

10

2d. That the South could have choked them off and brought them to terms in three months, for the want of supplies, if the members of Congress had retained their seats.

3d. That there would not have been any war but for the attack on Fort Sumter.

4th. That the Democratic party of the North had placed the game in their hands, which they threw away by re-signing their seats in Congress.

However, we beg pardon of the reader for troubling him so much about the editor of this paper and his opin-ions. We trust it will not be necessary to trouble them in future, however active our neighbor's devils may be in the use of their black-balls.

Finally, the best answer to give is to refer to the Jack Tar's remarks to an observer who expressed surprise when he witnessed Mr. Barker attending, personally, to the sale and delivery of a bale of hay to a drayman, in the plentitude of his business in New York : "It is not of any consequence, his dimensions have been taken."

———

[From the Advocate, September 8, 1862.]

TWENTY-FIVE PER CENT. TAX ON AGRICULTURAL PRODUCTS.

The Confederate Congress appears to be about im-posing an export duty of twenty-five per cent. on cotton, tobacco, sugar and other products of our soil. Those wise legislators should have thought of this before they authorized the burning of cotton and discouraged its further cultivation. Had they done this, allowing the planters to obtain supplies for their slaves in exchange for their sugar and cotton, the stock on hand to accumulate in the ordinary course of cultivation, there would have been a tempting boon for foreign intervention, for which they have been so long panting; and when exportation should be allowed, the twenty-five per cent., if collected, would have gone far to have paid the interest on the frightful debt which is augmenting with the speed of the crazy engineer when on his voyage to the moon.

Such a duty would, however, have been a two-edged sword, and might not have been easily collected in gold and silver. The planters would not have quietly submitted to such an inroad on their hard earnings after all their sufferings by the war, however much they may have consoled themselves with the notion that it would ultimately come out of the consumer; and this idea might have induced France and England to consider it war on their manufactories, and have indisposed them to taking part in our family quarrel. ·

All these things will doubtless be considered by those wiseacres, who hold the destinies of their constituents between their thumb and finger, before they thus burthen the agricultural interests of the country, about which we have no opinion to offer, beyond that which we have often proclaimed, viz: all legitimate trade should be left as free as air.

There appears to be another important measure pending before the said Congress, which is, to make its treasury notes a legal tender. This may be well enough as a political necessity, so far as it may apply to contracts entered into or made subsequent to the passage of such a law; while it would be a direct fraud on existing creditors if applied to them, particularly on those who hold bank notes, or mortgage or other collateral securities, all which, with a single dash of the pen, would be reduced to the value of Confederate Treasury notes, and ultimately to the value of old Continental paper.

If this measure should be brought about it will be done by bank influence, as furnishing the most convenient means of paying off their bank note issues.

<hr />

[From the Advocate, September 10, 1862.]

MAINTAINING THE CONSTITUTION.

The President is apparently determined to adhere to a strictly constitutional policy as the only path of safety for the country. Mr. Lincoln may lack the polish and statesmanship of some of his predecessors, and be somewhat *outre* in manners, but of one thing the people are now receiving almost daily assurances from Washington—he can be firm. He is not ignorant of the sentiments of the great masses of the people, and, assured of their support, he has the courage to resist boldly the terrible pressure of the radicals, seeing, as he does, that their course is ruinous and its end anarchy. He is opposed to extremists on either hand, and has on frequent occasions declared his purpose, while prosecuting the war vigorously, to carry it on solely and exclusively for the restoration of the Union and the maintenance of the Government.

———

[From the Advocate, September 15, 1862.]

We have uniformly contended for the Union and the Constitution; and if the terms of the compact had been promptly, honestly and fairly carried out, the Nation would have been saved the great misfortune it is now encountering, North and South, for no good. We say for no good, as we rarely meet an individual who does not complain of being worse off, with worse prospects for the future than before the war, and no one pretends that his condition will, when peace takes place, be improved from what it was before the war.

All this on the pretence of benefiting the colored race. We say pretence, because we religiously believe that all interference with their condition by the white man is prejudicial to their morals, their comfort and their happiness.

Slaves, in the eye of the law are, according to the Constitution, *property*, and whatever forfeiture of property those embarked in the Confederacy may incur, it cannot apply to the property of good loyal men; and so thought Major General Butler and General Shepley, and but for the last law passed by Congress on the subject, they would restore to the rightful loyal owners all their slaves coming within the lines. That law forbids such action; hence, all they can do is to refuse to receive, quarter or protect those who run away from good loyal citizens.

[From the Advocate, September 25, 1862.]

The editor of the Delta says, or rather broadly insinu-ates, that the publication of the Advocate should not be allowed. For once in his life he is honest in thus stating what he thinks. No one doubts that he thinks so. He should, however, remember that there is a tale connected with its origin as yet untold.

The wagoner of antiquity, when the wheels of his vehicle sunk deep into the mire, called on Jupiter for aid, instead of putting his shoulder to the wheel. We would impress upon the editor's memory that Major Gen-eral Butler has other fish to fry than to waste his valuable time in vain attempts to help this Cape Cod journalist out of the mud into which he has inextricably plunged his editorial ambulance.

If he should succeed in thus muzzling the press, it would not be a cause of much regret to the editor of this paper on his own account, however much he might regret the privation of their morning's entertainment which such a proceeding would impose upon the ladies—God bless them!

————

[From the Advocate, October 3, 1862.]

We thank the Delta for giving place to Mr. Barker's remarks which appeared in our paper of Tuesday. If by ascribing to him egotism the Delta supposed that he claimed to have an influence with the community, the editor was in error. Mr. Barker does not put forth any such pretension, while he insists that the truth, and facts fairly stated, are entitled to and have had a towering influence; and so far as he is concerned, he has endeavored, both now and in past time, to dispel the mist in which designing men have uniformly exerted themselves to involve all political subjects; and if the result has been favorable to his views, it has arisen from the imposing influence of the facts, and the conclusions therefrom, and not from any personal influence of Mr. Barker.

As to his considering "the institution of slavery of more importance than the Union," the Delta knows the folly of repining at an evil which cannot be cured.

If the Union is lost, it has been thrown away by the violation of the Constitution on the part of the North. The South should have held fast and resisted all innovation, in place of unwisely yielding the rights which they are now endeavoring to regain at the cost of men and money without stint.

Impossibilities cannot be accomplished. Consequently the Union cannot be preserved or restored until the North abandons its war on the Constitution.

He wrote to a friend in Philadelphia who had sent him the speech of Andrew Johnson, of Tennessee. as follows:

[EXTRACT.]

"NEW YORK, August 17, 1861.

"I have heard read the whole of Mr. Johnson's speech· It is a very able *expose*, and however correct his history may be, and however logical his legal and Constitutional deductions are, to enforce and carry them out will cost too many lives, too much money, and be fraught with too disastrous consequences for practical men to approve. The old saying is that gold may be bought too dear. Suppose it were possible to crush the South, what would dominion over so warlike a people, so restless as they would become, be worth at the end of a seven years' war? The best way is to let them go, and have a separate Confederacy. Bad as this would be, sooner or later you will come to that conclusion. Why not, then, do it at once, and save the further effusion of human blood and the waste of countless millions, for posterity to pay?"

For these opinions the Delta asserts that Mr. Barker considers "the institution of slavery of more importance than the Union," which is not the fact. What he does most implicitly believe is, that it is impossible to preserve or restore the Union without settling the slave question satisfactorily to the South.

———

[From the Advocate, October 11, 1862.]

Our Army and Navy came here to fight for the Union and Constitution, not for the negroes. Coming on so laudable a mission, they were welcomed by all good Union men, and by the women too. The latter were not so numerous as the former, because their superior quickness of perception led them to doubt the sincerity of those who sent them here, while declaiming for the Union and the Constitution; they thought they were proclaiming security for our peculiar institutions, when they were panting for an opportunity to invade our dearest rights, secured by that glorious Constitution, to maintain which the war of 1812 was declared, and sustained throughout by the whole country, in which the editor of this paper contributed to the extent of his ability, and did not expect to see the Star Spangled Banner furled so near the close of his long life.

———

COTTON.—The most remarkable thing that has occurred since the war commenced is the continued exportation of cotton from Great Britain to all parts of the world, including the United States. It was to have been supposed that the first act of that far-seeing nation would have been the prohibition of its exportation. Had this been done, it would have retained a supply for a season of the material so essential for the employment of her laboring classes. Not having done so, shows her obstinate determination to defy King Cotton, no matter at what cost.

Those who hazarded the very existence of this Nation on the expectation of foreign intervention should have known better.

———

Having announced our entire failure in accomplishing the main object for which this paper was established, our readers cannot expect us to discuss that subject much further. The evil has come upon us and on the world, and we cannot help ourselves until the ballot-boxes shall be freely opened to us. Then we shall speak in the thundering tones that become freemen. In the meantime we shall submit with all due humility and obedience

to the authorities placed over us, endeavoring to make
our paper interesting by the publication of such news as
may be received, without undertaking to control. public
opinion. That being irrevocably fixed, it could not be
changed if we had a disposition to do so.

———

[From the Advocate, November 7, 1862.]
FOREIGN INTERVENTION.

So great is the desire for peace that the foreign news
published in our Wednesday's extra was hailed with general joy and exultation. As sincerely as we wish for
peace, we are not without serious apprehension that the
intervention which that news foreshadows will not prove
acceptable. Not believing in the disposition of the rulers
of England and France to foster and cherish our form of
government, we have already said "hands off; we prefer
to manage our own affairs in our own way." We say so
still, and did not believe that either nation would hazard
such a measure, until the President's emancipation proclamation appeared. So strange, uncalled-for and unexpected a proceeding led us to believe that it was brought
about by some secret influence hostile to the South. The
mystery is now unveiled. We fear it resulted from a
disposition to meet the abolition views of England, in
which the Emperor of France has acquiesced. In such a
case their intervention will be a cause of regret rather
than of rejoicing. Let us wait.

The paper continued to flourish, becoming the most popular paper ever published in Louisiana—particularly with the ladies—until the 15th of November, when its publication was suspended for a *single day* by a special order from Major General Butler, from a misapprehension of the editor's views in relation to Foreign Intervention. This being explained to the General's satisfaction, the publication was resumed on Monday, the 17th November, as appears from the following exulting announcement which appeared in that paper on that day :

THE STARS AND STRIPES UNFURLED—THE CANDLE RELIGHTED.

HEADQUARTERS DEPARTMENT OF THE GULF, ⎱
, NEW ORLEANS, November 14, 1862. ⎰

Special Order No. 513.

The Daily Advocate having, after warning, published the following article :

"*The Ballot-Box.*—This palladium of our liberties, this charter of our rights, this emblem of Democracy, has been speaking in a voice of thunder, as we knew it would if the people could be aroused from their slumber· It has been our unceasing endeavor to awake them throughout the Nation.

"We were the first to tell our readers of its success in Pennsylvania, Ohio and Indiana; and now we have gratifying reports from Illinois, New Jersey and New York. If these reports be confirmed, an armistice will soon follow. Negotiations once commenced, there will not be any more fighting. Whether an armistice results from the Democratic success, or from foreign intervention, we shall hail it as a peace measure—to be welcomed by all parties."

The publication of that journal will be discontinued from this date.

By command of   MAJOR GENERAL BUTLER.
GEO. C. STRONG, A. A. General.

———

NEW ORLEANS, November 15, 1862.

Major Gen. Butler, Com'g Dept. of the Gulf:

General—I take pleasure in stating to you in this note what I have explained to you personally, that the purport of the objectionable article which is the basis of your order for the suppression of the Advocate, has been understood entirely different from the intention of the writer. The design of the article was to express the ardent desire of the editor of this paper for peace. The religion in which I was educated was peace and good will to my fellow men, and I have always advocated peace. Nothing, of course, can be more ardently sought by every well wisher to the country. "Foreign intervention" was inadvertantly mentioned as one means through which peace might be obtained, and the article would certainly bear the interpretation that I desired such intervention as the means of obtaining peace. This I regret. I have never been in favor of any intervention by any foreign power in this war; my whole thought has been opposed to it. I can point to many articles in my paper expressing that thought   I am entirely opposed to any intervention by foreigners with the affairs of this country, and, if permitted, the paper will most fully show that opposition.

I am, respectfully, your obedient servant,

JACOB BARKER.

HEADQUARTERS DEPARTMENT OF THE GULF, }
NEW ORLEANS, November 15th.   }

Sir—Your note upon the subject of the article in the Advocate is satisfactory, and its publication is permitted. I can have no objection to any proper advocacy of peace. To obtain it the United States are making war. But peace can never be obtained by "armed intervention" of a foreign power. That would be an act of war, and its possible effect would 'only be to put away the day of peace.

No more delusively treasonable idea can be entertained than the advocacy of foreign intervention, which can never be permitted, either directly or covertly, in this Department. Whosoever desires foreign aids to rebellion, and expresses that desire, is a traitor and an enemy to the Government, and will be so treated.

Respectfully,

BENJ. F. BUTLER, Major Gen. Com'g.

Jacob Barker, Esq.

Long before peace was restored President Lincoln was anxious to see civil authority re-established in such parts of Louisiana as had been conquered, and that that State should be represented in the Congress of the United States by her permanent citizens. For this purpose he recommended an election, saying : if one-tenth of the qualified electors of the whole State should cast their votes, their authority should be recognized; and, on the 21st November, 1862, he addressed a letter to General Shepley, as follows :

"Executive Mansion, }
" Washington, November 21, 1862. }

"*Dear Sir*—Dr. Kennedy, bearer of this, has some apprehension that Federal officers, not citizens of Louisiana, may be set up as candidates for Congress in that State. In my view there could be no possible object in such an election. We do not particularly need members of Congress from those States to enable us to get along with legislation here. What we do want is the conclusive evidence that respectable citizens of Louisiana are willing to be members of Congress, and to swear to support the Constitution, and that other respectable citizens there are willing to vote for them and send them. To send a parcel of Northern men here as Representatives, elected, as would be understood, (and perhaps really so,) at the point of the bayonet, would be disgraceful and outrageous, and were I a member of Congress here, I would vote against admitting any such man to a seat. ·

"Yours, very truly,   A. Lincoln.
" Hon. G. F. Shepley."

When the day of election was approaching, Major Gen

Banks informed Mr. Barker that he was very anxious that the required number of votes should be cast. Mr. Barker replied that his political friends were unwilling to take any part in the election; that, although anxious for the resumption of civil authority and the success of the Democratic party, that he had not, under existing circumstances, any hope of a fair election; that if they should call a public meeting, they apprehended that its deliberations would be interrupted by the new-comers. The General's reply was, that he was determined that no such interruption should take place; that if the political opponents of the ruling powers thought proper to call a public meeting, he would, if necessary, send a military guard to preserve order; that he wished all parties to bring forward their own candidates; that he was indifferent as to the success of any party; that his great object was to have the required number of votes cast to secure the recognition of the State. With this assurance, the Democratic party embarked in the election, and although it was conducted without mob violence or the anticipated interruptions, they were defeated by the receipt of illegal votes at the polls, and the application of money sent here from the North by the Abolitionists, to be refunded by taxing those thus defeated, as will be seen by the following letter:

MR. HAMILTON'S LETTER.

Nevis, Dobb's Ferry P. O., Jan. 5, 1864.

Thomas J. Durant, Esq., New Orleans:

Dear Sir—Your letter of the 20th ult. was received yesterday, with the accompanying papers.

Your account of the formation of *the Free State General Committee*, of which you are chairman, composed of delegates from all the Union Associations, whose object is to call upon the loyal Union citizens of your State to elect delegates to a Convention to form a Constitutional Gov-. ernment, making Louisiana a *Free State*, and loyally to declare that the people thereof owe allegiance to the Constitution of the United States as a paramount duty. A more patriotic effort could not be devised; nor one more deserving of the sympathy and aid of the loyal people of the United States, and the protection of the National Government.

Your Committee have been pleased to ask me to act as their agent; and to procure funds for them in New York. I feel honored that you should thus have connected my name with this great *first* step in the true direction to restore the Unity of the States, the Brotherhood of the People, and the Authority of the National Government over all the people within its jurisdiction.

Go on in your great and patriotic work—you must be successful. Your devotion to the great principle of liberty on which our system is founded, and your energy will be rewarded by the consciousness of having restored civil government and harmony among your fellow-citizens; and of having given a new development to the great material resources of your State. Further, you will have the distinguished honor of having been the pioneer of the States in rebellion in that great Christian duty of elevating the social condition of a feeble and much oppressed race by making them free.

Your example will lead the loyal Union men in States now in rebellion to take the same wise and beneficent course, and through its influence you will soon see the loyal citizens of Tennessee, of Arkansas, of North Carolina, and of Texas, forming *free* and loyal State governments, and thus wheeling into line in obedience to their national and supreme allegiance, and then sternly exerting the repressive energies of their civil State governments in aid of the military power of the United States "to reduce the refractory into obedience to the laws."

As to funds—I will not only contribute, but I will endeavor to induce others to do so. Allow me to state that in order to carry on the election for a Convention; to provide for the members and officers; stationery and printing for that Convention when in session; to submit the Constitution to the people, and carry on an election for that purpose; to provide for the expense of an election of State officers and the members of the Legislature; and the expenses of the departments of State and of the Legislature at its first session, you will require certainly not less than $20,000.

To obtain that sum, I submit that it is better to *borrow* than to *beg.* Call your *free* State delegates together; appoint a committee of finance—three or five of your best men; next, pass a *resolution* authorizing this committee to borrow, not over $20,000, on the *plighted faith of the loyal Union people of the State of Louisiana;* that the understanding is that the amount so borrowed shall be recognized in your Constitution as a debt of your State, to be

11

assumed and provided for by the Legislature at its first session. Having passed such a resolution, pass another authorizing the finance committee to prepare not over two hundred certificates of indebtedness of one hundred dollars each, payable with interest at ten per cent. per annum, within one year after the inauguration of your free State Government.

Such course will give you all the funds you may require, because it will give your friends, who are the loyal men throughout the country, the highest assurance of your earnestness and confidence of success; and because it will be understood that the members of the Convention who shall be elected are pledged to provide for this indebtedness as the price paid to restore the people to their legal rights, privileges and duties.

Such is my confidence in your efforts to restore your State to its true condition under the Constitution of the United States, that I am confident there will be found here more than one man of substance who will endorse your certificates, should that be necessary to give them credit.

I am, with great respect, your obedient servant,

JAMES A. HAMILTON.

Very many of the electors who had taken the oath of allegiance to the United States, and were otherwise qualified, by the laws of Louisiana, to cast their votes, being unwilling to take the "Iron-clad Oath," which obliged them to obey and support proclamations to be thereafter issued, and which consequently they had not seen, Mr. Barker, believing the President only meant to require it of those who had offended, solicited such an explanation from him, to which he did not receive a reply.

The Conservative Committee made application to Major General Banks on the same subject. His reply put an end to all hope of Conservative success in the election. It was nevertheless deemed expedient to bring out as large a vote as possible to restore the State to the glorious Union.

———

MR. BARKER'S LETTER TO THE PRESIDENT.

NEW ORLEANS, January 22, 1864.

Abraham Lincoln, President of the United States :

Dear Sir—Will you permit me to ask you to modify or explain your proclamation in relation to the return of the State to the Union, for which I am equally anxious with yourself. If enforced according to its literal construction, our best men cannot be induced to become candidates, and the votes cast will be of a very limited number, although probably enough, say one-tenth, to secure the main object of the election.

As to myself I have not the least objection to the oath if it does not invade a vested right, nor do I wish to vote. I do not, for myself, or any member of my family, desire any office or political situation. All we wish is good government.

I think you meant only to require the oath which

accompanies your proclamation of those who had not pre-
viously taken the oath of allegiance to the United States.

Those whose names were registered and who took the
oath and voted at the last Congressional election, which
election was recognized by Congress, think you did not
intend by your proclamation to disfranchise them when
they had all the qualifications required by the laws and
Constitution of Louisiana, they not having done anything
in violation of the oath of allegiance taken.

If the President will so modify or explain by proclamation, or authorize Major General Banks to do so in season
to be known through our lower parishes before election
day, he will greatly subserve the question to be decided
by the approaching election in this State. Citizens who
have not sinned cannot honorably accept a pardon.

Very respectfully, I have the honor to subscribe myself
your obedient servant,   JACOB BARKER.

LETTER FROM THE CONSERVATIVE COMMITTEE TO MAJOR
GENERAL BANKS.

NEW ORLEANS, Feb. 8, 1864.

Maj. Gen. N. P. Banks, Com'g Dept. of the Gulf:

General—We are particularly anxious to be informed
whether any oath will be required at the election to be
held on the 22d inst., from the loyal citizens who took
the oath of allegiance prior to the date of President
Lincoln's proclamation, the 8th day of December, 1863,
and who were then qualified voters according to the laws
of Louisiana.

In our opinion, if the last published oath should be required of those otherwise qualified, the number of votes will be so small as to be likely to defeat the proposed State organization.

We respectfully solicit an early answer for publication. Permit us to say that we take the liberty of making these inquiries with a view to aid in the best way the views of the Administration in an early restoration of the State government.

With great respect, we have the honor to subscribe ourselves,

Your obedient servants,

C. ROSELIUS,
WM. L. ADAMS,
JACOB BARKER,
J. MORGAN HALL.

GENERAL BANKS'S REPLY TO THE CONSERVATIVE COMMITTEE.

HEADQUARTERS DEPARTMENT OF THE GULF, ⟩
NEW ORLEANS, February 14, 1864.   ⟨

Gentlemen—I have the honor to acknowledge the receipt of your letter of February 8, and to enclose as a general answer thereto a copy of an order issued this day. It would have given me great pleasure to have found among those professing a willingness to support the Government in all the measures deemed necessary for the suppression of the rebellion, a coincidence of opinion as to the substantive qualification for a voter in the election which has been ordered. This I have not been able to obtain. There seems to exist an unnecessary diversity of opinion upon this most important subject. I have, therefore, as indicated in a letter published some time since, followed the course directed by the President in his proclamation of the 8th of December. After much reflection upon this topic I am satisfied that the course pursued is wisest and best. Sooner or later, all men must come to the declaration which is contained in the order of this date. The election of the 22d of February is not of so much importance as others which will follow in the full restoration of the Government of the State of Louisiana. It is necessary that those who participate in this, the first election, as in those that follow, should make public their purpose in regard to the measures of the Government. If this is not done in the declaration of private assemblies, in the organization of parties, or in the presentation of candidates, the only opportunity that is left is in establishing the qualifications of the voters. Acting upon this view, I have been unable to comply with the suggestions contained in your letter, which, under other circumstances, I should gladly have done; and I commend to the citizens you represent an earnest consideration of the condition of public affairs, and appeal to them to make at once that declaration of purpose— which in the end must be required of all men—to support the measures of the Government necessary for the suppression of the rebellion. Though they have suffered much from the war, they have received important favors from the Government, which is still desirous of restoring the general prosperity that attends successful industry and extended trade, and every effort will be made to strengthen these important interests. Assuredly, it is not too much to require of them in return an oath of allegiance to the Government, attended with such explanatory declarations as remove the suspicion of reservation or evasion, and places the citizen who takes it upon a platform of open, unreserved and unconditional loyalty. It is plainly inconsistent with any sound public policy, that an oath of allegiance, which implies a qualified dissent to the measures of the Government imposing the obligation, should be administered to any class of citizens.

This may not be a correct interpretation of the course you recommend, but there is just ground of apprehension that it will be so understood.

With sincere regret that I have been unable to comply with your request, and an earnest hope that those you represent may accept the views herein presented,

I have the honor to be, with much respect,

Your obedient servant,

N. P. BANKS, Major Gen. Com'g.

To Messrs. Jacob Barker, C. Roselius, J. Morgan Hall and W. L. Adams.

———

HIGHLY IMPORTANT ORDER—QUALIFICATIONS OF ELECTORS.

HEADQUARTERS DEPARTMENT OF THE GULF, }
NEW ORLEANS, Feb. 13, 1864. }

General Orders, No. 24.

I. Every free white male twenty-one years of age, who has been a resident of the State twelve months, and six months in the parish in which he offers to vote, who is a citizen of the United States, and who shall have taken the oath prescribed by the President in his proclamation of the 8th December, 1863, shall have the right to vote in the election of State officers on the 22d day of February, 1864.

II. Citizens of the State who have been expelled from their homes by the public enemy on account of their devotion to the Union, and who would be qualified voters in the parishes to which they belong, will be allowed to vote for State officers only, in the election precincts in which, for the time being, they may reside.

III. Citizens of the State who have volunteered for the defence of the country in the army or navy, and who are otherwise qualified voters, will be allowed to vote in the election precincts in which they may be found on the day of election. And if the exigencies of the public service be such as to prevent their attendance at any established precinct, then commissioners fairly representing the interests involved in the election will be appointed to receive their votes wherever they may be stationed for that day, and to make due returns thereof, as well as their own votes, to the Military Governor of the State, as provided for other commissioners of election.

IV. The commissioners of election, at any election precinct, are authorized to administer the oath of allegiance, as prescribed by the President, to any person otherwise qualified to vote, and to register the name of such voter in New Orleans where a register is required, or to receive it in other parishes when no register is required, at any time before the polls are closed on the day of election.

V. The commissioners of election in the several parishes will make prompt returns of the votes given to the sheriff of the parish, as provided by law, or in his absence to the Provost Marshal, who will immediately return the same to the Military Governor of the State.

VI. The sheriffs of the several parishes, and in their absence, the Provost Marshals, will take especial care that the polls are properly opened, and that suitable judges of election and other officers are appointed. It is desirable that all persons properly qualified shall vote, but it is more important that illegal or fraudulent votes shall not vitiate the election.

VII. The situation of Louisiana is not identical with that of other States designated by the President, but the test of loyalty required by him as a basis for the restoration of Government is unequivocal. Full opportunity has been given to the people for the suggestion of any obligation more in accordance, if possible, with the condition of this State, but no general unity of sentiment appears to exist as to the test of fealty which should be demanded. The inference is irresistible that all parties prefer the form prescribed by the President to any other than their own.

The oath prescribed by him offers amnesty and pardon only to those who have committed treason. To all others it is a simple pledge of continued fealty to the Government. The oath of allegiance cannot be materially strengthened or impaired by the language in which it is clothed, but it may be accompanied by such explanations as to make known to the public the sense in which it is administered and received.   Allegiance cannot be more or less than unreserved, unconditional loyalty:

The repetition of an oath once taken, or when unnecessarily clothed in unusual language, may well cause hesitation, but if it be identified with the restoration of a government, at a time when secret evasions and reservations have sapped public integrity, and endangered the safety of the nation, it is an unsound patriotism that criticises the form or hesitates at its removal.

In times of public danger the Government has a right to demand an unreserved declaration of the purposes of all its people, and to provide, if necessary, an iron-clad defence against the weapons of its enemies. Those who seek its favor and protection must yield to its just demands.   An exemption from all duties and an enjoyment of all privileges at the same time is a greater degree of happiness than is accorded to any man in this life.   Let the people of Louisiana look at things as they are, and base their political action upon a declaration of loyalty that cannot be misunderstood or misinterpreted.   Upon this depends the restoration of peace and private and public property.

By command of   MAJOR GENERAL BANKS.

RICHARD B. IRWIN, A. A. General.

The election resulted in favor of what was denominated the Union party, it being impossible to counteract the frauds practiced at Wood's Press.

The successful party, considering it expedient to celebrate the result, determined, among other things, that the city should be illuminated, inviting Mr. Barker to take part therein, as follows :

New Orleans, Feb. 27, 1864.

To Jacob Barker, Esq.:

In accordance with the resolution passed by the General Committee of Arrangements for the Inauguration of the Governor elect, you were appointed on the Committe on Finance. Will you please meet the Committee at the Mayor's office, City Hall, this evening at 8 o'clock, or signify your acceptance in writing to the Secretary.

By order,   George A. Fosdick, Chairman.

J. W. Thomas, J. T. Tucker, J. F. Collins, Secretaries.

The subjoined letter from Mr. Barker was his answer :

New Orleans, February 27, 1864.

Geo. A. Fosdick, Chairman; J. W. Thomas, J. T. Tucker, J. F. Collins, Secretaries:

Dear Sirs—In reply to your kind notice of this date, that the honorable situation of a member of your committee of finance had been conferred on me, I have to remark that it is my practice to obey the laws and to respect those placed in power over me ; hence, I am disposed to do all honor to his Excellency Governor Hahn ; yet I cannot take part in the proposed illumination, lest it should be construed into an approval of the invasion of the vested rights of our citizens.

We were well satisfied with the rule of Governor Shepley and did not wish any change until peace took place; yet as it was determined on, I was anxious for the largest practical vote to give respectability to our return to the glorious Union.

Although the Iron-clad Oath had an unmerited influence on the canvass, the vote cast in the rural parishes, outside of the military stations, indicated the feeling of the permanent population of Louisiana, and it is therefore, in my opinion, best to submit in silence to the rule established over us, leaving the responsibility with the new comers, throwing no obstacles into their way, giving them every opportunity to establish a good government without any contest or unsolicited participation in the formation thereof—therefore I beg respectfully to decline the honor of the appointment.

Your obedient servant,   JACOB BARKER.

———

There were not any returns from about one-half the rural parishes, and those which came in indicated that a very light vote had been cast, viz: in the parish of St. John the Baptist only eighteen votes were polled—one-half for the successful candidate and one-half for the Conservative candidate—and the other returns are indicative of the feeling of the permanent inhabitants of the rural districts of Louisiana. Six parishes cast 1698 votes, of which 1415 were for the Conservative candidates, the residue, 283, were for the Abolition candidates.

[From the Advocate, January 3, 1863.]

"THE WAY WE LIVE."

" I invite thee to a calf's head, and if I do not carve it most curiously, say my knife's naught."

It is seldom, indeed, that we notice the diatribes of malignant spleen or besotted envy when directed against ourselves, but when the fair daughters of our city are again and again assailed with the most scandalous libels, we consider it our duty to hold the libeler as a thing of scorn before "the outstretched finger of time." Some weeks ago, when military rule was so strict as to make an answer impolitic, the editor of the Delta broadly asserted that the dark eyes of our Creole ladies were derived from impure sources—derived from an unacknowledged relationship to the children of Ham. Since then, on the first day of the New Year, he attempted to enlighten his readers as to "The Way We Live," in nearly a column of vile and dastardly insinuations against the morals of our Southern women.

We know that "to err is human," and therefore will not pretend to assert that every Southern woman is an angel of purity; but we will assert—challenging contradiction—that our Creole ladies are as elevated in their tastes and as free from the low taints of vice as any women to be found in the wide world. In the moral city of Boston, to which the editor of the Delta refers so frequently, and in such laudatory terms, there are institutions as detestable as any that can be found within the limits of the South. That is the city in which a peculiar

paper, known as "Life in Boston," is published, and from
the scurrillous character of many of the leading articles
in the Delta, since it could boast its moral military editor,
the conclusion as to where the moral military man received his editorial training, is altogether irresistible.

Though vile and false as anything can be, "The Way
We Live" displays a clerky skill in the use of words not
usually found among the Delta's slanders.   Possibly it
may have been stolen from some "Paul de Kock" of the
Northern press, for editorials, as well as paper, ink and
glue, are among the articles surreptitiously acquired by
that journal under its present management.   Versed only
in the polemics of paltroonery and the literature of degradation, the editor of the Delta carries a shingle for a
sword, and is only brave when protected by a row of
bayonets.   He has proved himself a bag of wind; prick
him, and nothing but vile gas escapes.   Appointed to
conciliate the people of this city, his editorial career has
been such as still further to estrange them.   Calling those
who took the oath of allegiance *perjurers*, and those who
did not *traitors*, he has proved false alike to the Government which employed him, and a disgrace to the naval
and military power of which he pretended to be the
mouthpiece.

Heaven forgive us, that we have stooped so low as to
notice him.

————

After the resumption of the publication, Mr. Barker was
careful not to write or to admit any article approbating

foreign intervention; nor had an armed foreign intervention ever been mentioned in the columns of the Advocate.

Mr. Barker was very solicitous that the paper should be conducted to the satisfaction of Major General Banks. The columns of the Delta, the organ of the Government, furnished abundant evidence that its editors were watching over him for evil, and the retiring General informed him, the evening before he left, that those editors had been incessant in their efforts to induce him to close his paper. Desirous as Mr. Barker was to exclude everything likely to be disapproved by Major General Banks, he was not entirely successful, therefore a file of soldiers took possession of the establishment on Saturday morning, the 3d of January, 1863, the officer in command of which announced the paper's suppression.

Mr. Barker was so incessantly applied to by the public, particularly the ladies, to solicit of Major General Banks the liberty of resuming the publication, that he was induced to pen several letters to that eminent civil and military gentleman for that purpose; but the General was inexorable, as will be seen:

.NEW ORLEANS, January 6th, 1863.

Major General Banks:

Respected Sir—It was to me a cause of deep regret that you should have found cause to suspend the publication of the National Advocate, not so much on account of my pecuniary interest as from the impression created that I am unfriendly to the Union cause, which is not now, nor has it ever been the case.

Although my efforts to exclude all articles not likely to be approved by the military authorities, after my interview with Col. Strother, were not entirely successful, I am of the opinion that if its publication be *resumed,* the care taken to reject all objectionable articles will in future be more successful.

This paper was the most flourishing in the city, and it seems to be a pity that any profitable establishment, in these dull and calamitous times, should be overthrown. As to myself, I have other and more agreeable employment, while there are twenty or thirty employees about the establishment who have no other means of earning bread for their families. If there is any person connected with the army likely to conduct a paper satisfactorily, whom you would wish to place over such an establishment, the National Advocate can be had on very advantageous terms, as I dislike such occupation; or, if not convenient or agreeable to make the purchase, he might be employed at the expense of the paper to perform the duties of editor.

In the event of its republication being permitted, every day's delay is of the utmost importance.

Very respectfully, your obedient servant,

JACOB BARKER.

———

NEW ORLEANS, January 8th, 1863.
Major General Banks:

Respected Sir—I had this honor on the 6th inst., to which I have not received any reply.

If you should not have decided the question in relation to the publication of the National Advocate, I will thank you to peruse the article herewith, which appeared from my pen in that paper on the 15th ultimo, from which a more correct view of my sentiments and the principles that always governed that paper can be known, than from fugitive articles which have occasionally appeared in its columns, some of which have been disapproved of by me.

My excuse for thus troubling you is an unwillingness to be supposed unfriendly to the Union, which I made great sacrifices to sustain against a foreign foe in 1814, which attachment continues.

Very respectfully, your obedient servant,

JACOB BARKER.

NEW ORLEANS, January 13th, 1863.

Major General Banks:

Respected Sir—From the conversation I had the honor to have with you on Sunday, I was induced to believe that you would favor me with an early decision in relation to the further publication of the National Advocate, which, on many accounts, I am anxious to receive.

You remarked that you disliked to undo what had been done. As no order has appeared in print, closing the office, it will not be necessary to publish any order for its future publication. The guard being withdrawn, it can proceed without further explanation.

Had you honored me with an opportunity for a per-

12

sonal explanation, which I sought several times before the publication was suspended, I am of the opinion that you would have been convinced that public good did not require its suspension.

Public opinion is everywhere regulated by the ladies, and in this city they consider the loss of the Advocate a great privation; while the Delta is tolerated, a paper that villified them without stint—an unpardonable crime.

Soon after your arrival I presented a statement of the frauds of the editors of that paper in relation to the sale of the Crescent. I hope the other numerous and pressing claims on your valuable time did not prevent their perusal.

Very respectfully, your obedient servant,

JACOB BARKER.

To these letters and to a proposition to sell him the paper the General very courteously replied, orally, that he did not wish the paper, that he had not any use for it, that the guard might be withdrawn—which was done—and in relation to its publication he did not like to undo what had been done.

When conversing with Major General Banks on the subject of resuming the publication of the National Advocate, the General suggested to Mr. Barker that he had better put his views on paper, which was done in the words following:

NEW ORLEANS, 3d August, 1863.

Major General Banks:

Dear Sir—In compliance with your suggestion, I place on paper my views in relation to the affairs of Louisiana.

I was required to take the oath to support the Constitution of the United States. I have done so to the best of my ability, and especially so through the columns of the National Advocate and other newspapers, by resisting its violation in relation to slaves and other property, confiscating the same without proof of disloyalty or even the forms of trial.

When the President's emancipation proclamation appeared, I suggested to the then Commanding General its extraordinary character in the following words : " We have sworn to support the Constitution of .the United States. Where shall we find troops with which to make battle; our Commander-in-Chief having by his emancipation proclamation arrayed those heretofore enlisted for that *avowed* object, against the fundamental principles of our faith?" All my exertions having failed, utterly failed, I placed before the world, in pamphlet form, the opinions I have entertained and promulgated, and there wish to leave the subject.

The ship of State being wrecked, it will be the part of wisdom to endeavor to construct a new bark. Our slaves have been rendered valueless and placed in a position not only dangerous but offensive. They must be clothed and fed; they can only live in a Southern climate; they should be made to earn their own livelihood, and their owners had better abandon their claim to their services, and look to the United States for a pecuniary remuneration.

Let those who wish to leave and join the army do so—

the more the better. In this way fifty thousand could soon be organized and marched into Texas with facilities for their women and children to accompany or follow them; there they could be supported for one-half the amount it would cost in a Northern climate.

The United States have an abundance of vacant land there, where they could be colonized when the war is over, and such an army of fifty thousand able-bodied men would present a towering argument in favor of the Monroe doctrine. A suitable police should be placed over those who did not wish to join the army, and they required to labor faithfully for a stipulated compensation, to be paid from the produce of their labor.

They have been so thoroughly demoralized that without such a police their labor, in most cases, whether employed by the United States or by others, would be valueless.

What proceedings will be most likely to bring Louisiana back into the United States is a difficult problem to solve. Kindness and confidence in each other beget similar feelings, and until the public feel that they will be secure from further interruption, they will not be in a state of mind to form a new Constitution that would prove satisfactory to the people after peace shall be restored.

The old Constitution and laws of the State being ignored by military law, an election can be held in November for members of Congress under such regulations as the military authorities think proper to establish.

By the new census Louisiana is entitled to five members. Let them be elected on a general ticket to be voted for by every white loyal citizen who has resided in the State a required period, and at the proper time let there be a Convention to form a new Constitution, providing for an immediate or ultimate emancipation of slaves.

If the publication of the National Advocate should be resumed, nothing will appear in it at variance with the opinions herein expressed. How far it will be deemed profitable to advocate these doctrines before the public are prepared for them, is very questionable.

If the paper should lose its influence it would be valueless to the proprietor as well as to the Government, or to any party to which it might be attached. The great change wished for in the public mind can only be brought about by degrees.

I was greatly disappointed that you did not allow me to issue an "extra" this morning with the news we brought to the city, and if it is your determination to continue the suppression, I shall be obliged by your saying so, that I may not trouble you further on the subject.

Our intercourse on other matters has been so agreeable to me that I dislike very much to have the Advocate concern always hovering about our thoughts.

Very respectfully, your obedient servant,

(Signed)   JACOB BARKER.

Not receiving any reply to this letter, application was

again made, when the reply was that certain persons were opposed, alleging that the object of the paper was to favor speculation in stocks, currency and money, and that its tendency was to produce excitement prejudicial to public good. This being an entire mistake, the following letter was addressed to the Commanding General:

NEW ORLEANS, August 16th, 1863.

Major General N. P. Banks:

Dear Sir—You mentioned to me that there was an objection to the publication of the National Advocate on account of the excitement it occasioned, and its object being to affect the price of stocks.

As to the excitement produced, it was only confined to the newsboys who throng about all the newspaper offices when an "extra" is coming out, and make merry at the prospect of profitable employment; their innocent mirth did not harm any one, and continued to be equally boisterous about the other papers after the suppression of the Advocate.

The employees of the Advocate were generally more successful in obtaining the latest news than others; this gave rise to the excess of the joy of the boys over that than the other papers. This evidence of enterprise and industry I think merits applause rather than censure.

The editorials which appeared in the Advocate did not in any case produce the least excitement, nor were they intended to do so. As to the other questions, I have not been a stock dealer for years, nor have I purchased or sold a dollar's worth of United States or bank stock since the first establishment of the Advocate, nor written a line with a view to affect the market price. I deal principally in United States Treasury notes, gold and silver coin, exchange and bank notes; and nothing has ever appeared in the editorials influencing the market price of either.

The money articles were written by a person hired for that purpose, whose business has been, and continues to be, to collect information on the subject for different newspapers—he gets his information from others, not from me. I never interfered with his duties further than to require him to avoid personalities, and under no circumstance to criticise the conduct of the incorporated banks; if he did so, however just his criticisms, it might be ascribed to selfish motives. An inspection of these money articles, although somewhat prosing, will establish them to have been free from all speculative purposes. So far as the United States currency is concerned I have done, and am doing more than all others to sustain its market price. In support of this fact the numerous officers of the army and navy who have dealings at my bank, can give abundant testimony.

The persons who have made representations to you unfavorable to the Advocate, have done so in ignorance of the facts about which they undertook to speak, or from an apprehension that its publication would militate against their pecuniary interest.

Very respectfully, your obedient servant,

(Signed)   JACOB BARKER.

In reply, the General remarked that his secretary, Mr. Tucker, would examine the matter. For this purpose two periods were fixed between Mr. Tucker and the Editor for the examination of the files of the Advocate and hear explanations. Mr. Tucker not finding it convenient to attend, no examination took place, yet General Banks came to the conclusion that the publication of the paper could not be allowed, which determined the Editor to sell the press and materials of a newspaper which has been devoted to the cause of truth, honor, the Constitution and Union of these United States, circulating the latest reliable information received, foreign and domestic, for which purpose a negotiation was commenced.

Immediately before closing the sale Mr. Barker had occasion to call on Col. Holabird on other business. The Colonel, introducing the subject of the Advocate, expressed the opinion that its publication would be permitted if its Money Articles were not renewed. The Editor replied that he would not object to their omission. The Colonel responded, saying this had better be suggested to General Banks. The reply was, no further application could be made to him on the subject by Mr. Barker, except at the General's request. The Colonel then said. "Address me such a letter;" which was done, as follows:

New Orleans, September 14, 1863.
Colonel S. B. Holabird:

Dear Sir—Considering the question of the republication of the National Advocate settled by General Banks, without the opportunity of refuting the charges made, although he appointed his secretary, Mr. Tucker, to investigate the matter, I determined never again to trouble the General on the subject.

The paper had been suspended for more than eight months—too long for a man of my advanced age. Had the General come quickly to that determination I should have submitted without complaining, as I have ever felt for him, personally, the most sincere regard.

Notwithstanding that I considered the paper dead, and had written its epitaph, yet, at your suggestion, I have to remark that if republished the Money Articles, which you say were objectionable, shall be excluded from its columns.

Very respectfully, your obedient servant,

(Signed)   JACOB BARKER.

The letter was delivered to the Colonel with the understanding that he would see General Banks on the subject that afternoon or the next day. No reply being received, and Col. Holabird being too much indisposed to attend to the matter, the pending negotiation for the sale was consummated, and thus the attempt to bring the paper back into life was terminated, forever emancipating Mr. Barker from such duties as its publication imposed on him.

There is no doubt that General Banks, in the matter of the suppression of the Advocate, acted from a conscientious belief that the influence of the paper was prejudicial to the policy of the Administration, particularly of the emancipation and confiscation features, and perhaps of the great cause for the support of which he had been sent here—therefore, Mr. Barker did not complain. As to the latter branch Mr. Barker differed with the General in opinion. He then thought that the only way to reunite the South with the North was in a scrupulous respect for individual rights, as secured by the Constitution, which all loyal citizens had been required to take the oath to maintain. As a firm and consistent supporter of the Union as it was and the Constitution as it is, the National Advocate had no rival in this military department, and the editor therefore respectfully demurs to the imputation to the contrary, which is implied by the military suspension of the paper, and considered by Mr. Barker as an uncalled for infringement of the freedom of the press. The special order of General Butler, No. 2513, made the opinions of Mr. Barker a matter of history.

SENATOR WILSON.

The Hon. Henry Wilson, member of the United States Senate, from Massachusetts, stated to that body, among other things, that "Louisiana, reorganized under Mr. Lincoln by her few loyal men, passed, under the policy of Mr. Johnson, into the hands of her leading secessionists; that she elected to the House of Representatives Jacob Barker, editor of the Advocate, twice suppressed for disloyalty." Whoever takes the trouble to read this publication will perceive that the honorable Senator is totally mistaken in supposing that the Advocate had been suppressed for disloyalty. It advocated the Union and the Constitution, and opposed the war from its birth to its death. The letter of General Butler on page 157 establishes the error as to its first suspension, and the letters of Mr. Barker to General Banks, on pages 175 to 183 establish the error as to its final suspension. Its first suspension, it will be seen, took place on the 15th November, 1862, and its publication was resumed on the 17th, and continued until January 3d, 1863, when it was suspended by a military order from Major Gen. Banks, and taken possession of by a military guard, without there being any reason assigned therefor. It had been particularly fortunate in obtaining the earliest and most reliable information from the armies and from foreign nations, presenting the same to the public as it came, without any other object than to be the first to herald forth a truthful narrative of passing events, exposing the falsehood of our calumniators, for which the paper was indebted for its unequaled popularity. In accomplishing these objects the editor was under great obligations to his assistant, Wm. H. C. King, Esq., the present proprietor and editor of the New Orleans Times newspaper.

If Major General Butler, on his arrival, had pursued a mild, generous and conciliatory course in other matters, Mr. Barker is confident that New Orleans would have become the most loyal city in the Nation.

Major General Butler described his views in relation to arming slaves, thus :

"But I am to act hereafter, it may be, in an enemy's country, among a servile population, when the question may arise, as it has not arisen, as well in a moral and Christian as in a political and military point of view. What shall I then do ? Will your Excellency (Gov. Andrew, of Massachusetts) ·bear with me a moment while this question is discussed ?

"I appreciate fully your Excellency's suggestion as to the inherent weakness of the rebels, arising from the preponderance of their servile population. The question then is : in what manner shall we take advantage of that weakness? By allowing, and, of course, arming that population to rise upon the defenceless women and children of the country, carrying rapine, arson and murder— all the horrors of St. Domingo a million times magnified— among those we hope to reunite with us as brethren, many of whom already are so, and all who are worth preserving will be so when this horrid madness shall have passed away or be thrashed out of them ? Would your Excellency advise the troops under my command to make war in person upon the defenceless women and children of any part of the Union, accompanied with the brutalities too horrible to be named? You will say, "God forbid !" If we may not do so in person, shall we arm others so to do, over whom we have no restraint, exercise no control, and who, when once they have tasted blood, may turn the very arms we put in their hands against ourselves, as a part of the oppressing white race ?

The reading of history, so familiar to your Excellency, will tell you the bitterest cause of complaint which our fathers had against Great Britain in the war of the Revolution was the arming by the British Ministry of the red man with the tomahawk and the scalping knife, against women and children of the colonies, so that the phrase ' May we not use all the means which God and nature have put in our power to subjugate the colonies?' has passed into a legend of infamy against the leader of that Ministry who used it in Parliament. Shall history teach us in vain? Could we justify ourselves to ourselves, although with arms in our hands, amid the savage wilderness of camps and fields, we may have blunted many of the finer moral sensibilities in letting loose more than four millions of worse than savages upon the homes and hearths of the South? Could we be justified to the Christian community of Massachusetts? Would such a course be consonant with the teachings of our holy religion? I have a very decided opinion upon the subject and if any one desires, as I know your Excellency does not, this unhappy contest to be prosecuted in that manner, some instrument, other than myself, must be found to carry it on."

Gen. Butler came here to respect Southern rights in relation to slavery and acted in accordance therewith, so far as it could be done consistent with the action of Congress and of the President of the United States, until he was superceded by Major-General Banks, and then he threw himself, body and soul, into the arms of the Abolition party.

The war spirit predominates through the land. We may therefore look for a military chieftain to rule over us the next term. General Butler aspired to that high honor, and if he had kept clear of the Abolition faction, he might have been the man.

———

THE EDUCATION OF EMANCIPATED SLAVES.

After all their slaves had been emancipated, without compensation, their former owners—most of whom were made insolvent by such emancipation—were called on to pay a tax, termed the "school tax," on the assessed value of their property before such emancipation took place, under General Order No. 38, issued by Major Gen. Banks, which was not acted on by the General, but allowed to sleep on the shelves of the Department until September, 1865, when notice was published in the New Orleans Times to all those whose names commenced with the initial A., to appear at the office of the Provost Marshal, parish of Orleans, and there deposit the amount of tax levied upon them in pursuance of the said order No. 38, notifying the public that the publication of the names of those taxed would be continued daily in alphabetical order. Mr. Barker protested against such an exposure of the private affairs of individuals, as well as against the enormous expense—the names of those commencing with the initial A. having more than filled a column of the newspaper—whereupon such publications were discontinued, and the sending of individual notices, at a charge of fifty cents for each, was substituted, thus :

OFFICE ASST. PROVOST MARSHAL GEN. OF FREEDMEN, }
No. 32 Carondelet street.
820. NEW ORLEANS, October 7th, 1865. }
[Bring this notice with you.]

Mr. Jacob Barker—You are hereby notified to appear at this office immediately and deposit the tax levied upon you in accordance with General Order No. 38, series of 1864, amounting to one hundred and forty-four dollars, in default of which seizure and sale will be made to cover the amount and costs.

[Notice 50 cents.]   T. W. FOSTER, JR.,
1st Lieut. and Asst. Prov. Marshal Gen. of Freedmen.

———

Mr. Barker, who had always favored universal education, considered that the cost of educating emancipated slaves should be born by the United States Treasury, and not by any particular class or district of country, in as much as the Constitution provides that all taxation shall be equal, and particularly not by those who, without fault, had been deprived of their all; and if compelled to pay, nothing could be more unjust than to estimate the amount of tax on the value of property which no longer existed. He drew a petition to Major General Canby, invoking his interference to stay the execution of the unlawful and unconstitutional measure, fraught with injustice and oppression, which petition received the signatures of many hundreds of our citizens and was presented to General Canby, who declining to grant the solicited relief, transmitted it, by request, to the War Department at Washington.

His Excellency Governor Wells addressed a letter to General Canby on this subject, viz :

[Copy.]

STATE OF LOUISIANA, EXECUTIVE DEPARTMENT, }
NEW ORLEANS, October 13, 1866.   }

Major Gen. E. R. S. Canby, Com'g Dept. of Louisiana:

General—It is with some reluctance that I address you on the subject of General Orders No. 38, relating to the education of freedmen, because I am aware you have a petition before you from a number of tax-payers of the city, complaining of the tax levied, as illegal, both in a civil and military sense, and praying you to revoke said order. I was willing to await your action on said petition before interfering, but as a peremptory order has been issued for the collection of this tax, and regarding the same, as not sanctioned by any law of the United States and therefore is an infringement on the power of the State, I feel it my duty as the Chief Executive thereof to respectfully protest against the levy of the tax embraced in said order, for the reason assigned. I would state, I have carefully read the act of Congress creating the Freedmen's Bureau, as well as the various circulars issued by Major General Howard, Chief Commissioner, prescribing the rules and regulations relating to the same. In the act of Congress I find no allusion whatever to schools. In Circular No. 11, issued by General Howard, I find the following extract :

"The Assistant Commissioner will designate one or more of his agents to act as the General Superintendent of Schools (one for each State) for Refugees and Freedmen. This officer will work as much as possible in conjunction with State officers who may have school matters in charge. If a general system can be adopted for a State, it is well; but if not, he will at least take cognizance of all that is being done to educate refugees and freedmen," etc.

No reference is here made to any tax for the support of such schools, nor do I hear of any tax being levied in other States for such purposes. I would further remark that the imposition of this tax is in contravention of the Constitution of our State. (See Article 141.) I have no doubt that at the meeting of the Legislature provision will be made by law for the education of colored children, in pursuance of that section.

Trusting, sir, that you will give the matter your attention, and by revoking the order referred to, thus save me the trouble of appealing to Washington for redress.

I have the honor to remain,

Very truly your obedient servant,

(Signed) J. MADISON WELLS,

Governor of Louisiana.

———

REPLY OF GENERAL CANBY.

HEADQUARTERS DEPARTMENT OF LOUISIANA, }
NEW ORLEANS, Oct. 18, 1865. }

To His Excellency the Governor of Louisiana,

New Orleans, La.:

I have the honor to acknowledge the receipt of your

13

communication of the 13th inst. in relation to the taxes for school purposes, levied and now being collected under General orders No. 38, of 1864.

This order was issued by competent authority, and was within the legal discretion of the Commander who issued it. It was one of a series of measures dating from the first occupation of the city by the forces of the United States, forced upon the army by military exigencies, and adopted by it for the purpose of relieving the citizens of New Orleans from grievous burdens, and disembarrassing the army from encumbrances that would have hampered its movements and emasculated its efficiency.

The city of New Orleans was in no condition to feed the forty thousand of its inhabitants who were then fed, or of the gradually diminishing numbers in the intermediate periods to the present time, to the twelve thousand that are in part still fed by the army. It was in no condition to sustain the public charities that have been and are still, to a considerable extent, relieved by the army; nor for the care and education of the several thousand colored children which, but for the assistance rendered by the army, would have been, to a material extent, a charge upon the city treasury or a burden upon the public and private charities of its inhabitants.

It is not pertinent to this question to discuss the wisdom of these measures. It is sufficient to say that they were adopted at a time of great public and military exigency, and that as a practical result they have relieved the city and people of New Orleans, independent of the contributions that have been levied especially for that purpose, of an expenditure of more than $2,000,000, and that some of the exigencies have fallen upon us by a natural and inevitable inheritance, which we must meet as we may best meet them.

I have already advised your Excellency, both orally and in writing, that the necessities above indicated have outrun the means at the disposal of the military authorities for their relief, and that advances have been made not authorized by law or regulations, that should be reimbursed in order to save the officers who made them from pecuniary accountability at the Treasury of the United States. These amount in the aggregate to between $375,000 and $400,000, and have been made in the interest and for the benefit of the people of New Orleans. The collection of the particular tax to which your communication refers is one of these cases.

Under the law of March 3d, 1865, and the order of the President, of June 2d, 1865, the subject was transferred to the Bureau of Refugees, Freedmen and Abandoned Lands, and is now under control of that Bureau, except so far as military authority may be necessary to enforce its collection, and that collection is necessary in order to reimburse advances made to the Freedmen's Bureau, and for that reason is urged by Commissioner General Howard, at the head of that Bureau.

Its remission at this time will necessarily throw upon the State and city much greater burdens than they are now bearing. But while I cannot concede that the points

made by the petitioners have been well considered by
them or that the remission can properly be claimed upon
any principle of justice or equity, I will very willingly
unite with your Excellency and General Fullerton in any
measure of relief that may be devised.

Very respectfully, sir, your obedient servant,

(Signed)   E. R. S. CANBY,
                                Major General Commanding.

———

In the meantime, General Fullerton arrived in this city
and took the place of the Rev. Thos. Conway at the head
of the Freedmen's Bureau.   He immediately suspended
the execution of the obnoxious order, by issuing the subjoined circular :

HEADQUARTERS BUREAU OF REFUGEES,
FREEDMEN AND ABANDONED LANDS,
State of Louisiana, New Orleans, Nov. 7, 1865.
Circular No. 27.

The collection of the school tax, levied by virtue of
General Orders No. 38, 1864, Headquarters Department
of the Gulf, and which is now being collected by officers
of this Bureau, is hereby suspended.

The officers who have been collecting this tax will,
without delay, forward to this office complete rolls, which
shall show the names of all persons from whom they
have collected the tax ; the amount of tax collected from
each of such persons, and the assessed value of their
property.

By order of Brevet Brigadier Gen. J. S. FULLERTON,

Assistant Commissioner, Bureau of Refugees, Freedmen and Abandoned Lands, State of Louisiana.

D. G. FENNO,

1st Lieutenant and A. A. A. G.

General Fullerton conducted the business of the Bureau to the entire satisfaction of this community, but he was not allowed to remain at the post many days, and his successors renewed proceedings for collecting the tax, until instructions were received from Washington discontinuing its further collection, when the following order was issued by General Howard. It will be observed that this order omits to order a restitution of the money collected:

WAR DEPARTMENT, NEW ORLEANS, April 12, 1866.

Brevet Major Gen. Baird, Asst. Commissioner:

By direction of the Secretary of War the collection of the school tax referred to in the resolutions of the Louisiana Legislature, approved by the Governor March 22d, 1866, to be suspended until further orders.

O. O. HOWARD, Major General.

The New Orleans Times spoke thus of Gen. Fullerton :

[From the New Orleans Times.]

JUDICIOUS CIRCULARS.

Since his arrival in New Orleans Gen. Fullerton has won golden opinions from all of our people whose good opinions are worth having. Familiar with the President, and faithfully determined to carry out his views, he unostentatiously stepped into the Commissionership vacated by the removal of Mr. Conway, and at once, by the application of practical judgment and a common sense appreciation of the fitness of things, brought order out of chaos. Before he came among us "the bayonet in the hands of the negro" was rapidly becoming our only law. The crushing of the rebellion was not enough for the fanatical herd who set themselves up as the prophets and priests of universal equality; they clamored for the utter crushing out of those who, under a mistaken notion of political rights, had joined in the rebellion, and the raising up in their stead of an inferior race, for whom they demanded the highest privileges of citizenship. Freedmen who saw in *freedom* a vast array of magnificent yet indescribable privileges, but who knew nothing of that "eternal vigilance" which is its price, were to be raised above the white people of the South who always had been, and of right should be, part and parcel of the Government.

Under a government of the people there can be no rebellion, as the term is understood in monarchical and despotic lands. The people here are their own rulers, and they cannot rebel against themselves in the same sense that subjects may rebel against Emperors who claim "a right divine to govern wrong.". There may be grave quarrels under our form of government about disputed rights, but the weaker party must of necessity submit to the stronger, just as in our late election, the "Union Conservatives" and radicals had to submit to the "unterrified Democracy." To those who attempted a revolution in the South the cost was truly fearful. They lost the accumulations of half a century, and among them the servant for a time became privileged above his master. Under the teachings of incendiary missionaries, who had gone among them to preach anything but peace, the negroes became insolent, defiant and generally demoralized. Urged to convert Louisiana into another St. Domingo, unless the property of their old masters were divided among them and electoral privileges were at once conceded, it is strange indeed that their demoralization did not assume a more violent and decided shape. Had they been of the same temper of their teachers the consequences might have been of the most fearful character.

When General Fullerton arrived here ruin stared Louisiana in the face. The labor system was so disorganized and surrounded by artificial restrictions that planters were ready to abandon their plantations rather than undertake their cultivation. But within a few weeks a great change has been wrought. One judicious circular after another has been issued from the headquarters of the Freedmen's Bureau in this city, till the people have become inspired with new hopes, and they are now resolved to battle bravely with the difficulties of their situation. The considerate course pursued by General Fullerton has increased the confidence of our citizens in the Government, strengthened their loyalty, and enlarged their respect for human nature. Among the most important of the Bureau Circulars recently issued, is that

in regard to freedmen's contracts. With a stroke of his
pen General Fullerton has swept away those complicated
and confused restrictions which were left as a legacy by
General Banks, when he shook off the dust of Louisiana
from his feet, and labor and capital are now left to adjust
their relations according to the natural laws of supply
and demand. This recognition of the generally received
principles of political economy will have an immediate
effect in advancing the agricultural interests of the State,
and will also prevent a great deal of misery among the
less provident members of our late servile population.
Another important circular suspends the collection of an
arbitrary, unequal, and illegal tax for the alleged support
of colored schools. This circular was, as we are led to
understand, issued under direct instructions from President Johnson ; but the unequal character of the tax, and
other facts in relation to it, were doubtless communicated
to our worthy Chief Magistrate by General Fullerton
himself. Under the circumstances, the citizens of Louisiana owe to General Fullerton a debt of gratitude which
they cannot readily repay.

TREATMENT OF LOYAL NORTHENERS.

The Radicals complain at the treatment their friends
receive here. They are imposed on by those who come
here for plunder. (See the letter published in the New
York Tribune, dated February 13, 1866, purporting to

be signed by a citizen of New Orleans, calumniating Gen. Fullerton for accepting civilities from our citizens.) Strange that they did not impugn the motives of Generals Butler, Banks, Bowen, Sherman and Shepley for receiving hospitalities from Mr. Jacob Barker and others. What is more strange is that they are not satisfied with the citizens of New Orleans for having selected a uniform Unionist, born in Maine, to represent them in Congress. They remind us of Robinson Crusoe's story about blowing hot and cold with the same breath.

RECOGNITION.

The Louisiana Senate Committee on Federal Relations, to whom was referred the House "joint resolutions expressive of the sentiments of the people of Louisiana relative to the National Government" beg leave, respectfully to report that they find among the records of the Senate "joint resolutions relative to Federal relations," (numbered in the Senate "No 8," and in the House "No. 26,") which passed the Senate on the 2d of December, 1865, and was unanimously concurred in by the House of Representatives on the same day; which resolutions, in the opinion of the committee, briefly, comprehensively and truthfully express "the sentiments of the people of Louisiana, relative to the National Government," and renders unnecessary the action contemplated by the resolutions now under consideration.

For which reason the committee respectfully report the joint resolution expressive of the sentiments of the people of Louisiana, relative to the General Government as unnecessary. As, however, the Senate resolutions of the extra session alluded to do not appear in the printed journals, and have, no doubt, for that reason been overlooked, your committee respectfully recommend that they be now spread upon the minutes, in connection with and as a part of this report, to be published in the journal of this session, and for that purpose they annex a copy of said resolutions. In regard to that particular feature of the House "joint resolutions" now under consideration by your committee, which refers to the condition of the freedmen in Louisiana, they further considered the action would be unnecessary in view of the humane provisions of the law of Louisiana which existed long anterior to the events of the late war, and which extend to all free persons of color alike, the right to acquire education, to testify in courts of justice, the right to hold property, to possess the same by deed or will, descent or otherwise— the general laws of succession and marriage, husband and wife, parent and child, tutorship, minority, etc., etc., and the same protection of person and property accorded to the white man—in a word, the guarantees of law for life, liberty and the pursuit of happinesss. In these respects the laws of Louisiana are and always have been different and exceptional, among those of the other States; and as all these provisions apply as well to the recently emancipated, at the moment of freedom, as to any other class of free colored persons in our State, your committee have not found it necessary to profess, in the form of resolutions, a purpose to accord to the freedmen rights guaranteed them by the laws of the State already in existence. Such resolutions, in the opinion of your committee, would do injustice to the humane system of laws referred to, which has so long adorned our statute books, and sufficiently indicates the sentiments of our people, and would at the same time convey to the world impressions unfavorable to ourselves and inconsistent with those just claims to peculiar consideration, at this time, which the laws of Louisiana in this respect entitle her to. In conclusion, your committee would respectfully recommend that a copy of this report be furnished to the House of Representatives. All of which is respectfully submitted. M. A. FOUTE,

Chairman Committee on Federal Relations.

JOINT RESOLUTIONS RELATIVE TO FEDERAL RELATIONS.

WHEREAS, It is eminently proper and due to our constituents and the Government, that this representative body, fresh from the people of the whole State, the first that has assembled in Louisiana since the surrender, should give a public and unmistakable expression of sentiment with regard to the "situation," therefore

1. *Be it resolved by the Senate and House of Representatives of the State of Louisiana in General Assembly convened,* That there is no spirit of resistance to Federal authority among the people of Louisiana; that they

frankly avowed their purposes and objects in the late struggle for separate government, and having failed in that, they now with equal frankness accept as an inevitable result the present situation, including the abolition of slavery, the re-establishment of which they do not expect.

2. *Be it further resolved, etc.*, That in the expression that "the Southern people must be trusted," President Johnson exhibited a thorough acquaintance with Southern character and eminent wisdom and statesmanship, and that it is our firm resolve to justify this confidence, and to sustain the President in his efforts to restore these States to representation in Congress, and a position of political equality in the Union.

3. *Be it further resolved, etc.*, That the people of Louisiana are unreserved in their purpose of loyalty, and if permitted, that to the Constitution of the United States and the Union of the States thereunder, do they look for their future happiness and prosperity.

(Signed)   DUNCAN S. CAGE,
          Speaker of the House of Representatives.
(Signed)   ALBERT VOORHIES,
Lieutenant Governor and President of the Senate.
Approved December 6, 1865.
(Signed)   J. MADISON WELLS,
                    Governor of Louisiana.

NATIONAL UNION CONVENTION.

A National Union Convention, of at least two delegates from each congressional district of all the States, two from each Territory, two from the District of Columbia, and four delegates at large from each State, will be held at the city of Philadelphia, on the second Tuesday (14th) of August next.

Such delegates will be chosen by the electors of the several States, who sustain the Administration in maintaining unbroken the Union of the States, under the Constitution which our fathers established, and who agree in the following propositions, viz:

The Union of the States is, in every case, indissoluble, and is perpetual; and the Constitution of the United States, and the laws passed by Congress in pursuance thereof, supreme, and constant, and universal in their obligation;

The rights, the dignity and the equality of the States in the Union, including the right of representation in Congress, are solemnly guaranteed by that Constitution, to save which from overthrow so much blood and treasure were expended in the late civil war;

There is no right, anywhere, to dissolve the Union, or to separate States from the Union, either by voluntary withdrawal, by force of arms, or by congressional action; neither by the secession of the States, nor by the exclusion of their loyal and qualified representatives, nor by the National Government in any other form;

Slavery is abolished, and neither can, nor ought to be,

re-established in any State or Territory within our jurisdiction ;

Each State has the undoubted right to prescribe the
qualifications of its own electors, and no external power
rightfully can, or ought to dictate, control, or influence
the free and voluntary action of the States in the exercise
of that right;

The maintenance inviolate of the rights' of the States,
and especially of the right of each State to order and
control its own domestic concerns, according to its own
judgment exclusively, subject only to the Constitution of
the United States, is essential to that balance of power
on which the perfection and endurance of our political
fabric depend, and the overthrow of that system by the
usurpation and centralization of power in Congress would
be a revolution, dangerous to republican government and
destructive of liberty;

Each House of Congress is made, by the Constitution,
the sole judge of the elections, returns, and qualifications
of its members; but the exclusion of loyal Senators and
Representatives, properly chosen and qualified, under the
Constitution and laws, is unjust and revolutionary;

Every patriot should frown upon all those acts and
proceedings, everywhere, which can serve no other purpose than to rekindle the animosities of war, and the
effect of which upon our moral, social and material interests at home, and our standing abroad, differing only
in degree, is injurious like war itself;

The purpose of the war having been to preserve the

Union and the Constitution by putting down the rebellion, and the rebellion having been suppressed—all resistance to the authority of the General Government being at an end, and the war having ceased—war measures should also cease, and should be followed by measures of peaceful administration, so that union, harmony and concord may be encouraged, and industry, commerce, and the arts of peace revived and promoted; and the early restoration of all the States to the exercise of their constitutional powers in the National Government is indispensably necessary to the strength and defence of the Republic, and to the maintenance of the public credit;

All such electors in the thirty-six States and nine Territories of the United States, and in the District of Columbia, who in a spirit of patriotism and love for the Union, can rise above personal and sectional considerations, and who desire to see a truly National Union Convention, which shall represent all the States and Territories of the Union, assemble, as friends and brothers, under the national flag, to hold counsel together upon the state of the Union, and to take measures to avert possible danger from the same, are specially requested to take part in the choice of such delegates.

But no delegate will take a seat in such Convention who does not loyally accept the national situation and cordially endorse the principles above set forth, and who is not attached, in true allegiance, to the Constitution, the Union, and the Government of the United States.

Washington, June 25, 1866.

> A. W. RANDALL, Pres't.
> J. R. DOOLITTLE,
> O. H. BROWNING,
> EDGAR COWAN,
> CHARLES KNAP,
> SAMUEL FOWLER,
> Executive Committee National Union Club.

We recommend the holding of the above Convention, and endorse the call therefor.

> DANIEL S. NORTON,
> J. W. NESMITH,
> JAMES DIXON,
> D. A. HENDRICKS.

HEADQUARTERS NATIONAL UNION CLUB, 490 TWELFTH ST., WASHINGTON, D. C., June 25, 1866.

Sir—Preceding this you will find a "call" for a National Union Convention, issued by the National Union Club of this city, representing all the States in the Union.

If this call meets your approbation, you will be good enough to signify it by a brief letter, with authority to publish the same. Very respectfully, etc.,

> A. W. RANDALL, President.

[For Publication.]

NEW ORLEANS, July 4, 1866.

A. W. Randall, Esq., President
National Union Club, Washington:

SIR : I have had the honor to receive your letter of the 25th ult., with the accompanying documents. Approving of them, I have caused them to be published, confident that my constituents will send delegates to the Philadelphia Convention, they being, so far as I am informed, unanimously in favor of President Johnson's reconstruction policy, with a firm reliance that the ballot-box will restore to the agricultural, commercial, manufacturing and mechanical interests of the country their wonted prosperity, which is now very much depressed by unwise legislation.

I have the honor to subscribe myself,

Very respectfully your obd't serv't,

JACOB BARKER.

THE TAMMANY HALL PLATFORM.

Tammany Society has issued an invitation to prominent Democrats of the country, containing the platform of Tammany Hall on the great issues of the day, and asking them to participate in celebrating the coming Fourth of July. It sets forth that the exclusion of eleven States from participation in Congress, is not less treasonable, morally, when effected by partizan votes, than when attempted by rebellious resort to arms, and invites to co-operate those who believe that the Union was intended to be perpetual, and that the States are equal under the Constitution, and that the restoration of the Union by

14

the recent war ought to be acknowledged and recognized by all departments of the Federal Government, that a spirit of fraternity and magnanimity should prevail in all our councils and our policy, and that the South having accepted lessons from us, and relinquished the heresies of secession, should be entitled to immediate representation.

———

[From the National Advocate of the 15th of December, 1862.]
SECESSION.

Our people are now feeling the effects of this rash and inconsiderate measure, and however unpalatable it may be to its advocates, it is proper that an impartial view of the subject should be kept before the public. This is our intention, regardless of our popularity, in the hope that it will soon soften the asperity of both sides, and by possibility dispose all for peace.

The great Father of the Universe has not blessed man with any other discriminating power than that of comparison. We have, therefore, to compare our present condition and prospects for the future with what they were before the public mind was seriously agitated with the idea of secession; also to inquire into the causes which led to its adoption, the remedies for the evils on our hands, the arguments used to induce the people to acquiesce in and to support the measure, and finally, where and how a remedy is to be found.

The last proposition is easily solved. Let all endeavor to cultivate kindness towards each other, confiding in the ballot-box as the most safe, reliable, and least expensive remedy that can be found; both of which have been lamentably overlooked or neglected in Louisiana.

So far as we were personally concerned, we heartily rejoice at the result of the late election. So far as the public are concerned, we have to wait and see how far the question of Southern institutions will be sustained by our representatives. That should be the controlling question in all our actions; that is the heart of our body politic, and should be guarded as we would guard the apple of our eye.

We had a government that none felt—so gently were we governed that no one knew we had a government. The great question seemed to be with the politicians on all sides, who should have the offices, how the spoils should be divided.

A few slaves absconded from the border States, fleeing into the free States, where they found protection, and some of the States passed laws in violation of the Constitution, not only protecting such runaways, but encouraging others to follow their example.

Such outrages called for prompt and efficient measures to check further infractions of our constitutional rights. Our fathers provided a remedy in the Constitution: free discussion, free speech and the ballot-box, with a provision for amending that instrument when its operation should fail to perform all the offices intended. It having failed, by allowing a minority President to be elected, the first measure to have been adopted was an amend-

ment requiring a majority of all the votes cast to constitute an election, and in case of a failure, for the President
of the Senate or the Speaker of the House of Representatives to fill the office until another election could be had
giving a candidate the required majority, giving the
election to the people direct, without the intervention of
electors or State authorities, extending the period to six
or ten years, no citizen to be eligible for a second term;
a board of commissioners to be established at Washington to award damages for all absconding slaves not
restored, to be paid out of the U. S. Treasury.

Our fellow-citizens at the North took the matter in
hand and elected a sufficient number of new members
not only to extinguish the thirty majority the Abolition
party had in Congress under Mr. Buchanan, but to give
the Democratic party coming into power with Mr.
Lincoln (the Southern members retaining their seats) a
majority in the House of Representatives of seven. With
this majority they could have refused supplies until
justice had been obtained; the Abolitionists would have
been brought to terms in a very short period. Without
supplies an army could not have been formed or a navy
equipped; consequently there could not have been any
blockade or war.

Refusing supplies was considered, truly considered, a
harsh, high-handed measure, but not so much so as war.
Look at the loss of human life by sickness incident to the
camp and to battle. Look at the loss of commerce and
the loss of employment which constitutes the indepen-

dence of man, allowing each to earn his own livelihood by the sweat of his brow, in place of being dependent, as too many now are, on others for the daily bread of themselves and families. Look at the appetite infused into the rising generation for military life. Look at the destitution of a million of men, without employment or the means of subsistence when peace shall be restored. Look at the derangement of business, the destruction of property and the frightful amount of debt arising from this unnatural and ruinous war, and compare our present condition and future prospects with the evils that could possibly have resulted from refusing supplies. This will enable the reader to decide which would have been preferable, secession or the refusal of supplies.

President Lincoln could not have got a dinner without Democratic votes, nor could an office have been filled by an individual not approved by them, had our Southern members retained their seats. By resigning they threw away the game, which we held in our own hands.

South Carolina and Mississippi were bent on secession, and designing politicians availed of the aforesaid injustice of the Abolitionists to induce their people to pass ordinances of secession. Other slave States reluctantly joined them, because they considered it would be ruinous to the institution of the South for them not to hang together. These political leaders, these short-sighted mortals, vainly supposed the want of employment, for the want of cotton, in the Northern States, in England and in France, would produce such riots as would compel

the North to yield to their requirements and foreign
powers to interfere to force a compliance on the part of
the North. Not one of such results has been realized.
We told them that the effects of a short supply of cotton
would be to cause foreigners to redouble their exertions
to procure it elsewhere. This done, and the war over,
the cotton growers of the United States would long feel
the disastrous effects of the new source from which a
supply of the article could be obtained; farther, that if
foreigners once recognized the doctrine that King Cotton
is supreme, on future occasions it might be wielded
against them; hence they could not be expected to
acknowledge that it was such an omnipotent power even
if it existed. Again, they should have remembered that
each nation could have supported their hungry population in idleness for one-fourth the cost of a war. We
often expostulated with these deluded men. Considering
us old, too old, they would not heed our admonition.
They imagined that we were behind the age of Young
America.

The industry and prosperity of this city was suspended
by the anticipation of secession many months before the
fatal ordinance was passed; to which subject we called
public attention at a large meeting held at Odd Fellows'
Hall, suggesting that no remuneration therefor could in
any event be anticipated; that the anticipation of such a
calamity had inflicted damage to the amount of millions;
that there would be no limit to the extent of our suffering if the reality should take place.

The certain consequences of secession came, and we are now realizing its sad effects. What did its advocates expect to gain?—a new contract with the same parties who had violated the original contract? We would ask what better security would this have afforded? The expense of the war for a single month would more than have paid for all the slaves who have absconded during our existence as a Nation.   .

———

The following notice and receipt establishes that the Freedmen's Bureau proceeded to enforce Order 38 after the promulgation of the order of General Fullerton to be found on page 196:

Bring with this Notice City Tax Receipts.

353.   OFFICE AGENT B. R. F. & A. L. ⎱
                     PARISHES ORLEANS AND JEFFERSON, L. B. ⎰

Office Hours 9 to 3.]   (No. 211 JULIA STREET.)

NEW ORLEANS, February 13, 1866.

Mr. Thos. H. Barker—You are hereby notified to appear at this office immediately and deposit the tax levied on you in accordance with General Orders No. 38, Department of the Gulf, series 1864, amounting to $102 30, in default of which seizure and sale will be made to the amount and costs.

[Notice 50 cents.]   JAMES LEWIS,

1st Lt. V. R. C. and Agent B. R. F. and A. L.

[Endorsement.]

Paid by Mr. Jacob Barker, Feb. 6, 1866.

H. C. SEYMOUR, Lieut. 81st U. S. C. I.

Provost Marshal.

[From the New Orleans Times.]

MASTERLY INACTIVITY.

The States which have been denied representation by the so-called Congress are now coolly asked to stultify themselves by ratifying an amendment to the Constitution, which would degrade them in their own eyes and before the world. They will, however, pause before obeying the behest of the radical task-masters. There is no force in the decrees of the Council of Fifteen which can make either men or States sign away their own birthright, with all the high prerogatives of manhood and citizenship, at the bidding of the sectional tyrants of the hour. With honorable alacrity the Southern States accepted the binding issues of the war as soon as closed, but the more eager they were to return to their father's house the more persistently their seats were denied them. There was no fatted calf killed on the occasion—no generous tender of forgiveness. The olive branch held up was stained with gall, and the enmity of war was continued after all armed opposition to the Government had ceased.

Never was a more sublime spectacle presented to the world than that exhibited by the armies of the Confederacy when they surrendered in good faith on a promise of general amnesty. If prompted solely by enmity and recklessness, they might have fought on for months, slaying and being slain; but as soon as it became apparent that the cause in which they had been engaged could not succeed, they laid down their arms forthwith, determined to have no act or part in the shedding of blood not sanctified by what to them seemed an honorable purpose.

In Gen. Lee's act of surrender there was more true heroism displayed than in all his battles. There was a moral grandeur in the sight which shadowed forth the supremacy of high intellect and moral sentiment over the baser passions. Conviction controlled resistance and laid the foundations of what might have towered up into a sublime temple of national fraternity, had the victors not been intoxicated by their unexpected success and clamorous for vindictive humiliations and for spoils.

At first, with some repining and mental protestations, the Southern States complied with the demands made by the Executive and Legislative departments of the General Government. With singular unanimity they ratified an amendment to the Constitution by which African slavery was prohibited in the States of the Union for all future time, and by which two thousand millions of dollars' worth of property, guaranteed by an express provision of the old Federal organic law, was lost to them forever. But this was not regarded as enough. The demands of the dominant sectional party were akin to the spleen of the green-eyed monster "which doth mock the meat it feeds on." They mocked at their own triumphs. Every success became the parent of a dozen new demands, till the cautious innovations which the sectional legislators were contented with at first, swelled up at length into bold, unblushing usurpations. All this was in a great measure brought about by the nervous anxiety which the

people of the South displayed in relation to the Union
and the Constitution—that Union which they found it
impossible to divide, and that Constitution which they
had ineffectually endeavored to overthrow. Wishing to
be restored to their proper places in the unbroken Union
and to preserve what is left of the Constitution, after it
had been amended to their prejudice, they humbled
themselves before the accidental masters of the situation;
but their humility was turned into contempt and their
calamity was mocked at. "He that humbleth himself
shall be exalted," saith the Scripture, but they humbled
themselves and their humility was made an excuse for
new humiliations and impositions. These facts have
taught the South bitter yet salutary lessons. She has
nothing to gain from humility; in her present helpless
condition she is incapable of exercising any power or
authority sufficient to right her wrongs; for her the magnanimity of the dominant party has proved altogether
unreliable. She must now await "the sober second
thought" of the great American people, who can make
and unmake rulers at a breath, and while waiting in
faith and hope, her true political policy is "masterly inactivity." In material matters—in commerce, agriculture
and manufacturing industry—our people may be as
active as they please; but the vexed question of Federal
politics, let them be sure to "make haste slowly." The
madness which invariably precedes destruction is clearly
exhibited by the disorganizing extremists of the so-called
Congress, and they will soon be pushed from their stools

by the ghosts of the moral Banquos they have murdered. Having failed in her respectful demands, the South should now try the virtue of masterly inactivity, ratifying no further amendments to a Constitution, the privileges of which are persistently denied to her people.

———

PRESIDENT'S MESSAGE ON THE PROPOSED CONSTITUTIONAL AMENDMENT.

On the 22d of June, 1866, the President sent in to Congress the following message in relation to the reconstruction amendment to the Constitution:

To the Senate and House of Representatives:

I submit to Congress a report of the Secretary of State to whom was referred the concurrent resolution of the 18th inst., respecting a submission to the Legislatures of the States of an additional article to the Constitution of the United States. It will be seen from this report that the Secretary of State had on the 16th transmitted to the Governors of the several States certified copies of the joint resolution passed on the 13th proposing an amenement to the Constitution. Even in ordinary times any question of amending the Constitution must be justly regarded as of paramount importance. This importance is at the present time enhanced by the fact that the joint resolution was not submitted by the House for the approval of the President, and that of the thirty-six States which constitute the Union, eleven are excluded from representation in either House of Congress, although, with the single exception of Texas, they have been entirely restored to all their functions as States in conformity with the organic law of the land, and have appeared at the National Capital by Senators, and have been refused admission to the vacant seats; nor have the sovereign people of the nation been afforded an opportunity of expressing their views upon the important question which the amendment involves. Grave doubts may naturally and justly arise whether the action of Congress is in harmony with the sentiments of the people, and whether to such issue they should be called upon by Congress to decide. Respecting the ratification of the proposed amendment, waiving the question as to the constitutional validity of the proceedings of Congress upon the joint resolution proposing the amendment, or as to the merits of the article which it submits through the Executive Department to the Legislatures of the States, I deem it proper to observe that the steps taken by the Secretary of State, as detailed in the accompanying report, are to be considered as purely ministerial, and in no sense whatever committing the Executive to an approval or recommendation of the amendment to the State Legislatures or to the people. On the contrary, a proper appreciation of the letter and spirit of the Constitution, as well as of the interests of national order and harmony and union, and a due deference for an enlightened public judgment, may at this time well suggest a doubt whether any amendment to the Constitution ought to be proposed by Congress, and pressed upon the legislatures of the

several States for final decision, until after the admission
of such loyal Senators and Representatives of the un-
represented States as have been, or may hereafter be
chosen, in conformity with the Constitution and laws of
the United States.

(Signed) ANDREW JOHNSON.
Washington, D. C., June 22, 1866.

———

The compiler of this book, in referring to the Convention of Louisiana which passed the Secession Ordinance,
unintentionally omitted the name of our distinguished
fellow-citizen Christian Roselius, Esq., the eminent jurist,
who lifted up his voice against that fatal measure. In
order to make amends for the omission, we give in full
his address as President of the Union Association, which
was read on the 7th July, 1866, before the Union and
Johnson Clubs, adopted and ordered to be published :

ADDRESS.

Fellow-Citizens—At a time when the great charter of
American liberty appears in imminent danger; when the
spirit of disorganization and anarchy is rife in the land,
and threatening to undermine the foundation of this
magnificent fabric, devised by the wisdom and cemented
by the blood of the fathers of the Republic; when dema-
gogues and politicians are openly assailing the sacred
rights which the Constitution of the United States has
secured to every citizen; it becomes the imperative duty
of the people of the United States to come to the rescue ;

to defend and vindicate those rights by every legal means in their power. To do this effectually, all mere party connections ought to be disregarded; the preservation and perpetuation of the constitutional Union alone should become the paramount object of the unceasing and united efforts of all.

It is for this purpose that the association called "the Constitutional Union Association" has been formed.

The sole end which it seeks to accomplish is to preserve the Constitution in its integrity, and the only influence which it will attempt to exercise will be in opposition to constitutional encroachments, come from what quarter they may.

We address ourselves to the ardent patriotism and sober judgment of our fellow-citizens, to enlist them in this great cause by which alone the Republic can be saved from impending danger.

The people of the United States recognize no majesty or power, except the majesty and power of the Constitution and laws.

All public officers are but ministers of the law and servants of the people. When any power is exercised in time of peace, which is not warranted by law, it is usurpation. Laws are supreme and subordinate, and whenever the latter conflict with the former they are utterly null and void, and it follows, as a matter of course, that the citizen is bound to disobey them.

In the clear and forcible language of Mr. Justice Patterson: "A constitution is the form of government delineated by the mighty hand of the people, and is the supreme law of the land; it is paramount to the law of the Legislature, and can be revoked or altered only by the power that made it.

"The Constitution is the work or will of the people themselves in their original, sovereign and unlimited capacity. Law is the work or will of the Legislature, in its derivative and subordinate capacity.

"The Constitution fixes limits to the exercise of legislative authority, and prescribes the orbit in which it must move. In short, the Constitution is the sun of the political system, around which legislative, executive and judicial bodies revolve."

The people of the United States have delegated their powers and attributes of sovereignty to two distinct governments, viz: Federal and State governments.

The respective powers of each are established and limited by constitutions emanating equally from the only legitimate source of all power.

The Constitution of the United States was ordained and established not by the States in their sovereign capacities, but emphatically as the preamble declares, "by the people of the United States;" or, in the language of Chief Justice Marshall, in McCulloch vs. the State of Maryland, "the government of the Union is emphatically and truly a government of the people in form and substance, and it emanates from them. Its powers are granted by them, and are to be exercised directly on them and for their benefit. This government is acknowledged by all to be one of enumerated powers; though limited, it is supreme within its sphere of action. It is the government of all, with powers delegated by all, it represents all and acts for all."

Power incident to the nature of the specified powers is necessarily vested in the General Government. This constitutes the implied power necessary to carry the express powers into execution. All other power not delegated by the people to the Government of the United States, is reserved to the States respectively, and with regard to these, the sovereignty of the States is absolute. A difference of opinion upon this subject, connected with local interests, culminated in civil war, which the Government of the United States was forced to carry on for the maintenance of the integrity of the Union.

The war being ended, and the great object for which it was waged, attained, we consider it of the utmost importance for the final settlement of our unfortunate domestic difficulties, that the disturbing element of sectional and party views and prejudices, should not be permitted to exercise its baneful influence by preventing that harmony of feeling as citizens of a common country, which is the very corner stone on which our free government rests.

Can this end be attained by pursuing a course of policy evidently dictated by party prejudice, and in open opposition to the plainest principles of justice?

When, for example, the Constitution of the United States was to be amended, the Southern States were consulted, and their votes counted for the purpose of adopting the amendment; then, no one questioned their status.

But when the people of these same States sent their Senators and Representatives, duly elected, the doors of Congress were closed to them, on the pretext that they are out of the Union.

The Constitution declares that the Government of the United States is a unit, composed of the people of all the States, and that the people of each State shall be entitled to an equal representation in the Senate, and to the same ratio of representation in the House of Representatives.

The great boast of the American people is, that their form of government is the most perfect in theory and practical operation ever framed. The history of the world furnishes no parallel to the United States in growth of population, wealth or power; no example of such rapid and astounding development of inexhaustible resources.

The source of all this prosperity and greatness is a profound reverence for, and implicit obedience to, the Constitution and laws of the country. When this cardinal principle of our political conduct was abandoned, and the destructive rule of the sword substituted for the benign and protecting control of law and justice, the charm was broken, and the dreadful ravages of civil war, with its concomitant suffering, was the consequence. The blessings of peace are now once more restored to the country, and the empire of law and order was naturally anticipated. But in this fond hope we have thus far been sadly disappointed.

By the action of Congress eleven States are deprived of any representation. No one can dispute the exclusive right of each branch of the Legislature to judge of the qualifications, elections, etc., of its members; but in the decision of these questions, these bodies act in a judicial character, and are not allowed to travel out of the record for the purpose of disfranchising States, by excluding them from representation. Such a power of destruction has never been delegated to them—its assumption is mere arbitrary usurpation.

A general distrust of the consequences of this course has seized the public mind, and a universal alarm is spreading among all classes of the community.

The experience of the last four years causes them to be apprehensive of calamity, which they most ardently desire to avert. In our opinion, it can be done by the force of public sentiment, forcibly and energetically expressed.

The Constitution is our platform, upon which Andrew Johnson, the Chief Magistrate of the United States, has placed himself.

It is our duty to uphold the Constitution, and, with it, the President; and we call upon all having faith in our glorious institutions, to step forward and show, by their acts, as well as words, their repugnance to the mutilation of the Constitution, the ground work of our institutions.

C. ROSELIUS,
President National Union Association.

LETTER FROM SECRETARY WELLES.

WASHINGTON, D. C., July 11, 1866.

Sir: Your note of the 10th inst. was received yesterday. I cordially approve the movement which has been instituted to "sustain the Administration in maintaining unbroken the Union of the States," and I recognize in the call which you have sent me the principles and views by which the Administration has been governed.

The attempt made to destroy the national integrity by secession, or the voluntary withdrawal of a State from the Union has been defeated. War has forever extinguished the heresy of secession. On the suppression of the rebellion measures were promptly commenced to re-establish those fraternal relations which for four years had been interrupted.

The policy initiated by President Lincoln to restore national unity was adopted and carried forward by President Johnson; the States which had been in rebellion were, under this benign policy, resuming their legitimate functions; the people had laid down their arms, and those who had been in insurrection were returning to their allegiance; the Constitution had been vindicated and the Union was supposed to be restored, when a check was put upon the progress to national harmony and prosperity thus dawning upon the country. On the assembling of Congress all efforts towards union and nationality became suddenly paralyzed; the measures of reconciliation which the President had, from the time he entered upon his duties, pursued with eminent success, were assailed, and their beneficent purpose, to a great extent, defeated ; attempts were made to impose conditions precedent upon States before permitting them to exercise their constitutional rights ; loyal Senators and Representatives from the States which had been in rebellion were refused admittance into Congress—the people were denied rightful constitutional representation—and even States were and are excluded from all participation in the Government. These proceedings, which conflict with the fundamental principles on which our whole governmental system is founded, are generating and consolidating sectional animosity, and, if long persisted in, must eventuate in permanent alienation. I rejoice, therefore, in a movement which has for its object the union in one bond of love of our country, and which invites to counsel and to political action the citizens of every State and Territory, from the Atlantic to the Pacific, and from the Lakes to the Gulf. The centralizing theory that the loyal and qualified Senators and Representatives from eleven States shall be excluded from Congress, and that those States and the people of those States shall not participate in the Government, is scarcely less repugnant than that of secession itself.

Propositions to change the Constitution and unsettle some of the foundation principles of our organic law—to change our judicial system in such a manner as to destroy the independence of the States by insiduously transferring to the Federal tribunals all questions relating to the "life, liberty and property of the citizen "—to change the basis of representation, which was one of the difficult and delicate compromises of the convention of 1787, when no States were excluded from representation—to change the existing and wisely adjusted distribution of powers between the different departments of the Government, by transferring the pardoning power in certain cases from the executive, where it properly belongs, to Congress or the legislative branch of the Government, to which it does not legitimately pertain—to incorporate into our Constitution, which is to stand through all time, a proscription of citizens who have erred, and who are liable to penalties under existing enactments, by disqualifications, partaking of the nature of *ex post facto* laws and bills of attainder—these propositions or changes, aggregated as one and called an amendment to the Constitution, designed to operate on the people and States which are denied all representation or voice in the Congress which originates them, are of a radical, if not revolutionary character.

These and other proceedings, and the political crisis which they have tended to produce, justify and demand a convocation of the people by delegates from all the States and from the whole country.

The President has labored with devoted assiduity and fidelity to promote union, harmony, prosperity, and happiness among the States and people, but has met with resistence, misrepresentation, and calumny where he had a right to expect co-operation and friendly support. That the great body of our countrymen are earnestly and cordially with him in his efforts to promote the national welfare. I have never doubted, notwithstanding the hostility of malevolent partisans, stimulated by perverted party organizations; and I rejoice that the convention which shall represent all true Union men of our whole country has been called to sustain him.

Very respectfully,

GIDEON WELLES.

Hon. J. R. Doolittle, Washington, D. C.

———

CONCLUSION.

The object of this publication is to exhibit Mr. Barker's uniform devotion to the Union, his reliance on commercial restrictions to'redress wrongs, in preference to war. He has not any new opinions to put forth—those of others embraced in this book are promulgated for reason that they are in furtherance of the great principles for which he has always contended. An original and consistent Democrat, and consequently politically opposed to the Abolition party in power at Washington, his reliance is on the ballot-box, and the watchword at the coming election should be, "no taxation without representation." He protests against "reconstruction," demanding recognition as one of the States of this glorious Union.

The perusal of this book will convince the reader that Mr. Barker, from childhood, has been a friend of the colored race; that he considers their emancipation the removal of a blemish from our national escutcheon; that he would not have slavery restored if he could; that he totally disapproved of the manner it was brought about; that it could have been effected by purchase at half the cost of the war; that the battle should have been fought in Congress, and not at the cannon's mouth. The reader will also be convinced that the National Advocate was a loyal paper, and that its suspension was an infringement of the freedom of the press, which every freeman is bound to defend.

INVESTIGATOR.

APPENDIX.

The reader of the preceding pages will perceive, on the perusal of the resolutions of the National Union Convention held at Philadelphia, the Hon. Reverdy Johnson's address and the President's reply which follows, that Mr. Barker foreshadowed public opinion with remarkable accuracy.

ADDRESS

OF THE

PHILADELPHIA CONVENTION

TO THE PEOPLE.

[Special Dispatch to the Chicago Republican.]
PHILADELPHIA, August 17.

To the People of the United States:

Having met in a convention at the city of Philadelphia, in the State of Pennsylvania, this 16th day of August, 1866, as the representatives of the people in all sections, and from all the States and Territories of the Union, to consult upon the condition and the wants of our common country, we address to you this declaration of our principles, and of the political purposes we seek to promote

Since the meeting of the last National Convention, in the year 1860, events have occurred which have changed the character of our internal politics, and given the United States a new place among the nations of the earth. Our Government has passed through the vicissitudes and the perils of civil war—a war which, though mainly sectional in its character, has nevertheless decided political influences that from the very beginning of the Government has threatened the unity of our national existence, and has left its impress deep and ineffaceable upon all the interests and sentiments and the destiny of the Republic. While it has inflicted upon the whole country severe losses in life and in property, and has imposed burdens which must weigh on its resources for generations to come, it has developed a degree of national courage in the presence of national dangers, a capacity for military organization and achievement, and a devotion on the part of the people to the form of government which they have ordained, and to the principles of liberty which that government was designed

to promote, which must confirm the confidence of the nation in the perpetuity of its republican institutions, and command the respect of the civilized world Like all great contests which rouse the passions and test the endurance of nations, this war has given new scope to the ambition of political parties and fresh impulse to plans of innovation and reform.

Amid the chaos of conflicting sentiments inseparable from such an era; while the public heart is keenly alive to all the passions that can sway the public judgment and affect the public action; while the wounds of war are still fresh and bleeding on either side, and fears for the future take unjust proportions from the memories and resentments of the past, it is a difficult but an imperative duty which, on your behalf, we, who are here assembled, have undertaken to perform.

For the first time, after six long years of alienation and of conflict, we have come together from every State and every section of our land as citizens of a common country under that flag, the symbol again of a common glory, to consult together how best to cement and perpetuate that Union which is again the object of our common love, and thus securing the blessings of liberty to ourselves and our posterity.

In the first place we invoke you to remember always and everywhere, that the war is ended, and the nation is again at peace. The shock of contending arms no longer assails the shuddering heart of the Republic. The insurrection against the supreme authority of the nation has been suppressed, and that authority has been again acknowledged by word and act, in every State, and by every citizen within its jurisdiction. We are no longer required or permitted to regard or treat each other as enemies. Not only have the acts of war been discontinued, and the weapons of war laid aside, but the state of war no longer exists, and the sentiments, the passions, the relations of war have no longer lawful or rightful place anywhere throughout our broad domain.

We are again people of the United States, fellow-citizens of one country, bound by the duties and obligations of a common patriotism, and having neither rights nor interests apart from a common destiny. The duties that devolve upon us now are the duties of peace, and no longer the duties of war. We have assembled here to take counsel concerning the interests of peace, to decide how we may most wisely and effectually heal the wounds the war has made, and to perfect and perpetuate the benefits it has secured, and the blessings which, under a wise and benign providence, have sprung up in its track. This is the work, not of passion, but of calm and sober judgment, not of resentment for past offences prolonged beyond the limits which justice and reason prescribe, but of a liberal statesmanship which tolerates what it cannot prevent, and builds its plans and its hopes for the future, rather than upon a community of interest and ambition than upon distrust, and the weapons of force.

In the next place, we call upon you to recognize in their full significance, and to accept with all their legitimate consequences, the political results of the war just closed. In two most important particulars the victory achieved by the National Government has been final and decisive. First, it has established, beyond all further controversy, and by the highest of all human sanctions, the absolute supremacy of the National Government as defined and limited by the constitution of the United States, and the permanent integrity and indissolubility of the Federal Union as a necessary consequence; and second, it has put an end, finally and forever, to the existence of slavery upon the soil or within the jurisdiction of the United States. Both these points became directly involved in the contest and controversy. Upon both depended, absolutely and finally, the result.

In the third place, we deem it of the utmost importance that the real character of the war, and the victory by which it was closed, should be clearly understood. The war was carried on by the Government of the United States in maintenance of its own authority and in defence of its own existence; both of which were menaced by the insurrection which it sought to suppress. The suppression of the insurrection accomplished that result. The Government of the United States maintained by force of arms the supreme authority over all the territory and over all the States and people within its jurisdiction which the constitution confers upon it: but it acquired thereby no new power, no enlarged jurisdiction, no rights, either of territorial possession or of civil authority, which it did not possess before the rebellion broke out. All the rightful power it can ever possess is that which is conferred upon it, either in express terms or by fair and necessary implication, by the constitution of the United States. It was that, however, and that authority which the

rebellion sought to overthrow; and the victory of the Federal arms was simply the defeat of that attempt.

The Government of the United States acted throughout the war on the defensive. It sought only to hold possession of what was already its own. Neither the war nor the victory by which it was closed, changed in any way the constitution of the United States. The war was carried on by virtue of its provisions and under the limitations which they prescribe, and the result of the war did not either enlarge, abridge, or in any way change or affect the powers it confers upon the Federal Government, or release that Government from the restrictions which it has imposed. The constitution of the United States is to-day precisely as it was before the war, the supreme law of the land, anything in the constitution or laws of any State to the contrary notwithstanding. To-day, also, precisely as before the war, all the powers not conferred by the constitution upon the General Government, nor prohibited by it to the States, are reserved to the several States, or to the people thereof. This position is vindicated, not only by the essential nature of our Government and the language and spirit of the constitution, but by all the acts and the language of our Government in all its departments, and at all times, from the outbreak of the rebellion to its final overthrow. In every message and proclamation of the Executive, it was explicitly declared that the sole object and purpose of the war was " to maintain the authority of the constitution and to preserve the integrity of the Union; ' and Congress more than once reiterated this solemn declaration, and added the assurance that " whenever that object should be attained the war should cease," and all the States should retain their equal rights and dignity unimpaired. It is only since the war was closed that other rights have been asserted in behalf of one department of the General Government. It has been proclaimed by Congress that, in addition to the powers conferred upon it by the constitution, the Federal Government may now claim over the States, the territory, and the people, involved in the insurrection, the rights of war, the right of conquest and of confiscation; the right to abrogate all existing governments, constitutions and laws, and to subject the territory conquered, and its inhabitants, to such laws, regulations, and deprivations as the Legislative Department of the Government may see fit to impose.

Under this broad and sweeping claim, that clause of the constitution which provides that no State shall, without its consent, be deprived of its equal suffrage in the Senate of the United States, has been annulled. Ten States have been refused, and are still refused, representation altogether in both branches of the Federal Congress; and the Congress, in which only a part of the States and of the people of the Union are represented, has asserted the right thus to exclude the rest from representation, and from all share in making their own laws and choosing their own rulers, until they shall comply with such conditions, and perform such acts as this Congress, thus composed, may itself prescribe. That right has not only been asserted, but it has been exercised, and is practically enforced at the present time.

Nor does it find any support in the theory that the States thus excluded are in rebellion against the Government, and are, therefore, precluded from sharing its authority. They are not thus in rebellion. They are, one and all, in an attitude of loyalty toward the Government, and of sworn allegiance to the constitution of the United States. In no one of them is there the slightest indication of resistance to this authority, or the slightest protest against its just and binding obligation. This condition of renewed loyalty has been officially recognized by common proclamation of the Executive Department. The laws of the United States have been extended by Congress over all these States and the people thereof. Federal courts have been reopened, and Federal taxes imposed and levied; and in every respect, except that they are denied representation in Congress and the Electoral College, the States once in rebellion are recognized as holding the same position, as owing the same obligations, and subject to the same duties, as the other States of our common Union. It seems to us, in the exercise of the calmest and most candid judgment we can bring to the subject, that such a claim, so enforced, involves as fatal an overthrow of the authority of the constitution, and as complete a destruction of the Government and Union, as that which was sought to be effected by the States and people in armed insurrection against them both.

It cannot escape observation that the power thus asserted to exclude certain States from representation, is made to rest wholly in the will and discretion of the Congress that asserts it. It is not made to depend upon any specified conditions or circumstances, nor to be subject to any rules or regulations whatever. The right asserted and exercised is absolute, without qualification or restriction—not confined to States in rebellion, nor to States that have rebelled. It is the right of any Congress, in formal possession of legislative authority, to exclude any State or States, or any portion of the people thereof, at any time, from representation in Congress and in the Electoral College, at its own discretion, and until they shall perform such acts and comply with such conditions as it may dictate. Obviously, the reasons for such exclusion, being wholly within the discretion of Congress, may change as the Congress itself may change. One Congress may exclude a State from all share in the Government for one reason, and, that reason removed, the next Congress may exclude it for another. One

State may be excluded on one ground, to-day, and another may be excluded on the opposite ground, to-morrow. Northern ascendancy may exclude Southern States from our Congress; the ascendancy of Western or Southern interests, or of both combined, may exclude the Northern or the Eastern States from the next. Improbable as such usurpations may seem, the establishment of the principle now asserted and acted upon by Congress will render them by no means impossible.

The character, indeed the very existence of Congress and the Union, is thus made dependent, solely and entirely, upon the party and sectional exigences and forbearance of the hour. We need not stop to show that such action not only finds no warrant in the constitution, but is at war with every principle of our Government, and with the very existence of our free institutions. It is, indeed, the identical practice which has rendered fruitless all attempts hitherto to establish and maintain free governments in Mexico and the States of South America. Party necessities assert themselves as superior to the fundamental law, which is set aside in reckless obedience to their behests. Stability, whether in the exercise of power in the administration of the government, or in the enjoyment of rights, became impossible: and the conflicts of party, which, under constitutional governments, are the conditions and means of political progress, are merged in the conflicts of arms to which they directly and inevitably tend.

It was against this peril, so conspicuous and so fatal to all free governments, that our constitution was intended especially to provide. Not only the stability, but the very existence of the Government is made by its provisions to depend upon the right and the fact of representation.

The Congress, upon which is conferred all the legislative power of the national Government, consists of two branches, the Senate and House of Representatives, whose joint concurrence or assent is essential to the validity of any law. Of these, "the House of Representatives," says the constitution, article 1, section 2, "shall be composed of members chosen every second year by the people of the several States." Not only is the right of representation thus recognized as possessed by all the States, and by every State without restriction, qualification or distinction of any kind, but the duty of choosing Representatives is imposed upon the people of each and every State alike, without distinction, or the authority to make distinctions among them for any reason or upon any grounds whatever. And in the Senate, so careful is the constitution to secure to every State this right of representation, it is explicitly provided that no State shall, without consent, be deprived of its equal suffrage in that body, even by an amendment of the constitution itself. When, therefore, any State is excluded from such representation, not only is a right of a State denied, but the constitutional integrity of the Senate is impaired, and the validity of the Government itself is brought in question. But Congress, at the present moment, thus excludes from representation in both branches of Congress ten States of the Union, denying them all share in the enactment of laws by which they are to be governed, and all participation in the election of officers by which those laws are to be enforced. In other words, a Congress in which only twenty six States are represented asserts the right to govern absolutely, in its own discretion, all the thirty-six States which compose the Union; to make their laws and choose their rulers, and to exclude the other ten from all share in their own Government, until it sees fit to admit them thereto. What is there to distinguish the power thus asserted and exercised from the most absolute and intolerable tyranny?

First.—Nor do these extravagant and unjust claims on the part of Congress to powers of authority never conferred upon the Government by the constitution, find any warrant in the arguments or excuses urged on their behalf. It is alleged, at first, that these States, by the act of rebellion, and by voluntarily withdrawing their members from Congress, forfeited their right of representation; and that they can only receive it again at the hands of the supreme legislative authority of the Government, on its own terms, and at its own discretion. If representation in Congress and participation in the Government were simply privileges conferred and held by favor, this statement might have the merit of plausibility; but representation is, under the constitution, not only expressly recognized as a right, but it is imposed as a duty; and it is essential, in both aspects, to the existence of the Government, and to the maintenance of its authority. In free government, fundamental and essential rights cannot be forfeited, except against individuals, by due process of law; nor can constitutional duties and obligations be discarded or laid aside. The enjoyment of rights may be for a time suspended by the failure to claim them, and duties may be evaded by the refusal to perform them. The withdrawal of their members from Congress, by the States which resisted the Government, was among their acts of insurrection—was one of the means and agencies by which they sought to impair the authority and defeat the action of the Government; and that act was annulled and rendered void when the insurrection itself was suppressed. Neither the right of representation, nor the duty to be represented, was in the least impaired by the fact of insurrection; but it may have been that, by reason of the insurrection, the conditions on which the enjoyment of that right, and the performance of that duty, for the time depended, could not be fulfilled. This was, in fact, the case. An insurgent power, in the exercise of usurped and unlawful authority,

had prohibited, within the territory under its control, that allegiance to the constitution and laws of the United States which is made, by that fundamental law, the essential condition of representation in its Government.

No man within the insurgent States was allowed to take the oath to support the constitution of the United States and, as a necessary consequence, no man could lawfully represent those States in the councils of the Union. But this was only an obstacle to the enjoyment of the right and to the discharge of a duty; it did not annul the one or abrogate the other; and it ceased to exist when the usurpation by which it was created had been overthrown, and the States had again resumed their allegiance to the constitution and laws of the United States.

Second.—But it is asserted, in support of the authority claimed by the Congress now in possession of power, that it flows directly from the laws of war; that it is among the rights which victorious war always confers upon the conquerors, and which the conqueror may exercise or waive in his own discretion. To this we reply, that the laws in question relate solely, so far as the rights they confer are concerned, to wars waged between alien and independent nations, and can have no place or force, in this regard, in a war waged by a government to suppress an insurrection of its own people, upon its own soil, against its authority. If we had carried on a successful war against any foreign nation, we might thereby have acquired possession and jurisdiction of their soil, with the right to enforce our laws upon their people, and to impose upon them such laws and such obligations as we might choose. But we had, before the war, complete jurisdiction over the soil of the Southern States, limited only by our own constitution. Our laws were the only national laws in force upon it. The Government of the United States was the only Government through which these States and their people had relations with foreign nations; and its flag was the only flag by which they were recognized or known anywhere on the face of the earth.

In all these respects, and in all other respects involving national interests and rights, our possession was perfect and complete. It did not need to be acquired, but only to be maintained; and victorious war against the rebellion could do nothing more than maintain it. It could only vindicate and re-establish the disputed supremacy of the constitution. It could neither enlarge nor diminish the authority which that constitution confers upon the Government, by which it was achieved. Such an enlargement or abridgement of constitutional power can be effected only by the amendment of the constitution itself; and such amendment can be made only in the modes which the constitution itself prescribes.

The claim that the suppression of an insurrection against the Government gives additional authority and power to that Government, especially that it enlarges the jurisdiction of Congress, and gives that body the right to exclude States from representation in the national councils, without which the nation itself can have no authority and no existence, seems to us at variance alike with the principles of the constitution and with the public safety.

Third—But it is alleged that in certain particulars the constitution of the United States fails to secure the absolute justice and impartial equality which the principles of our Government require; that it was, in this respect, the result of the compromises and concessions to which, however necessary when the constitution was formed, we are no longer compelled to submit; and that now, having the power through successful war, and just warrant for its exercise in the hostile conduct of the insurgent section, the actual Government of the United States may impose its own conditions, and make the constitution conform in all its provisions to its own ideas of equality and the rights of man. Congress, at its last session, proposed amendments to the constitution, enlarging in some very important particulars the authority of the General Government over that of the several States, and reducing by indirect disfranchisement the representative power of the States in which slavery formerly existed; and it is claimed that these amendments may be voted as parts of the original constitution without the concurrence of the States to be most seriously affected by them, or may be imposed upon those States by three-fourths of the remaining States, as conditions of their readmission to representation in Congress and in the Electoral College

It is the unquestionable right of the people of the United States to make such changes in the constitution as they, upon due deliberation, may deem expedient; but we insist that they shall be made in the mode which the constitution itself points out, in conformity with the letter and spirit of that instrument and with the principles of self-government and of equal rights, which lie at the basis of our republican institutions. We deny the right of Congress to make these changes in the fundamental law without the concurrence of three-fourths of all the States, including especially those to be seriously affected by them, or to impose them upon States or people as conditions of representation, or of admission to any of the rights, duties, or obligations which belong, under the constitution, to all the States alike; and with still greater emphasis do we deny the right of any portion of the States to exclude the rest of the States from any share in their councils, to propose or sanction change in the constitution which are to affect permanently their political relations, and control or coerce the legitimate action of the several members of the common Union. Such an exercise of power is simply an usurpation, just as warrantable when exercised by Southern States, and not to be fortified or

palliated by anything in the past history either of those by whom it is attempted, or of those upon whose rights and liberties it is to take effect. It finds no warrant in the constitution. It is at war with the fundamental principles of our form of government. If tolerated in one instance, it becomes the precedent for future invasions of liberty and constitutional right, dependent solely on the will of the party in power; and thus leads, by direct and necessary sequence, to the most intolerable and fatal of all tyrannies—the tyranny of shifting, irresponsible factions. It is against this, the most formidable of all dangers which menace the stability of free government, that the constitution of the United States was intended most carefully to provide. We demand a strict adherence to its provisions. In this, and this alone, can be found a basis of permanent union and peace.

Fourth—But it is alleged, in justification of the usurpation which we condemn, that the condition of the Southern States and people is not such as renders safe their readmission to a share in the Government of the country; that they are still disloyal in sentiment and purpose, and that neither the honor, the credit, nor interest of the nation would be safe, were they admitted to the councils of the nation.

We reply to this, First—That we have no right, for such reasons, to deny to any portion of the States or people any right conferred upon them by the constitution of the United States. Second, that so long as their acts are those of loyalty, so long as they conform in all their public conduct to the requirements of the constitution and laws, we have no right to distrust the purpose or the ability of the people of the Union to protect or defend, under all contingencies, and by whatever means may be required, its honor and its welfare.

These would, in our judgment, be full and conclusive answers to the plea thus advanced for the exclusion of these States from the Union; but we say, further, that this plea rests on a complete misapprehension or an unjust perversion of existing facts. We do not hesitate to affirm that there is no section of the country where the constitution and laws of the United States find more entire or prompt obedience than among those people who were lately in arms against them, or where there is less purpose or danger of any further attempt to overthrow their authority. It would seem to be more natural and inevitable that in States so recently swept by the whirlwind of war where all ordinary modes of organized industry have been broken up, and the bonds and influences that guarantee social order have been destroyed; where thousands and tens of thousands of turbulent spirits have been suddenly released from the discipline of war, and thrown without resources or restraint upon a disorganized and chaotic society, and where the keen sense of defeat is united to the overthrow of ambition and hope—scenes of violence should defy, for a time, the imperfect discipline of law, and excite anew the fears and forebodings of the patriotic and well disposed. It is unquestionably true that local disturbances of this kind, accompanied by more or less violence, do occur; but they are confined to the large cities of the South, where different interests are most closely in contact, and where passious and resentments are most easily fed and fanned into outbreak, and even there they are quite as much the fruit of untimely and hurtful political agitation as of any hostility on the part of the people to the National Government. But the concurrent testimony of those best acquainted with the condition of society and state of public sentiment in the South, including its representation in this convention, establishes the fact that the great mass of the Southern people accept, with as full and sincere submission as do the other States, the reestablished supremacy of the national authority, and are prepared, in a most liberal spirit, and with a zeal quickened alike by their interest and their pride, to co operate with other States and sections in whatever may be necessary to maintain the right, promote the welfare, and sustain the honor of our common country. History presents no instance when a people so powerful in numbers, in resources and in public spirit, after a war so long in its duration, so destructive in its progress and so adverse in its issue, have accepted defeat and its consequences with so much of good faith as has marked the conduct of the people lately in insurrection against the United States. Beyond all question, this has been mainly due to the wise generosity with which their intoreed surrender was accepted by the President of the United States and the generals in immediate command, and the liberal measures which were afterwards taken to restore order, tranquility and law to the States where before all had been overthrown. No steps could have been better calculated to win the respect, revive the patriotism and secure the permanent support of the people of the South to the constitution and Union than those which have been so firmly taken and steadfastly pursued by the President of the United States; and if that confidence and loyalty has been impaired; if the people to-day are less firm in their allegiance than at the close of the war, we believe it is due to the changed tone of the legislation toward them. Congress has endeavored to supplant and defeat the President's wise and beneficent policy of restoration; to their exclusion from all participation in our common Government; to the withdrawal from them of rights conferred and guaranteed by the constitution, and to the evident purpose of Congress, in the exercise of usurped and unlawful authority, so reduce them from the rank of free and equal members of a Republic of States, with rights and dignities unimpaired, to the condition of conquered provinces and conquered people, in all things subordinate and subject to the will of their conquerors, free only to obey laws in making

which they are not allowed to share. No people have ever yet existed whose loyalty and faith such treatment, long continued, would not alienate and impair; and the ten millions of Americans who live in the South would be unworthy citizens of a free country degenerate sons of an heroic ancestry, unfit ever to become guardians of the rights and liberties bequeathed to us by the fathers and founders of this Republic, if they could accept, with uncomplaining submissiveness, the conditions thus sought to be imposed upon them. Resentment of injustice is always and everywhere essential to freedom; and the spirit which prompts the States and people lately in insurrection, but insurgent no longer, to protest against the imposition of unjust and degrading conditions, makes them all the more worthy to share in the Government of a free commonwealth, and gives still firmer assurance of the future power and freedom of the Republic. For whatever responsibility the Southern people may have incurred in resisting the authority of the National Government, and in taking up arms for its overthrow, they may be held to answer as individuals, before the judicial tribunals of the land; and for that conduct, as societies and organized communities, they have already paid the most fearful penalties that can fall on offending States, in the losses, the sufferings, and humiliations of unsuccessful war. But whatever may be the guilt or the punishment of the conscious authors of the insurrection, candor and common justice demand the concession that the great mass of those who became involved in its responsibility acted upon what they believed to be their duty, in defence of what they had been taught to believe their rights, or under a compulsion, physical and moral, which they were powerless to resist.

Nor can it be amiss to remember that terrible as have been the bereavements and the losses of the war, they have fallen exclusively upon neither section and upon neither party; that they have fallen, indeed, with far greater weight upon those with whom the war began. That in the death of relatives and friends; the dispersion of families; the disruption of social systems and social ties; the overthrow of governments of law and order; the destruction of property, and of forms, and modes, and means of industry; the loss of political, commercial and moral influence in every shape and form which great calamities can assume —the States and people which engaged in the war against the Government of the United States have suffered tenfold more than those who remained in allegiance to its constitution and laws.

These considerations may not, as they certainly do not, justify the action of the people of the insurgent States; but no just or generous mind will refuse to them very considerable weight in determining the line of conduct which the Government of the United States should pursue towards them. They accept, if not with alacrity, certainly without sullen resentment, the defeat and overthrow they have sustained. They acknowledge and acquiesce in the results, to themselves and the country, which that defeat involves. They no longer claim for any State the right to secede from the Union. They no longer assert for any State an allegiance paramount to that which is due the General Government. They have accepted the destruction of slavery, abolished it by their State constitutions, and concurred with the States and people of the whole Union in prohibiting its existence forever upon the soil, or within the jurisdiction of the United States. They indicate and evince their purpose, just as fast as may be possible and safe, to adapt their domestic laws to the changed condition of their society, and to secure, by the law and its tribunals, equal and impartial justice to all of its inhabitants They admit the invalidity of all acts of resistance to the national authority, and of debts incurred in attempting its overthrow. They avow their willingness to share the burdens and discharge all the duties and obligations which rest upon them, in common with other States and other sections of the Union; and they renew, through their representatives in this Convention, by their public conduct in every way, and by the most solemn acts by which States and societies can pledge their faith, their engagement to bear true faith and allegiance, through all time to come, to the constitution of the United States, and to all laws that may be made in pursuance thereof.

Fellow countrymen, we call upon you, in full reliance upon your intelligence and your patriotism, to accept, with generous and ungrudging confidence, this full surrender on the part of those lately in arms against your authority, and to share with them the honor and renown that await those who bring back peace and concord to jarring States.

The war just closed, with all its sorrows and disasters, has opened a new career of glory to the nation it has saved. It has swept away the hostilities of sentiment and of interest which were a standing menace to its peace. It has destroyed the institution of slavery, always the cause of sectional agitation and strife, and has opened for our country the way to unity of interest, of principle, and of action, through all time to come. It has developed, in both sections, a military capacity, an aptitude for achievements of war both by sea and land, before unknown even to ourselves, and destined to exercise hereafter, under united councils, an important influence upon the character and destiny of the continent and the world. And while it has thus revealed, disciplined, and compacted our power, it has proved to us, beyond controversy or doubt, by the course pursued toward both contending sections by foreign powers, that we must be the guardians of our own independence, and that the principles of republican freedom we represent can find among the nations of the earth no friends or defenders but ourselves. We call upon you, therefore, by every consideration of your own dignity and safety, and in the name of liberty throughout the world, to complete the work of restoration and peace which the President of the United States has so well begun, and which the policy adopted and the principles asserted by the present Congress alone obstruct.

The time is close at hand when members of a new Congress are to be elected. If that Congress shall perpetuate this policy, and, by excluding loyal States and people from representation in its halls, shall continue the usurpation by which the legislative powers of the Government are exercised, common prudence compels us to anticipate augmented discontentment; a sullen withdrawal from the duties and obligations of the Federal Government; internal dissension, and a general collision of sentiments and pretensions, which may renew, in a still more fearful shape, the civil war from which we have just emerged.

We call upon you to interpose your power to prevent the recurrence of so transcendent a calamity. We call upon you, in every Congressional district of every State, to secure the election of members who, whatever other differences may characterize their political action, will unite in recognizing the right of every State in the Union to representation in Congress, and who will admit to seats, in either branch, every loyal representative from every State in allegiance to the Government who may be found by each House in the exercise of the power conferred upon it by the constitution, to have been duly elected, returned, and qualified for a seat therein. When this shall have been done, the Government will have been restored to its integrity; the constitution of the United States will have been reestablished in its full supremacy, and the American Union will again have become what it was designed to be by those who formed it. a sovereign nation, composed of separate States, each, like itself, moving in a distinct and independent sphere, exercising powers defined and reserved by a common constitution, and resting upon the assent, the confidence and co-operation of all the States and all the people subject to its authority. Thus reorganized and restored to their constitutional relations, the States and the General Government can enter, in a fraternal spirit, with a common purpose and a common interest, upon whatever reforms the security of personal rights, the enlargement of popular liberty, and the perfection of our republican institutions may demand.

THE PRESIDENT AND THE PHILADELPHIA CONVENTION.

VASHINGTON, Aug. 18.—The committee, appointed by the National Union Convention to wait on the President for the purpose of presenting him an official copy of the proceedings of the invention, held a meeting this morning and postponed until 1 o'clock the time for so doing. It was originally intended that 10 A. M. should be the hour at which their reception would be had. The committee, followed by the delegates to the late invention, and after them in regular order, at '30 o'clock, proceeds to the executive mansion. About 1 o'clock the committee, headed by a body of music, reached the White House. They were conducted into the East Room by Marshal Gooding, and so arranged as to form a circle. The delegates to the convention were then ushered in, and took a position in the rear of the committee, and President Johnson appeared, accompanied by Secretaries McCulloch, Welles, Browning and Postmaster-General Randall.

The Hon. Reverdy Johnson then advanced and said:

Mr. President—We are before you as a Committee of the National Union Convention which met in Philadelphia on Tuesday the 14th instant, charged with the duty of presenting you with an authenticated copy of the proceedings. Before acting in your hands, you will permit me to congratulate you, that in the object for which the convention was called, in the enthusiasm with which every State and Territory responded to the call, the unbroken harmony of its deliberations, in the unanimity with which the principles it has declared were adopted, and more especially the patriotic and constitutional character of the principles themselves, we are confident that you and the country, will find gratifying and cheering evidence that there exists amongst us a public sentiment which renders an early and complete restoration of the union, as established by the Constitution, certain and inevitable. Party faction, seeking the continuance of its misrule, may momentarily delay it, but the principles of political liberty for which our fathers successfully contended, and to secure which they adopted the Constitution, are so glaringly inconsistent with the condition in which the country has been placed by such misrule, that it will not be permitted a much longer duration. We wish, Mr. President, you could have witnessed the spirit of concord and brotherly affection which was manifested by every member of the convention. Great as your confidence ever has been in the intelligence and patriotism of our fellow-citizens, in their deep devotion to the Union, and in their present determination to reinstate and maintain it, that confidence would have become a positive conviction, if you could have seen and heard all that was done and said on the occasion. Every heart was evidently full of joy; every eye beamed with patriotic ani-

mation. Despondency gave place to the assurance that our late dreadful civil strife was ended; that the blissful reign of peace, under the protection, not of arms, but the Constitution and laws, would have sway and be in every part of our land cheerfully acknowledged, and in perfect good faith obeyed. You would not have doubted that the recurrence of dangerous domestic insurrection in the future is not to be apprehended. If you could have seen, sir, the men of Massachusetts and South Carolina coming into the convention on the first day of its meeting, hand in hand, amidst the rapturous applause of the whole body, awakened by the heartfelt gratification of joy at the event, filling the eyes of thousands with tears, which they neither could nor desired to repress, you would have felt as every person present felt that the time had arrived when all sectional or other perilous dissensions had ceased, and that nothing would be heard in the future, but the voice of harmony proclaiming their devotion to a common country—of a pride in being bound together by a common union existing and protected by forms of government proved by experience to be eminently fitted for the exigencies of either war or peace. In the principles announced by the convention, and in the feelings there manifested, and we may have every assurance that harmony throughout our entire land will soon prevail. We know that, as in former days, as was eloquently declared by Webster, the nation's most gifted statesman, Massachusetts and South Carolina went shoulder to shoulder through the revolution, and stood hand in hand around the administration of Washington, and felt his own great arm lean on them for support, so will they again, with like devotion and power, stand around your administration and cause you to feel that you mean also to lean on them for support. In the proceedings, Mr. President, which we are about to place in your hands, you will find that the convention performed the duty imposed upon them by their knowledge of your devotion to the Constitution, the laws and interests of your country, as illustrated by your entire Presidential career, of declaring that in you they recognise the chief magistrate of the nation, and equal to the great crisis in which your lot is cast. It gives us unmixed pleasure to add we are confident that the convention have but spoken the intelligent and patriotic sentiment of the country, ever inaccessible to the low influences which often control mere partizan governing, knowing no constitutional obligations and rights, nor the duty of looking solely to the true interest, safety and honor of a nation. Such a class is incapable of resorting to any stress for popularity at the expense of public good. In the measures which you have adopted for the restoration of the Union, the committee of the Union convention saw only a continuance of the policy which for the same purpose was inaugurated by your immediate predecessor. His re-election by the people, after that policy had been fully indicated, and had been made one of the issues of the contest, those of his political friends who are now assailing you for sternly pursuing it, forgetful or regardless of the opinion which their support of his re-election necessarily so far as they could accomplish in the condition of subjected provinces, denying to them the right to be represented, whilst subjecting their people to every species of legislation, including that of taxation. That such a state of things is at war with the very genius of our government, inconsistent with every idea of political freedom, and most perilous to the safety of the country, no reflecting man can fail to believe. We hope, sir, that the proceedings of the convention will involved, being upon the same ticket with that much lamented public servant, whose foul assassination touched the heart of the civilized world with grief and horror. You have been false if you have not endeavored to carry out the same policy; and, judge now by the opposite one which Congress has pursued, its wisdom and patriotism are vindicated by the fact that Congress has but continued a broken Union by keeping ten of the States in which at one time the insurrection existed cause you to adhere if possible with even greater firmness to the course which you are pursuing, by satisfying you that the people are with you, and that the wish which lies nearest the hearts, is that a perfect restoration of our Union at the earliest moment be attained, and a conviction that that result can be only accomplished by the measures which you are pursuing, and in discharge of duties which these measures devolve, we as it did every member of the convention, again, for ourselves individually, tender our profound respect and assurance of our cordial and sincere support. With a reunited Union, with no foot but a freedman's to be permitted to tread our soil, with industry redeemed, with a nation's faith, pledged forever to a strict observance of all obligations, with the kindness of eternal love everywhere prevailing the desolations of war will soon be removed, its sacrifice of life sad, as they have been will with christian resignation be preferred to a providential purpose of fixing our bereaved country firm and endurable—which will forever place our liberty beyond reach of peril. Then and forever will our government challenge the admiration and receive the respect of the nations of the earth, and be in no danger of any efforts to impeach our honor. Permit me, sir, in conclusion to add that, great as is your solicitude for the restoration of our domestic peace and your labors to that end, you have also a watchful eye to the rights of the nation, and every attempt by an assumed or actual foreign power to enforce an illegal blockade against the government or good citizens of the United States, to use your own mild, but expressive words, "will be disregarded." In this determination I am sure you will receive the unanimous approval of your fellow-citizens.

Now, as the chairman of this committee and in behalf of the convention, I have the honor to present you with an authenticated copy of its proceedings.

The allusion in the above address to the determination of our government to disregard the attempt of an assumed or actual foreign power to enforce an illegal blockade caused loud and continued cheering. On the conclusion of Mr. Johnson's address, the president, received the authenticated copy of the proceedings of the convention, and said:

Mr. Chairman and gentlemen of the convention: Language is inadequate to express the emotions and feelings produced by this occasion. Perhaps I could express more by permitting silence to speak, and you to infer what I ought to say. I confess that notwithstanding the experience I have had in public life the words you have addressed to me on this occasion, and this assemblage, are well calculated to and do overwhelm me. As I have said, I have not language to convey adequately my present feelings and emotions. In listening to the address which your eloquent and distinguished chairman has just delivered, the proceedings of the convention as they transpired recalled to my mind seemingly and partook of the inspiration that prevailed in the convention. When I read a dispatch by two of its distinguished members conveying in terms the scene which has just been described of South Carolina and Massachusetts, arm and arm marching into the vast assemblage, and thus giving evidence that the extremes had come together, and that for the future they were united as they had been in the past for the preservation of the Union; when the dispatch informed me in that vast body of men distinguished for intellect and wisdom, every one was suffused with tears on beholding the scene, I could not finish reading the dispatch to one so associated with me in the office, for my own feelings overcome me (cheers); I think we may justly conclude, we are moving under a proper inspiration, and that we need not be mistaken, and that the favor of an overruling and unerring Providence is in this matter. (Loud cheers.) We have just passed through a mighty, a bloody and a momentous ordeal. Yet we do not find ourselves free from the difficulties and dangers that at first surrounded us. While our brave men have performed their duties, both officers and men, (turning to Gen. Grant, who stood on his right,) while they have won laurels imperishable, there are still greater and more important duties to perform, and while we have had their co-operation in the field, we now need their support in our efforts to perpetuate peace. (Loud cheers.) So far as the executive department of the government is concerned, the effort has been made to restore the Union, to heal the breach, to pour oil into the wounds which were consequent upon the struggle, and to speak in common phrase, to prepare as the learned physician would, a plaster, healing in character and co-extensive with the wound. (Loud cheers.) We thought, and yet think, we had partially succeeded. But as the work progressed, as reconciliation seemed to be taking place, and the country becoming united, we found a disturbing and warring element opposed to us. In alluding to that element I shall go no further than did your convention, and the distinguished gentleman who has delivered to me the report of its proceedings. I shall make no reference to it

hat I do not believe the time and the oc-
:asion justly. We have witnessed in one department of the government every effort, as it were, to
irevent the restoration of peace and harmony in
he Union. We have seen hanging upon the verge
.f the government, as it were, a body called, or
rhich assumed to be, the Congress of the United
States, and in fact a Congress of only part of the
States. We have seen this Congress assume and
pretend to be for the Union, when its every step
ind act tended to perpetuate disunion and make
t disruption of the States inevitable. Instead of
promoting reconstruction and harmony, its legis-
ation has partaken of the character of penalties
retaliation and revenge. This has been the curse
ind policy of one department of our government.
The humble individual who is now addressing you
stands the representative of another department
of the government. The manner in which he was
called upon to occupy that position, I shall not
allude to on this occasion. Suffice it to say that he
s here under the Constitution of the country, and
being here by virtue of its provisions, he takes his
stand upon the charter of our liberties as the great
rampart of civil and religious liberty. (Prolonged
cheering.) Having been taught in my early life to
hold it sacred, and having practised upon it during my whole public career, I shall ever continue
to reverence that Constitution—the Constitution
of the fathers of our country, and to make it my
guide. (Enthusiastic cheers.) I know it has
been said, (and I must be permitted to indulge in
the remark) that the executive department of
the government has been tyrannical. Let me ask
this audience of distinguished gentlemen around
me here to-day, to point to a vote I ever gave, or
to a speech I ever made, to a single act in my
whole public life, that has not been against the
tyranny and despotism which has been exercised.
As to myself, the elements of my nature, or the
pursuits of my life, have not made me either
in my feelings or in my practice, aggressive. My
nature, on the contrary, is rather defensive in its
character. But I will say that, having taken my
stand upon the broad principles of liberty and the
Constitution, there is not power enough on earth
to drive me from it. (Prolonged cheering.) Having pledged myself on that broad platform, I
have not been awed, dismayed or intimi-
dated by either threats or encroachments
but have stood there in conjunction with
patriotic spirits, sounding the tocsin of alarm
whenever I deemed the citadel of liberty in danger. (Great applause.) I said on a previous occasion, and repeat now, that all that was necessary in the great struggle against tyranny and
oppression was that the struggle should be sufficiently audible for the American people to hear
and understand. They did hear, and looking on
and seeing who the contestants were, and what
that struggle was about, they determined that
they would settle this question on the side of the
Constitution and of principles. (Cries of that's
so and applause.) I proclaim here to-day, as I
have on other occasions, that my faith is abiding
in the great masses of the people. In the darkest
moment of the struggle, when clouds seemed to
be most lowering, my faith, instead of giving way,
looked up through the dark clouds. Far beyond

I saw that all would be safe in the end. (Cheers.)
My countrymen, we all know that, in the language of Thomas Jefferson, tyranny and despotism even can be exercised and executed more
effectually by the many than the one. We have
seen a Congress gradually encroach, step by step,
upon constitutional rights, and violate, day after
day, and month after month, the fundamental
principles of the government. We have seen a
Congress that seemed to forget that there was a
Constitution, and that there was a limit to the
sphere and scope of legislation. (Renewed cries
of "that's so.") We have seen a Congress in a
minority assume to exercise powers which, if
allowed to be carried out, would result in
despotism or monarchy itself. (Cries of
"that's so," and most enthusiastic cheers
given for the President.) This is truth; and because others as well as myself, have seen proper
to appeal to the patriotism and republican feeling of the country, we have been denounced in
the most severe terms. Slander upon slander,
vituperation upon vituperation, of the most vil-
lainous character, has made its way through the
public press. What, gentlemen, has been your and
my sin? What has been the cause of our offending? I will tell you. Daring to stand by
the Constitution of our fathers. (Cheers.)
The President here approached the spot where
Senator Johnson was standing, and said: "I consider the proceedings of this convention, sir, as
more important than those of any convention that
ever assembled in the United States. (Great applause.) When I look with my mind's eye upon that
collection of citizens, coming together voluntarily,
and sitting in counsel with ideas, with principles and
views commensurate with all the States, and co-extensive with the whole people, and contrast them
with the collection of gentlemen who are trying to
destroy the country, I regard it as more important
than any convention that sat, at least since 1787.
(Loud cheers.) I think I may say, also, that the
declarations that were there made are equal to
the Declaration of Independence itself. And
I here to-day pronounce it "a second declaration
of independence." (Cries of "glorious," and the
most enthusiastic and prolonged applause.)
Your address and declarations are nothing
more nor less than a reaffirmation of the Constitution of the United States. (Cries of "good,"
and cheers.) Yes, I will go further and say
that the declarations you have enunciated in
your address are a second proclamation of emancipation to the people of the United States. (Renewed applause.) For, in proclaiming and repro-
claiming these great truths, you have laid down a
constitutional platform upon which all can make
common cause, and stand together, for the
restoration of the States and the preservation of the government, without any
reference to party questions, which only
is the salvation of the country; for our country rises above all party considerations or influences. (Cries of "Good" and cheers.) How many
are in the United States that now require to be
free that have the shackles upon their limbs, and
are bound as rigidly as though they were in fact
in slavery? I repeat, then your declaration is the
second proclamation of emancipation to the peo-

[212]

ple of the United States, and offers a common ground upon which all patriots can stand.

Mr. Chairman and gentlemen, let me, in this connection, ask you what have I to gain more than the advancement of the public welfare? I am as much opposed to the indulgence of egotism as any one. But here in a conversational manner, while formally reviewing the proceedings of this convention, I may be permitted again to ask what have I to gain, consulting human ambition, more than I have gained. Except in one thing my race is nearly run. I have been placed in the high office which I occupy under the Constitution of the country, and I may say I have held from lowest to highest—almost every position to which a man may attain in our government; I have passed through every position from an alderman of a village to the presidency, and surely, gentlemen, this should be enough to gratify a reasonable ambition. If I wanted authority, or if I wished to perpetuate my own power, how easy it would have been to hold and wield that which was placed in my hands by measures called freedmen's bureau bills (Laughter and applause.) With an army which it placed at my discretion I could have remained at the capital of the United States and with its 50 or 60,000,000 of appropriations at my disposal, with the machinery to be worked with my own hands, with satraps and dependents in every town, and village, and then, with the civil rights bill following as an auxilary (Laughter) in connection with all the other appliances of the government, I could have proclaimed myself dictator. (Cries of "that's true," and three cheers for the President.)

But, gentlemen, my pride and my ambition have been to occupy that position which retains all power in the hands of the people. (Great cheering.) It is upon that I have always relied. It is upon that I rely now. (A voice, "and the people will not disappoint you.") And I repeat that neither the taunts nor jeers of Congress, nor of a calumniating press, can drive me from my purpose. (Great applause.) I acknowledge no superior, except my God and the author of my existence, the people of the United States. (Prolonged and enthusiastic cheers.) For the one I try to obey all his commands as best as I can compatible with my poor humanity. For the other in a political and representative sense the high behests of the people have always been respected and obeyed by me. (Loud cheers.)

Mr. Chairman, I have said more than I intended. For kind allusions to myself contained in your address and in resolutions adopted by the convention, let me remark that in this crisis and at this period of my public life, I hold above all price and shall ever recur with feelings of profound gratification to the last resolution containing the indorsement of the convention, emanating spontaneously from the great mass of the people. (Loud cheers.) I trust and I hope that my future action may be such that you and the convention may not regret the assurance of confidence you have expressed to me. (Cries of " We are sure of it.")

Before separating, my friends, one and all, committee and strangers, please accept my sincere thanks for the kind manifestations of regard and respect you have exhibited on this occasion. I repeat, I shall always continue to be governed by a firm and conscientious conviction of duty (and that always gives one courage) under the Constitution, which I make my guide.

At the conclusion of the President's remarks, three cheers were enthusiastically given for Andrew Johnson, and three more for Gen. Grant. The President and Gen. Grant then retired arm in arm, and the committee and the audience commenced to disperse.

DISRUPTURE OF THE PRETENDED CONVENTION.

statements which have been pur-
h concerning the occurrences of
30th July last, are calculated to
ic generally. Whether such state-
igned to perpetuate military rule
ffusions of ignorance, they are
s to the fair fame of Louisiana.

serts, without fear of contradic-
sidents of New Orleans, as a gen-
iot take any part therein, nor did
iing about it until it was over. It
ke a thunder-gust, and passed over
l time to learn what it was all

im reliable information, that a
ve us was concocted at Washing-
e police had full information, and
conspirators, with their deluded
attempted to execute their nefari-
cy were interrupted by the police
of the community. A few hun-
cted about the scene of action, as
e done about a fire, or to observe
he moon. or to witness a donkey
ibitants, however, white and col-
remained quietly at their homes or
ss ; they deeply regret the sacrifice
inocent or deluded men, and should
suffer for the indiscretion of the
for the criminal conduct of the
premeditated invasion of our cou-
s.—*Aug.* 25, 1866.

OF THE GRAND JURY.

bell, Judge of the First District Court of

rors of the parish of Orleans have
deration the subject of the terri-
urred in this city on the 30th of
ow come into court and ask leave

ised to be summoned before them
of citizens. whose testimony they
med was material to show the
i, manner and close of the bloody
th of July ; and in order to secure
npartial history of the bloody day,
stain and justify the conclusions to
e arrived, and have embodied in
have caused the testimony of the
ned by them to be carefully reduced
to writing, which testimony they submit herewith,
and from which it appears—

That, on the 30th day of July last, there was a
conflict at and near the Mechanics' Institute, in
this city, which resulted in the death of about
forty persons, white and black, and in the wound-
ing, slightly and severely, of about two hundred
more.

The first question naturally presenting itself is,
what caused, in a time of profound peace, so terrible a conflict? What aroused our usually quiet
and peaceable population to so dire and fierce a
struggle? It could be no trifling or ordinary cause
that could bring on such deathly collision upon the
members of a community hitherto moving so har-
moniously together. The question, however, is
not difficult of solution.

Some four weeks since a meeting of about
thirty persons met in secret caucus in this city,
elected Rufus K. Howell president pro tem., resolved that he should convoke the convention of
1864, to meet on the 30th of July last, and that
the governor of the State should be requested to
issue his proclamation for elections to fill the vacancies in the convention. These men claimed to
have the right and power, and very undisguisedly
expressed the intention to remodel the Constitution of the State to suit their purposes, and to
take possession or control of the State government. It is unnecessary to enter into a discussion here of the question of the pretensions of
this body of men. Suffice it to say that there
never was a more impudent and audacious claim
set up to assume power than this pretended right
to meet in convention. It had not the slightest
foundation whatever. even under the resolutions
of the convention of 1864, under which it was
claimed they could meet, which, construed together, as well as by the interpretation of their
author, never contemplated that the power of
calling the convention together should be conferred on the president of the body, except in the
case of the rejection of the Constitution by the
people. The second resolution, on the contrary,
clearly and explicitly confers the power on the
legislature at its first session to reconvoke the
members of the convention—in case of the rejection of the Constitution by the people. Again, even
if the construction that the president of the convention had the power to call the convention together'
be correct, he alone possesses that power, and he
(E. H. Durell) refused to exercise it. The idea of a
caucus of twenty-nine, of a body whose quorum is
seventy-six, undertaking to elect a president,
is a palpable absurdity, as in fact is the whole
thing. For admitting that the convention of 1864
had undertaken to perpetuate their own existence
by a resolution not a part of the Constitution, it
would have been a ridiculous pretension without
binding effect, and necessarily a nullity. This as-

sumption of power, then, on the part of these men, was a flagrant, open, defiant violation of law. It was an insolent and lawless attempt to subvert the government and destroy the Constitution, and under the laws of most countries, would have amounted to high treason, and would be punishable with death. Fortunately for them, the only offense for which, under the laws of Louisiana, they could be indicted and punished for simply meeting with the object professed of destroying the government of the State, is for making and knowingly assisting at an unlawful assembly, of which they were guilty as soon as they met in convention, and for which offense, those who met in convention on the 30th of July, have been indicted by the grand jury.

On the 30th of July, then, this body, according to public announcement, was to meet. On Friday night, 27th July, a meeting of the friends of universal suffrage, irrespective of color, took place in this city. At this meeting inflammatory speeches were made to the colored people, who attended in large numbers. They were advised to come to the convention on Monday, "to come in their might, to come prepared."

They were exhorted to exterminate the whites, who were called hell-born and hell-bound villains, and were told that unless the rights of loyal citizens and their colored brethren were conceded, the streets of New Orleans would run with rebel blood.

On Monday morning, the 30th July, at an early hour, the colored people commenced gathering in and about the place designated for the meeting of the convention, many of them armed. About 12 o'clock a procession of negroes came marching up toward the place of sitting of the convention, with colors flying and drums beating; and these armed with heavy sticks or other weapons. As they came up they hallooed and shouted, and, according to some witnesses, jostled and pushed the bystanders on the streets out of their way. The crowd of white people gave way as they passed along. There was but slight disturbance as the crowd passed up, (one arrest made) and the procession passed on to the place where the convention sat. During this disturbance there were pistols fired—the first two by negroes in the procession.

The condition of things now presented is an unlawful assembly in session, arrogating to themselves without even the shadow of right, the power to overturn the government of the State—a body of usurpers conspiring for the subversion of the Constitution and laws of the State; and they surrounded by a crowd of negroes, brought there by previous invitation, and armed for the protection of the "unlawful assembly" in their lawlessness.

Under these circumstances, what was the legal right as well as the palpable duty of the conservators of the peace, both State and municipal? It clearly was to disperse the violators of the law, and to arrest and hold them for trial. The offence being complete, as soon as the "unlawful assembly" took place, the ministers of the law were not compelled to await an attack to be made on them by the disturbers of the public peace before they proceeded to do their duty in dispersing and arresting them. They were authorized by the law to take the initiative, using such force as was necessary, and only such to break up the unlawful assembly, and secure the persons of the offenders for punishment. This, however, was not done, and why? It appears that the civil authorities found that the military authorities would not only not co-operate with them in making the arrests, but would protect the convention from being interfered with by either the municipal or State authorities. Mayor Monroe was informed that he would not be allowed to arrest the members of the convention, and the general in command at the time was equally explicit in asserting that the sheriff of the parish, after indictment found by the grand jury, would not be allowed to arrest the members of the pretended convention. Unwilling to bring about a collision between the military and civil authorities, Mayor Monroe desisted entirely from his intention of arresting the members, and it was agreed and distinctly understood between the general commanding at the time and Lieut. Gov. Voorhies, that in case the Grand Jury should indict the members of the convention, that the sheriff, instead of making the arrests, should take his writ for the arrest of the persons indicted directly to the general, who would indorse thereon his refusal to allow the execution thereof, and would forward the whole matter to the President of the United States for direction and specific instruction in the premises. In the meantime the convention was to remain undisturbed, and in order to secure peace and quiet a small military force was to be used in conjunction with some of the police. It is evident to this Grand Jury that, in pursuance to this arrangement, the municipal authorities sedulously and carefully avoided everything that could possibly lead to collision between the police and the armed negro force assembled for the protection of the usurping convention. It appears that in furtherance of these pacific views, at the request of a number of respectable citizens, the mayor issued a proclamation calling on citizens to so behave themselves as to avert all danger of riot and difficulty, which they appear to have heeded, as evidenced by the uninterrupted passage, through their midst, of the noisy, turbulent, menacing and insulting procession of armed negroes on their way to the place of the assembling convention.

The military force promised to assist in maintaining order, from some cause or other not forthcoming—a fact much to be lamented, as there can be no doubt its timely arrival could easily have averted all disturbance, and the dreadfully bloody scenes of the day would thereby have been avoided. The military never did arrive until the riot was entirely quelled by the police. The evidence shows that the conflict, which terminated so fatally to themselves, was begun by the negroes in front of the place where the convention sat. After the first attack the negroes fell back, and, many of them taking cover in the Mechanics' Institute, the fight was continued by them from the building, and the police force and some persons in citizens' clothes, from the street. It is needless to go into the details of the struggle—they will be found in the accompanying testimony; suffice it to say, the police succeeded in arresting many persons, white and black, who were placed in confinement, and in entirely quelling the riot. There appears to have been some unnecessary sacrifice of life, and some unnecessary ferocity and brutality in the closing scenes of this lamentable tragedy, by persons in the crowd, until now unidentified. Some of these persons were arrested by order of the mayor and chief of police, but were all, together with all the other persons arrested by the police at the time of the riot, discharged, as far as we have been informed, without examination, by the military authorities, who had, on the evening of the 30th of July, taken possession of the city by virtue of a declaration of martial law; hence the impossibility of identifying parties engaged in the riot, as well as those who were guilty of unnecessary cruelty in attempting to suppress it. The evidence is all concurrent to the fact that the police, with a few exceptions, and these not identified, behaved with humanity, used no unnecessary violence towards the rioters, and protected persons arrested by them, in many instances at the risk of their own lives.

One fact connected with this unfortunate affair we would leave untold, did we deem its suppression consistent with the full and faithful discharge of our duty to the public. It is the course pursued in this whole matter by J. Madison Wells, the governor of the State. We find him co-operating with the usurping convention, for the purpose of destroying the government under which he holds his power and position.

We find him on the day of this disastrous riot in his office, in the same building where the unlawful assembly was held, where he remains until a very short time before the rioting begun. On leaving his office he had to pass through the mob of armed negroes assembled to sustain the usurpers. He must have known the evident danger of riot and bloodshed, yet not one word have we heard from him, the sworn protector of the laws, to prevent the impending consequences of the threatened trouble, evidences of which were all around him. The first thing that we hear from his excellency is a published manifesto, in which he attempts to justify his giving aid and comfort to the usurpers, and villifies and slanders the people who have elevated him to his present position.

The testimony before the Grand Jury shows that the feeling of the people of the city is one of sympathy for the unfortunate colored people who have fallen the deluded victims to the lawless ambition for place and power of bad and unscrupulous white men, whose great interest in the welfare of the blacks is all feigned for the purpose of accomplishing their own nefarious ends. To the colored people, as a class, there is no hostility. On the contrary, there is a disposition entertained very generally to see that even-handed and impartial justice is done to them in every respect.

In conclusion, as these troubles have been brought amongst us by political tricksters, in an attempt to deprive us of our proper participation in our own government, and as the events of the 30th of July are sought to be tortured and misrepresented to our injury, we deem it not out of place to express our strong conviction that the people of New Orleans have in good faith renewed their allegiance to the government of the United States, and are now, in the fullest sense, loyal to the Constitution and the Union.

FRANCIS RAWLE, Foreman.

L. F. CHARBONNET,
PHILIP POWER, Jr.,
JOHN R. CONWAY,
J. VIOSCA,
ISAAC N. PHILIPS,
S. B. FROST,
VICTOR DAVID,

B. P. VOORHIES,
CHAS. W. HOPKINS,
VICTOR J. FORSTALL,
ANTHONY PRADOS, Jr.
CHARLES ROUYER,
H. B. FLORES,
HENRY AUBERT,

J. G. VIENNE.

www.ingramcontent.com/pod-product-compliance
Lightning Source LLC
Chambersburg PA
CBHW030812020726
47499CB00006B/1877